Ark of Love by Lauralee Bliss
Brian Davis is indebted to his best friend Bob for helping him start his pet store business, and in gratitude, he takes on Bob's sister, Rachel, as an employee. Rachel's skills in the pet store leave much to be desired, and her many mistakes could cost Brian his reputation and his business. Can love turn the situation around before it's too late?

Walk, Don't Run by Pamela Griffin
Frenzied barking leads Jake to Kerry's rescue when she accidentally locks herself outside on her sister's balcony. After a dual case of mistaken identity is cleared up, the two call a truce, but it doesn't last long. Later, Kerry finds an injured dog and seeks a veterinarian—who turns out to be Jake. A dog brought them together; can another dog reunite them when all else has failed?

Dog Park by Dina Leonhardt Koehly
When a Welsh corgi bites Matt's Great Dane in the leg, Matt demands the owner pay the vet's bill. Lynne refuses, claiming her sweet Bamboo wouldn't bite a flea, let alone a Great Dane. Her confidence in her dog's innocence falls apart when she meets the new youth pastor, who just happens to be the Great Dane's owner. Lynne doesn't know what to do. As time passes more questions plague her: Instead of wondering about Brutus, why is she thinking about his owner?

The Neighbor's Fence by Gail Sattler
Fluffy doesn't particularly like Fido, and their owners don't differ much in their opinions of each other, either. Whenever Fluffy and Fido see each other, fur flies, likewise with Heather and Bill; yet something draws the two sides together and they can't stay apart. Then one day, Fluffy and Fido get lost, and Heather and Bill must unite to find them before it's too late. Usually, with cats and dogs, never the twain shall meet. Or shall they?

TAILS
of LOVE

*Pets Play Matchmakers
in Four Modern Romances*

Lauralee Bliss
Pamela Griffin
Dina Leonhardt Koehly
Gail Sattler

BARBOUR
PUBLISHING, INC.
Uhrichsville, Ohio

Ark of Love ©2001 by Lauralee Bliss.
Walk, Don't Run ©2001 by Pamela Griffin.
Dog Park ©2001 by Dina Leonhardt Koehly.
The Neighbor's Fence ©2001 by Gail Sattler.

Illustrations by Mari Goering.

ISBN 1-58660-112-1

All Scripture quotations, unless otherwise indicated, are taken from the HOLY BIBLE, NEW INTERNATIONAL VERSION®. NIV® Copyright ©1973, 1978, 1984 by International Bible Society. Used by permission of Zondervan Publishing House. All rights reserved.

Published by Barbour Publishing, Inc., P.O. Box 719, Uhrichsville, Ohio 44683 http://www.barbourbooks.com

Member of the
Evangelical Christian
Publishers Association

Printed in the United States of America.

TAILS
of LOVE

Ark
of Love

by Lauralee Bliss

Dedication

For Dad. His love of hound dogs, aquarium fish,
and a chameleon named Zeb rubbed off on me.

Godliness with contentment is great gain.
1 TIMOTHY 6:6

One

S ure, Bob, uh-huh, uh-huh."
Pause.
"No, I understand how it is. What? Sure, I can put her somewhere in the store." A flush filled his face. He gazed around the pet store at the small rodents scratching to get out of their cages, the squawks of cockatiels and parakeets, accompanied by the bubbling of aquarium aeration systems. "That didn't come out right. I don't mean I can put her here like she's an animal or something." *Lord, help me.* He shifted the phone to the other ear. "What I meant to say is, I'm sure I can use her help. Now look, she. . .uh. . . ," he hesitated, "she knows about animals, right? I don't mean that to sound derogatory or something. I just want to know how much training she needs. Yeah. Uh-huh. Sure, I mean I'll train her if I need to." He closed his eyes, thinking of the requisition slips that needed to be filled out, the boxes to be unpacked, and the receipts to be tallied. Where in the world would he get the time to train a new employee for the store?

Brian felt a twinge of pain shoot across his temple.

His hand reached for a mug of coffee decorated with species of tropical fish and took a sip, nearly spitting the contents on the floor. *Cold as ice. What else is new?* "What? I'm still here, Bob. Okay, so when do you want to bring her over?" He squinted his eyes at his calendar book in front of him until the dates wavered like ripples on water. "One-thirty?" *Just when I'm expecting a shipment of tropical fish. Great timing. How am I supposed to handle all this? What a time for Mac to take a business trip.* "Sure, one-thirty will be fine. See you then." He put down the phone and collapsed into a small swivel chair, grimacing when he recalled the conversation. *Sure, Bob, uh-huh, uh-huh. Sure, Bob, uh-huh, uh-huh.* It had all the sound of an oldies song, or better yet, a damaged CD. But if he had said, *No, Bob, nope, no sirree*, there would have gone his finances for managing Noah's Ark, right down the tubes.

Bob was the guy Brian met one afternoon in his college zoology class when his only friend at the time had been the lizard in the lab. . . Bob, the one Brian latched on to and developed a friendship that lasted through the years. . . Bob, who held the same vision for a pet store as Brian and whose money helped purchase tanks, food, critters, and half the down payment. . . Bob, who waved away his generosity, saying it was a good business venture with the town lacking a pet store. . . And Bob, who now said his sister could sure use a job.

"Sure, Bob, uh-huh, you bet," Brian said out loud. He was indebted to the man, no doubt about it. The least he could do was offer a small job to his sister. She could unpack boxes, sweep the floors, dust the shelves, and flick a few flakes of food into the aquariums. How dangerous could that be? "I just hope I know what I'm getting myself into," he grumbled. "Whenever Bob speaks I jump, just like one of those chameleons leaping for a dinner of mealworms. But I've got no choice. Without Bob, I wouldn't have my dream."

Long ago as a youngster growing up, Brian had cages of toads, lizards, and gerbils decorating every nook and cranny of his ever-shrinking bedroom. In the corner of the room stood a wooden box that housed an iguana. The room glowed red from a hot lamp that kept the lizard warm. Every week, Brian ventured home with a stray dog or cat he had found wandering around on the street. Once he came across a potbelly pig abandoned by its owner. The garage began taking on the appearance of a miniature SPCA. He even owned a bat for a day and chuckled in recollection of the bat flying in his grandmother's living room after it had flown down the chimney. He managed to capture the bat in a net and house it for a time until his mother caught wind of his newest pet.

"Brian Davis!" she cried. "You get rid of that thing this instant! Bats carry rabies and disease. I won't have it under my roof another minute."

Thankfully, the bat was the only creature out of the menagerie his mother insisted he dump. Animals were Brian's mainstay in life. They brought him comfort and purpose. When everyone in life abandoned him—family, friends, the world in general—the animals were here to stay. He knew all along what his life's work would be—operating his own pet store and sharing the enjoyment of animals with others.

Brian glanced out the plate glass window of his shop on Main Street to see the sign swinging in the gentle breeze. NOAH'S ARK PET STORE. He liked the name. It fit perfectly. After all, Noah was the first pet owner there ever was. He had every kind of mammal, bird, reptile, and insect known to mankind, housed in that ark of his for almost a year.

Brian winced when he told his younger sister, Cathy, about his dream of a pet store with the name of Noah's Ark. She pointed her nose in the air like only a middle school student could do. Earrings much too big for her petite earlobes swayed back and forth as she remarked, "Can you imagine the disgusting smell of that ark after a year of keeping dirty animals? Ugh."

"Every species of animal has its odor," he said in defense. "You smell too, you know. Many animal species find human odor offensive."

"How dare you say something like that about me!" She swatted his arm with her school notebook and strode off in a huff.

"It's true!"

"Well, this whole house stinks! I feel like we're living in the Brian Davis Zoo! I can't have any of my friends over because all they do is gawk at your collection. Not only are there dogs and cats, but that awful pig with flies buzzing around it, and those lizards that stick their tongues out whenever I come near."

"They're particular about the company they keep," he mumbled to himself.

"What was that?"

"Nothing, Cathy. Just a joke."

"You *are* a joke, Brian! Your whole life is a joke, filled with dirty, disgusting animals. Heaven help the one who ends up marrying you. She'll have to stumble over the animal cages just to get near you, that is, if she doesn't get sick instead."

At least one member of his family had respect for what he did in life. His beloved aunt Harriet, who owned her own assortment of cats and a cockatiel named Cheep, used to send him ten dollars every so often to help him feed his brood. She lived out in California. One day he hoped to have the money to finally meet her and tell her how much he appreciated her support.

Now the loud hum of some malfunctioning aquarium aeration unit disturbed his contemplation. Brian strode over to the tanks containing the various species of fish, watching them swim about in their environment without a care in the world. The colorful fins moved in rhythmic fashion to the gentle ripple of current generated by the aeration system. He stared for a time, watching the fish commune with each other. Nothing fascinated him more than seeing the unique life God had created. He knew of people in the medical field who spent a lifetime learning how the human body worked. Brian's interest rested in God's creatures, both great and small. He studied their every move and myriad habits until he knew them all like the back of his hand.

Brian detached the small plastic tube from the unit and looked over the aerator, wondering if he had the where-withal to take it apart and oil the motor. "We'll get you guys some air in no time," he said to the fish who swam about, ignoring his offers of assistance. Brian tipped his head to examine them. The fish were neon tetra with an unusual blue and red tint to their scales, that moved about in schools. When one decided to change direction, the others followed suit. He tapped gently on the tank. "Hey, are you listening to me? Or are you too busy playing follow the leader? I'm your pop, you know. I keep this tank going and feed you all that wonderful-tasting fish food. And remember that great brine shrimp I throw in for good measure? You won't get anything better in a gourmet restaurant, let me tell you."

Brian turned with the aerator unit in his hand, only to find himself face-to-face with an elderly woman, Mrs. Wilson, in to buy her weekly bag of premium dog food. She glared at him over a pair of spectacles. "Who are you talking to, young man?" she asked, staring first at Brian, then to the tank of fish, and back at him.

He coughed before managing a weak smile. "Oh, my friends here, Mrs. Wilson. Let's see. . ." He pointed them out. "Matthew, Mark, Luke, John, Bartholomew, Philip, and Andrew. Good Bible names, don't you think?"

Mrs. Wilson shook her head before pointing her walking cane to the aisle of pet food. "If you don't mind, I need another twenty-pound bag of dog food for Sparky."

"Sure, Ma'am, right away." Brian put down the aerator and hefted up a sack of food from the display. "Is your car parked out front?"

"I took the bus today. My arthritis is acting up something dreadful. I expect there's a storm on the way. Can you have it delivered to me? Sparky ate his last bowl of food

14

this morning and he will need more by this afternoon."

Ugh. Brian groaned with yet another duty added on to his ever-growing list. He could've kicked himself for giving his helper, Mac, the week off. "Uh, what time is good for you? I have a worker coming in at one-thirty and I'll get her to deliver the dog food."

"One-thirty is fine," she said, laying out a twenty-dollar bill on the counter, filled to capacity with containers of dog chews, fish pendants, animal bookmarks, and a donation jar for the SPCA.

"Could I make it a little after one-thirty? You see, she arrives at one-thirty."

Mrs. Wilson glared at him over the tops of her spectacles, gave a huff, and left the store. Brian sank his chin into a hand. It was not turning out to be a stellar day at the Noah's Ark Pet Store.

Brian shook the hand of his longtime friend, Bob, five minutes after the delivery man dropped off the containers of tropical fish. Bob appeared sleek and professional in a pinstripe suit. Gone were the strange clothes, acne, and the disheveled hair as if he had just risen out of bed. A businessman had emerged from his college friend, and one who had made it big in computer repair. Brian always knew Bob would excel at something, and he had done so beyond anything Brian expected. Computer repair was a far cry from the zoology work Bob often spoke of when he graduated.

"I really appreciate you giving Rachel this opportunity," said Bob.

"Of course." Brian dug his hands into the pockets of his jeans, giving a cautious once-over of the petite young woman who stood in the aisle, fingering the dog leashes for sale. From his initial inspection, she seemed pretty average. Her brown hair hung to her shoulders; her slight frame decked out in jeans and a rose-colored top. He suddenly panicked, wondering if she could handle a twenty-pound dog food delivery to Mrs. Wilson, due within the hour.

"What are you looking at?" Bob teased.

"Huh? Nothing. I was just wondering if. . .well. . .if your sister's been around animals much."

"Just Grandpa's farm during the summers. She was his right-hand lady. The animals loved her. Now she has a dog, a coonhound. He sits on the front lawn and howls at the moon."

Great. We don't happen to sell chickens, hogs, cows, or coonhounds in this small place. Brian continued wearing a grin on his face. "Well, good. At least she's been around animals a little."

"She's willing to work any hours." Bob took Brian by the arm and propelled him into the aisle filled with bird products. "I wouldn't have her work with your. . .uh, birds or anything. She got bitten by a bird once and has never been the same. Just give her simple stuff to do at first until she gets used to the place."

"I was actually going to start her off by delivering an order."

"Sounds good. You see, she needs this job to pay off her college debts. She's been looking everywhere for the right place to work. Her last job was at a toy store, but they went out of business."

"Why didn't you hire her to help you out?" Brian asked until he caught the strange look materializing in Bob's eyes.

"Computer repair is not her style. She's much more comfortable around. . .well, less expensive items, like these animals of yours. What does a fish go for? A few bucks at most. Computers run several thousand for the heftier models. A big difference, you know."

What's that supposed to mean? Brian gulped, wondering why he let himself get roped into this. He buried his feelings inside and continued to wear the plastic smile on his face. "All right, if you think she'll be okay here. I trust your judgment."

"Everything will be dandy. Hey, Sis!" he called. "Let me introduce you to my business partner. This is Brian Davis. Brian, my sister Rachel."

"Hi." She tucked strings of brown hair behind one ear and smiled.

Brian only nodded and turned to escort Bob out the door. "How long do you think she'll need. . .well, this job?"

"Don't know, Brian. 'Til she finds something better I suppose. Have a good day."

Brian watched Bob shuffle out the door, whistling a tune. He turned around to see his new charge standing there, looking forever like a little girl lost in the big city. "Okay, first order of business. I need you to make a delivery."

"Delivery?"

"I need you to deliver a sack of dog food to a customer.

She lives in the apartments on Cedar Road. You know where that is?"

She nodded.

"Okay. Did you drive a car to work?"

"Bob drove me."

Brian sighed. "Right. Take my car then. I assume you can drive. She lives in Building C, Room 203. When you enter, ring the bell for number 203 on the wall to your right. If she doesn't answer, just leave the bag at the door along with the receipt. Got it?"

Rachel nodded once more.

"Okay." He dug into his pocket. "Here are my keys. I'm parked in the back—the light blue compact."

She took the keys from his hand. Brian followed her out the rear door of the store with the bag in his hands and placed the dog food in the trunk. "You're all set."

"Bye." She waved before entering the car and starting the ignition.

Brian nearly waved back before thrusting his hand into the pocket of his jeans at the last minute. Talking to animals was one thing. Waving good-bye to a young woman he barely knew was something entirely different.

Brian tried to keep himself busy sorting out the tropical fish during Rachel's absence. After a half hour went by, he began to wonder if she'd gotten lost. When the telephone in the store rang and it was Mrs. Wilson calling about the delivery, Brian assured her the bag of dog food would appear on her doorstep at any moment. He sighed in relief when Rachel walked in ten minutes later, holding a cup of soda larger than a plastic milk jug. "Want some?" she asked. "I was thirsty."

He shook his head, averting his gaze to the sign prominently displayed on the wall that said, NO FOOD OR DRINK. "Did you make out okay?"

"Sure, no problem." She dug her hand into the pocket of her jeans and tossed his car keys on the counter. "What else can I do around here?"

"Let's see, how about—" The phone interrupted him. "Noah's Ark Pet Store." He held the receiver away from his ear, wincing at the shouts erupting from the other end. "But Mrs. Wilson, it has to be there. My delivery guy...uh, gal, just dropped it off. . . . Yes, I know you were expecting it. . . . I'm sure Sparky's hungry. Yes, I would be too if I didn't have lunch." He rolled his eyes. "All right, I'll deliver it myself." Brian slammed down the phone harder than he would have liked and whirled around in his swivel chair to face his employee. "Rachel, exactly where did you leave that bag of dog food?"

"At the address on Cedar Lane."

"Cedar Road, you mean."

She gulped. "I thought you meant Cedar Lane. There's a big office complex. I went to Building C, Room 203, just like you said. I searched for a bell but there wasn't any." She paused with a finger to her chin. "Now I know why the secretary gave me a funny look and said that Mr. Feldon didn't own a dog. In fact, she said he hates dogs and the only way Mr. Feldon prefers his dogs is roasted over a barbecue. Pretty crude if you ask me."

Brian slapped his forehead. *A nightmare come true,*

right before my eyes! "You delivered a bag of dog chow to Lester Feldon on the board of supervisors? And the receipt is on the bag, plain as anything. Rachel, how could you?" He began to tremble in a combination of fear and anger. *Feldon will think I did it for spite. He'll have me and my business in a noose for sure, hanging from the nearest lamp pole.* Brian wanted to yell and scream at her incompetence. Instead, he remembered Bob's cheerful face that afternoon, thanking him for giving his sweet little sister a job. Brian forced down the words until they became a brick in the pit of his stomach. *Facing a brick would be better than facing the consequences of this mistake,* he thought miserably.

Two

The rest of the day remained subdued. Rachel offered to return to the office building on Cedar Lane and retrieve the dog food. Brian informed her in a controlled voice that he would handle it after he closed the pet store. Normally he kept the store open for evening browsers, but after the calamity of the day, he shut down at five and headed directly for Mrs. Wilson's with another bag of food loaded in the trunk of his car. Passing the turnoff for Cedar Lane and the prominent brick buildings housing the elite of town, a lump lodged in his throat. He contemplated cruising over to Feldon's office and swiping the dog food before the supervisor noticed but realized the offices were probably closed by now. Instead, he headed for the apartment complex on Cedar Road and Mrs. Wilson, who met him at the door with a look of consternation painted on her worn face.

"I don't know what to do!" she cried. "Poor Sparky has been whimpering and whining all afternoon. I had no dog food here at all!"

"It's right here, Mrs. Wilson. I'm sorry about the

mix-up this afternoon."

"Whoever that incompetent person is that you hired, young man, I suggest you fire him immediately."

"Her," Brian corrected.

Mrs. Wilson raised an eyebrow. "You mean you sent some young girl to deliver the dog food? For goodness' sake, why didn't you do it yourself?"

Brian opened his mouth to defend his actions, but realized the fruitless gesture of debating work ethics of the twenty-first century with an eighty-year-old woman. She had lived in an earlier period, after all, where men did most of the hard labor. This was the new millennium and things were different. *Way too different*, he thought, lugging in the food.

"As long as you're here," Mrs. Wilson continued, "I could use a man to do some fixing around my apartment. Are you handy with a hammer?"

"I can use one, if that's what you mean." He frowned, wishing he didn't sound so impertinent. The day's events had already rubbed his nerves raw and he was not looking forward to tomorrow.

After two hours of hammering in fallen curtain rods, gluing down linoleum in the kitchen, fixing a door latch, taking out the garbage, and listening to Mrs. Wilson tell of Sparky's woes, Brian dragged himself back to the pet store for one final look at the critters. A bag of dog food stood propped up against the outside door. The receipt was taped on the bag with the words *Wrong Delivery* written in red pen.

"At least it didn't come with a pipe bomb attached,"

he said bitterly, carrying in the bag and placing it with the appropriate food in the aisle. He then went back to his desk to find a note waiting for him. Picking up the notepaper, he caught the fragrance of flowers. The scent made every hair stand at attention. He hadn't smelled anything that good in ages. Surrounded by the odor of animals, fish, and the like, this scent seemed to have come down from heaven. The letters on the note were formed in pretty handwriting.

> *Dear Mr. Davis,*
> *I'm very sorry about the mix-up with the dog food. If there is anything I can do to make it up to you, please let me know. Thank you again for giving me a job.*
>
> *Love,*
> *Rachel* ♡

Brian stared at the note. Love. . .perfume. . .hearts. . . what was this? It knocked his senses for a loop. He walked around in a daze after that, nearly dumping a whole container of fish food into an aquarium before catching himself in time. The note's scent followed him everywhere, as did the image of a soft-spoken Rachel, tucking a strand of loose hair behind her ear. Of course he would forgive her. As far as Brian was concerned, biblical principles applied. East or west, forgiveness is best. Anyone could have made the error. So long as Lester Feldon did not make an issue out of it, Brian was safe. So was Rachel, for that matter, with the pleasing scent and the heart attached to her name.

The next morning when Rachel arrived for work, Brian sniffed the air, hoping for a whiff of eau de toilette, a la flowerette. *Guess she forgot to put some on today*, he thought, surprised by his disappointment. Every so often, he would turn from his work to watch her unpack a crate of birdseed and place the boxes on the shelves. Her long fingers gently pushed each box into its rightful place, one on top of the other, neat as a pin, until suddenly an avalanche of boxes tumbled off the shelf. Boxes burst open, spraying birdseed everywhere.

"Oh no!" Rachel cried in distress when Brian arrived on the scene. "I'm so sorry. I guess I stacked them too high. Do you have a broom and dustpan?"

"In the storage closet," he said glumly. "How many boxes are wasted?"

"Well, this one." She lifted up a few. Her face brightened. "These look okay." She picked up another, only to have a fine stream of seed trickle out of a crushed corner. "This makes two. Three. Uh, five."

Brian felt his muscles tightening. *Relax, Davis. Don't lose it over spilt birdseed.*

"Seven in all," she noted. "Can we tape them or something? Maybe put a tag on them that says *Reduced Price, Damaged Goods?*"

"Why not." He picked up the damaged boxes, keeping fingers pressed against the ripped corners to prevent any further seed from escaping. *I'll just make sure to dock your paycheck to compensate for the loss.* After taping the corners shut and slapping a reduced tag on the items, he put them on a shelf with the other outdated products for sale. *I take it back. I won't make her pay for it. I don't sell a lot of birdseed anyway. I just hope we've gotten all the kinks out, now that the dog food has been delivered to the wrong address, and the store has been baptized in birdseed.*

"I'm sorry," came Rachel's soft voice behind him. He turned to find a pair of curly eyelashes lowering over a set of dark brown eyes in a picture of dejection. "I'll try to be more careful next time."

His anger dissipated. "That's okay. Go ahead and sweep up the mess. And while you're at it, sweep up the rest of the store. It needs it." *That should be harmless enough, unless she pokes a broom handle through an aquarium.* He shuddered at the thought of his beloved tank of neon tetra shattered with Matthew, Mark, Luke, John and all the rest gasping for breath on the cold floor. *Everything's going to be fine,* he reassured himself.

The rest of the morning proceeded smoothly. Brian was in a better mood after selling a customer a huge aquarium setup for over a hundred dollars. The birdseed issue faded into oblivion, as did the dog food under the essence of flowers. He looked at Rachel with new eyes after she had the floor all clean and even took a cloth to polish up the glass on the aquariums.

"Looks good," he noted approvingly when the phone rang. "Hey, Mac! How was your trip?" Pause. "Huh? So the trip turned out to be permanent? Uh. . .and I owe you a week's salary? Yeah. Well sure, if it's better for you, I can get along." *Somehow,* he added silently. *Right now I haven't a clue.* "What? . . . Okay, bye." The phone sank into the cradle with a *thump.*

"Bad news?" Rachel asked, running a cleaning cloth along the counter.

"My other employee, Mac, just found a new job. Super-de-duper." He thought of the hundred bucks he had pocketed that morning and realized all of it would have to go toward Mac's exiting salary. "I don't know how quick I can find someone to take his place."

Rachel paused, aiming the nozzle of the cleaning bottle at him like a weapon. "You hired me." She lowered the bottle and sprayed antibacterial fluid onto the smooth countertop, rubbing hard with a cloth to emphasize the point.

"I know, but just for certain jobs. Mac was responsible and. . ."

Rachel raised an eyebrow.

Careful Brian, ol' boy. Remember Bob. "Not to mean you aren't responsible or anything, it's just that Mac could open and close the store, perform sales, and help the customers with their selections."

"I can do all that. I've sold before."

"What?"

"Kids' toys, you know, at a toy store. I could get parents to buy anything for their kids."

"Well, this is *not* a toy store. I've got a lot of expensive merchandise in here. It takes responsibility and knowledge." Brian gazed at the shelves filled with stock, the aquariums loaded with fish, and the finches and other birds in their cages. He recalled his excitement when the first shipments for the new pet store arrived. It was like

Christmas Day, only the presents had been boxes of flea shampoo, chew toys, bird feeders, gerbil cages, and the like. Each box he ripped open revealed more of the merchandise that would line the brand-new steel shelving units, making Noah's Ark Pet Store what it was today. Scanning the huge inventory that cost thousands of dollars, he bit his lip. "I just can't afford to have all this. . ." He pressed his lips shut before the words slipped out. *I can't afford to have you messing up my inventory and costing me everything*. He cleared his throat. "I need someone who can take on a lot of responsibility. I don't think I can heap it all on you at one time. You just started here, after all."

"I can do it," Rachel insisted, tucking a loose strand of hair behind her ear. "Ask Bob. He says I'm very responsible."

Brian sensed the irritation build within him. *I don't want to ask Bob. I know just what he'll say. "Oh, Brian, give sweet Rachel a chance. She's excellent with the customers. And don't you think you owe it to me after the money I gave to help start this measly business?"* Brian cringed at the thoughts conceived in his mind.

"Is something wrong?" Rachel asked, staring at him critically. "You look sick."

Brian could just imagine what he looked like, as if he had sniffed an open bottle of vinegar. "I have a lot on my mind."

"I'm sure you do. I want to help and not make more work for you. It has to be tough, running a business on your own."

"It's no piece of cake, that's for sure."

"But I can tell you love what you do."

After this compliment, the icy block of irritation melted into a puddle of acceptance. "That's true. I've loved animals ever since I was a kid. There's just something about animals that's special. Of course, I drove my family crazy with my hobby. But I think it's good for Christians to take care of animals. Helps give us an appreciation for God's creation."

Rachel drew forward when he spoke these words. Her eyes widened in interest. "So you're a Christian! I should have known by the way you hired me on the spot like you did."

"Actually, it had to do with. . ." Brian stopped himself before he allowed the name of her brother to escape from his lips. He cleared his throat. "Ahem. I guess it was good timing with Mac quitting. I know eventually I'll have to hire additional help. I was counting on two full-time employees, besides you."

"Like I said, I'll gladly take Mac's place. You won't be sorry."

"Lord, I pray I won't be," Brian murmured to himself before leading Rachel over to the counter where he began explaining store procedures. She watched his every move, soaking in the information like a sponge to spilt milk. In turn, Brian studied her when she wasn't looking—the large inquisitive brown eyes framed by thick lashes, the ruddy-colored cheeks and small nose. Her lips were the most appealing—a natural cherry red color untainted by lipstick. For an instant, Brian wondered if those lips tasted as good as they looked when Rachel suddenly held up a requisition slip, blocking her lips from view.

"I'll take care of ordering stock," he told her. "If you can keep the customers happy, then the store will make profits and I'll be happy."

The bells on the shop door interrupted the lesson. "Okay, there's your first customer," Brian murmured to her, watching an older woman in her fifties meander in and move toward the fish aisle. "Break a leg."

Rachel put on her best smile and went over to help the lady while Brian returned to his desk, cluttered with bills and receipts. He sat down heavily to stare at the pile of bills and the check ledger resting beside them, realizing he should soon join the twenty-first century and get himself a decent computer system. After paying each bill, he took up a large red marker and wrote *Paid* in bright letters on the bills. The color of the marker made him think of Rachel and her lips like cherries in a deep-dish pie—or better yet, a cherry ice pop, refreshingly cool on a hot summer's day. Brian licked his own lips in response. *Man, get ahold of yourself, Davis,* he thought, sensing the perspiration build on the back of his neck. The caustic side continued, *Remember, she's the one who delivered the dog food to enemy number one and trashed the birdseed.*

The calm, mild-mannered side responded. *Yes, but she cares about animals, just like you. And she wants to help. Plus, she's a Christian. All this points to a winning combination.*

You mean a losing combination, retorted the dark side. *It's all feminine wiles. You witnessed it firsthand with Cathy. Remember how she treated her boyfriends—wrapped guys around her finger like they were bandages, then the next moment, dumped 'em in the trash.*

"Well, that wasn't so bad. I think I did pretty good, Brian."

The sweet voice made him jump, scattering bills all over the floor. "Feminine wiles," he muttered, stooping to gather up the bills, never noticing one that came to rest beside a file cabinet.

"What did you say?" Rachel inquired.

"Uh. . .I said, 'Thought it would take awhile.'" He shuddered at the lie that came out easier than it should. Heat flooded his face. "So what did the customer want?"

"She said her fish had white spots on them and wanted a cure. I pointed out several of the medications we had in stock."

"Good." He sat down in his chair, pushing back strands of his brown hair with his fingers. "This has been one crazy day. I'm beat already."

"Maybe you'd like to go for a walk after we close?" Rachel suggested. "Sometimes a walk around the block is just what you need to feel refreshed."

Brian felt the return of the sweat on his neck that now trickled down the back of his shirt. "A walk?"

"In the evening, I walk my dog Spot around the neighborhood. We'd love some company."

"Spot! I can't believe you would name a dog Spot." Brian laughed loudly, more from exhaustion than anything. "Bet your favorite book in grade school was *Run, Spot, Run.*" He straightened. "'See Spot run. Oh, Spot, don't run. Run fast, Spot.'"

"Spot runs all right," Rachel agreed with a smile. "Just you wait."

The cherry red lips beckoned to him, framing a pair of even, white rows of teeth that sparkled in the lights of the store. He licked his own lips that had dried up during the conversation. "So you really do have a dog named Spot?"

"Yes and I'm warning you, Spot loves to run."

Brian composed himself enough to return to the bills, now in disarray and sprinkled with dust balls carried from the floor. He blew the dust, sending both dust and bills flying in a whirlwind. A look of disgust crossed his face. "Before we do any running with Spot, this floor needs cleaning. And I'm going to get myself a computer so I won't have mountains of paper to deal with."

"I guess I forgot this area when I swept out the shop. I'll get the broom." Rachel marched back to the small closet containing the cleaning supplies. Her willingness to pitch in left another big impression on Brian, right up there with the cherry red lips and flowery perfume. He decided a walk with Rachel and Spot might do him a world of good.

Brian tousled the floppy ears of the coonhound that peered at him with a look of loving adoration in his dark brown eyes. A long red tongue dripped saliva on his sneakers. "Great dog, but he doesn't have any spots. I don't know why you named him that."

Rachel fastened the leash to the plaid collar around the dog's furry neck. "Haven't you seen the kids' show on television about a dog named Spot? He loves to play games and make friends. We used to sell the videos at the toy store where I worked. When I got this guy, I knew exactly what his name would be." Rachel pushed the leash into Brian's hand. "Okay."

"C'mon, Spot ol' boy, let's go for a waaaa—" Brian never finished the statement. The dog lurched and took off down the sidewalk at breakneck speed. "Whoa! Hold on! Stop, Spot, stop. Heel!"

Giggles floated in the air behind him. He glanced over his shoulder to find Rachel smiling broadly. "See? I don't walk Spot. Spot walks me."

"I guess," he gasped, finally bringing the dog to a fast-paced walk.

"He keeps me in shape," Rachel added, jogging beside Brian and the dog whose ears bounced up and down with each stride. "You must have had dogs in your life."

"I had seven at one time," he puffed, wondering where the dog got his super canine strength. *Must've had fortified kibbles in his breakfast bowl.*

"Seven dogs?"

"And when one barked, they all barked. I had my own dog chorus. I once tried to get them to bark to the tune of "Row, Row, Row Your Boat," but they didn't get the message. I've seen on television shows where owners can get dogs to do all sorts of tricks—ring bells, walk tight-ropes, ride unicycles. I had too many other animals to care for to try and train them. It was enough for me just to keep the kennels clean and give them fresh food."

"So what other animals did you have besides dogs?" Rachel asked after they plopped down together on the sidewalk for a quick breather. Miraculously, Spot sat on his haunches right along with them.

Brian watched her tighten the laces of her running shoes. She had perfectly shaped fingers with long nails—not stubby ones that looked like they had undergone a chewing contest. Her nails were well rounded at the tips and painted with sparkling nail polish. "You name it and I had it. Fish, gerbils, birds, snakes, an iguana. . ."

Rachel's head spun around. Huge brown eyes burrowed into his. "An iguana! Are you kidding?"

"No, but I was sure kidding myself when I thought it would only grow to a certain size. The thing kept getting bigger and ornerier. I kept it in this huge box with a plastic door. Charlie, I called him, used to strike the cage door with his tail. It made this awful rattling sound. Once Charlie even got out. Cathy screamed bloody murder."

"Cathy?"

"My sister. The iguana crawled underneath her bed and camped out there for awhile. Charlie would bang on the box springs and scratch. Cathy couldn't figure out what the noise was. She looked under her bed one night and was suddenly staring eyeball-to-eyeball at this thing with beady, yellow eyes. I'll tell you, the scream alone took ten years off my life. I checked the mirrors in the bathroom just to make sure they hadn't cracked."

"Oh, Brian, really." Rachel shook her head. "You can't blame her for screaming. I would have, too. Can you imagine staring face-to-face with an iguana in the middle of the night?" She trembled. "Makes me shiver just thinking about it."

"Cathy didn't sleep in her room for a month afterward. After that, Mom made me get rid of it. Charlie went to the happy iguana hunting ground. I tried to get him shipped to Central America, but I ran out of time. He died from a broken heart and shattered ear drums." Brian cracked a smile. "Well, maybe not that."

Rachel cupped a hand to her chin. The shiny fingernails tapped on a smooth velvety cheek. "That's too bad. I remember when I lost my first goldfish. It was such a tragedy. Bob made fun of Goldie. My mother had this tiny frying pan she used for melting butter, and he would bring it to the tank, pretending he was ready to fry up my goldfish. 'Mmm, Goldie and hush puppies tonight,' he'd say."

Brian raised an eyebrow. "I can't believe Bob would say something like that. In college he loved animals. We both got A's in zoology."

"He loves animals, but not as much as teasing. But he's been a good brother, in spite of himself. He was very comforting to me when Goldie died. He helped me find a little box to bury her in. Years later he told me the neighbor's cat had dug Goldie up. He hadn't had the heart to tell me at the time."

Brian gulped before staring down at Spot who rose up on all fours, ready for another sprint. He wondered how they'd gotten onto such strange topics like Charlie and Goldie. He rose to his feet and proceeded to jog down the sidewalk with Spot and Rachel by his side. Despite the conversation, he was enjoying the evening immensely. When they finished the walk—or rather the run—around the block, Rachel invited him into Bob's house for a glass of iced tea.

"How about an ice cream cone?" she inquired.

Brian barely heard the question. He hadn't set foot inside Bob's place in a long time. Everything seemed different. There were more plants decorating the place than he remembered. A large aquarium housed a multitude of tropical fish. He recalled the old-fashioned rolltop desk in the corner of the living room. There at that desk, Bob and he had drawn up the financial agreement for starting Noah's Ark Pet Store.

Brian whirled in a start when a finger tapped him on the shoulder. "The ice cream cone?"

"Huh? What ice cream cone?"

Rachel's cherry red lips broke open into a radiant smile. "The one I plan to fix for you."

"Oh, sure, sure." Brian stuffed his hands inside the pockets of his jeans. "It's been ages since I've been inside Bob's place. I see you've added a few touches."

"He's been real nice, letting me stay here until I can afford a place of my own," her voice sang from the kitchen.

Brian moseyed on over to the place where his life began. He patted the rolltop desk fondly. Here at this very place, the conception for Noah's Ark turned into a reality. He sighed, thinking back on those days, until he noticed a letter addressed to Bob sitting on the desk. The return address was Lester Feldon's. *Why would Feldon be contacting Bob?* Brian wondered. Glancing back to the doorway of the kitchen, he snatched up the envelope and held it to the light.

"Find anything interesting?"

Brian dropped the letter when Rachel came forward with two ice cream cones in her hands.

"Oh. . .uh, I was just curious why Feldon would be contacting Bob."

"I was wondering the same thing myself when I brought in the mail today." She handed him a cone before bending to pick up the letter. "I know from the mistake with the dog food that you and Mr. Feldon are not the best of friends."

Brian began to lick the chocolate chunk ice cream. He would have preferred strawberry but enjoyed the cold concoction sliding down his parched throat, especially after being caught red-handed meddling in other people's affairs. "Feldon hates animals."

Rachel lifted her eyebrows, making her eyes appear like the huge chunks of chocolate embedded in the ice cream. "I didn't know that. No wonder you were so upset when you found out I'd delivered the dog food to him."

"Yeah. He gave us a hassle about renting the space for a pet store. Feldon owns practically that whole block on Main Street, you see. When he found out that Bob and I wanted to put in a pet store, he was up in arms about it. Bad-mouthed the idea and everything. Bob was able to smooth things over. I think he offered Feldon free computer service if he simmered down. Whatever Bob said, it worked." Brian glanced back at the envelope. When he did, the ice cream trickled down his windpipe. He coughed, then felt a shiver race through him when a hand slapped him gently between the shoulder blades.

"The ice cream go down the wrong way?"

He only nodded. Rachel hastened to the kitchen for a glass of water. Watching her return with the water and a napkin to wipe the dribble off his chin, he could only marvel at her caring attitude. "Thanks. Anyway, seeing that letter from Feldon makes me think that something might be up."

"I'm sure it's just business. Maybe a request for computer repair service."

"You're probably right." Brian finished the ice cream. "Well, I need to check on a few things at the store and make sure the critters are tucked in for the night. Uh. . . thanks for the ice cream."

"Sure. Thanks for being a great boss."

Brian managed a smile before exiting the house, hoping there was no ice cream smeared across his face. Spot barked several good-byes from the yard while Brian headed for his car, still thinking about the letter sitting on the rolltop desk. "Rachel's right. It must be some kind of business thing between the two of them." He shrugged his shoulders and sped off toward the downtown area, thinking of Rachel's sweet face and cherry red lips.

Three

Brian hummed to himself, feeling better than he had in weeks or maybe even months. He owed it all to Rachel. She had been a godsend despite a few trivial mistakes on her part. Her love for the animals and her willingness to learn gave Brian a new outlook on life. Most of all, he admired her caring ways. For so long he had yearned for the love and devotion of another human being. He found acceptance with the animals, but since Rachel came along, he knew God had begun to open his eyes to the love and concern of people. Being around her was like fresh air in springtime. He hoped when she came in later today, she would be wearing his favorite perfume—the one that smelled like a garden of flowers.

The door jingled and a customer strode in. Brian glanced up and smiled, only to be greeted by the angry snarl of a middle-aged woman.

"You're going to have to pay for what you did!" she shouted.

Brian jumped out of his swivel chair at the accusatory tone. "W–what do you mean, Ma'am?"

"I mean this." She banged the small bottle on the counter. "I was told to buy this by some young thing working in your store last week. She said it would cure my fish. In less than a week, all my fish were dead!"

Brian picked up the bottle. "What were the initial symptoms, Ma'am?"

"I told her they had white spots all over them. She called it Ich."

"That's correct. This should have cleared the condition. What type of fish did you have?"

"Oh they were beautiful—a school of lovely neon tetra." She sniffed. "I used to love watching them swim together. N—now they're gone!"

Brian widened his eyes. "Tetra? Did she tell you to administer half the normal dosage?"

The woman shook her head. "No. I put in the ten drops, just like she told me. Why?"

"Tetra are very sensitive fish. They don't react well to this type of chemical. The smallest amount possible should have been used." Brian blew out a sigh that sent his set of wavy brown bangs flying in the air. "Exactly what did my assistant tell you to do?"

"Put in ten drops three times a day, if I'm not mistaken."

Anger replaced the joy Brian had felt over Rachel's presence in the store. *What was she thinking? You don't even use that amount with normal fish! And she even has an aquarium in her home!* "I'm very sorry this happened, Ma'am. Let me know how many fish you lost and I will gladly reimburse you for the damage."

"The tank is also ruined, you know. I had to discard the

water. The gravel is sitting in my driveway back home, so I'll need new gravel. And this beautiful bridge I had at the bottom of the tank—why, it even had a little tower that a few of the fish liked to hide in—it broke while I was trying to empty the tank." Brian could see a large teardrop hovering in the corner of her eye. "The bridge is irreplaceable."

Brian began adding up the figures in his head. More money wasted on account of Rachel. He took back every nice word he had been contemplating that morning. Rachel was sloppy, inept, not to mention downright embarrassing to him and his establishment. Brian buried his feelings for the moment and gave the woman his prized collection of neon tetra, a bag of gravel, and a decorative bridge for her aquarium. She added fish food and a new tank heater to the mound. Brian almost charged her for the additional items, but bit his lip and allowed her the materials for free.

When the woman left, slightly happier than when she arrived, Brian slumped down in his chair. A headache began teasing his temples. "I can't keep Rachel on like this," he told himself. "I just can't. This is the end of it."

The bell tinkled and a cheery greeting came from the front door. "Hi, Brian!"

He said nothing, but only stared blankly at his desk. Even the sweet scent of the flowery perfume failed to stir him.

"Is something wrong?"

"You bet it is," he said tightly before looking up at her. "Remember the customer who came in the other day, saying she had a tank of sick fish? You gave her an overdose of medication for the Ich. Her whole tank died. Yours truly had to replace the loss—not just with any fish, mind you." He sank his chin into a hand. "I had to give her my pals Matthew, Mark, Luke, John, Bartholomew, Philip, and Andrew."

Rachel's merry expression faded. "I–I don't understand how her fish could have died. I know I gave her the right medicine." She hurried to the fish supplies and came back with the small plastic bottle. "You see? The label says it cures the Ich."

"Read what else it says," he said in a monotone voice. He waited for a moment, watching the chocolate-colored eyes scan the label. "See where it says, 'Use half the normal dosage with tetra'?"

"She didn't tell me she had tetra."

"Did you ask?"

"Not specifically, but I thought all fish could—"

Brian flew to his feet. "You thought wrong. Only the smallest dosage, if any, should have been used. You told her to put in ten drops three times a day!"

"Brian, I didn't tell her to put in—"

"Look, I can't keep having all these mistakes. I didn't mention it, but the other day I found a whole cage of gerbils running loose because the cover wasn't replaced after the feeding. I went around on my hands and knees hunting for the things. Some boxes were chewed up. I didn't make a big deal out of it at the time because. . ." He paused. *Because I'm really attracted to you.* He forced down the words and said defiantly, "No, I'm not."

Rachel stared at him. "What?"

"What I mean is, I can't keep having sloppiness in the store. It's costing me business and money."

Her lower lip began to quiver. The tears began to pool, turning her eyes into chocolate syrup. "I'm so sorry about this, Brian. If you want, I'll quit right now and you can hire someone else."

Brian opened his mouth to accept the resignation, that is, until he imagined the face of Bob when he heard the news. *What? You fired my sister? After all I did for you, getting this rattrap going. Brian Davis, you ungrateful wretch. Some friend you turned out to be. I lend you all kinds of money, then you treat my sister like garbage you can toss out on collection day.*

"I'm not asking you to resign. But from now on, I need you to be more careful. Next week I have a new guy starting. Hopefully he will be able to take over some of the workload."

The tears grew heavy enough to drip down her cheeks. "I see." She turned on her heel. "Guess I'll start sweeping the floor and dusting the shelves. At least I can do that well enough."

Brian watched her shuffle off to the storage area for the broom with her shoulders slumped and her gaze fixed on the tile flooring. *What else can I do?* he thought miserably. *I'm doing the best I can, under the circumstances. I only wish Rachel would give her best at this job.*

The next several weeks in the pet store were active ones. A new guy named Stu began working, and to Brian's relief, brought with him a great deal of knowledge about

operating a pet store. The two of them would sit compan-
ionably in the office and discuss ways to make the store
more profitable. Stu recommended new sign displays,
weekly specials, placing ads in the paper, and other incen-
tives to bring in the customers. He also suggested an inex-
pensive computer system that made organization a snap.
After several days at the keyboard, Brian was able to set up
an inventory and billing screens that reduced his piles of
papers on the desk to practically nothing. "So this is what
the desk actually looks like!" he joked to himself when he
discovered the smooth wood finish of the desk beneath the
mounds of paper. He sat back and sighed in contentment.

Brian now adjusted the sign advertising twenty percent
off all pet food—another idea of Stu's—and stepped back
to view the results. He never noticed Rachel pass by with
a broom and dustpan filled with cedar chips from the animal cages. They had not spoken personally since the
escapade with the fish. Brian was too busy implementing
Stu's wonderful ideas to spend time thinking about Rachel,
Bob, Spot, or anything else.

At that moment, Stu burst into the pet shop, wearing
a huge grin on his face. In his hands he carried a large
metal cage that contained a squirming puppy. "Look
what I got, Brian!"

Brian gasped. "What are you doing with that?"

Stu placed the cage on the floor before looking for
newspapers to scatter underneath. "It's a new way to
attract business. Kids love puppies. You gotta start having
a couple of these guys in the store."

"I don't know about dogs, Stu."

"Look, when people see the sign for a pet store, they aren't thinking lizards. They're thinking about a puppy for little Joey or a kitten for Susie. Isn't this one great?"

"I guess. He looks pretty big to be a puppy."

Stu smirked. "Anyway, he is great—a Great Dane puppy, that is. A purebred, through and through. I have the papers."

"Must've cost a bundle."

"Not at all. Gotta shop around and get a good deal. I found someone willing to sell him to me cheap. You'll make more than double. I bought it for a hundred. You can easily sell this pup for two-fifty."

Brian straightened, instantly intrigued by these figures. "You did get a good deal. Guess we'd better make room. Rachel!"

Rachel scurried out from the dark room housing the lighted aquariums. "Yes? Oh, what a cute puppy!"

"Yeah, we're gonna start selling puppies. Clean out that corner over there for the cage." Brian pointed to a table filled with reduced items for sale. "Find another place to set up the display." He then turned to Stu and began discussing the puppy venture, shrugging off the look on Rachel's face when she scanned the many boxes and bottles arranged on the table. She slowly shuffled over to the display area and began dismantling it.

"I'm gonna call him Brownie," Brian said, chuckling as the puppy licked his finger with a pink tongue.

"Now don't get too attached," Stu warned him with a laugh. "You're supposed to sell him, you know."

"That could be a problem. I was really attached to my

neon tetra. I named them after the disciples in the Bible. I had to give them all away when Rachel gave a customer the wrong information about caring for Ich and ended up poisoning the whole tank."

"Oh, really?" Stu glanced over his shoulder, watching Rachel's mechanical motions as she tore down the display. "You should get rid of her," he whispered.

"She's not that bad to have around. Unfortunately, I'm beholden to her brother. He paid a chunk of the down payment to start this place."

"Uh-oh. You'd better find a way to get yourself off her brother's leash. Sell a bunch of these little guys," he suggested pointing to the puppy. "Then you can pay off the loan to her brother and have it made."

Brian glanced at Stu. "Would you happen to have the cash on you? I wouldn't mind you being a co-owner. You've only been here a few weeks, but already you've turned this place around. My business is up twenty percent."

"If I had the cash, I wouldn't be working here!" Stu said with laugh. "But thanks for the offer."

Despite the refusal, Brian felt elated over how well everything was going, that is, until he saw Rachel at closing time. She was still laboring over the new display, long after Stu had left for the day. One by one she stacked the bottles on the new shelving that Stu had pieced together with pieces of plywood. Brian marveled at the carpentry job. Not only did Stu have good business sense, he was also handy with a hammer and nails.

Brian strode over to where Rachel was finishing a stack of outdated flea and tick products. "You almost done?"

"I'm going as quick as I can. I don't dare spill anything, so it's taking me a little extra time."

Brian flinched at her remark. "Look, I'm not going to bark at you if you accidentally spill something."

She glanced over her shoulder. It had been a long time since he focused his attention on her brown eyes and cherry lips, only now the lips seemed pale. Dark circles rimmed her eyes. "That's all they were, you know. Accidents. I didn't do things wrong on purpose."

"I know. I'm not making a big deal about it anymore."

"You have Stu now. Everything's peachy, right?" She rose to her feet.

"Do I detect a little jealousy?"

"That he's perfect and I'm a slob? Maybe. Anyway, you might as well know, I'm quitting next week. This is my notice."

The news stunned him. Everything had been going so well in the store, he hadn't expected her to quit outright. "Why? Did you find a better job?"

"No. I just think it's for the best. As you can see, I'm not the model saleslady."

Brian caught her hand. The skin felt velvety soft in his. "Rachel, I don't think you should quit just because someone might be a little better than you at what he does."

She pulled her hand away from his. "I was never given a chance. The first mistake I made, you demote me to janitorial duty. Stu comes walking in here off the street and you hand him the cash register key. You hardly know him!"

"He came with an excellent resume. He's worked in pet stores before. Look Rachel, sometimes you have to start at the bottom to work your way up. I once heard a message like that at church. Sometimes the reason God doesn't put us in a position of responsibility is because we aren't ready. Sometimes the training for a position means we have to work in the trenches, like mopping floors or cleaning fish tanks. My training was my home-based zoo. Day after day I cleaned and cared for those animals. I didn't get thanks from anyone. In fact, I got a whole lot of ridicule. But I kept after it. Then God opened the door for me to own Noah's Ark. He knows when you'll be ready for a higher position. But right now, you need to do the best at what you're given." Brian scanned the display. "By the way, I think you're stacking things a whole lot neater than when you first came here."

"I didn't spill anything either," she added with a shy smile that quivered at the corner of her mouth.

"You see?" Brian stepped forward to embrace her. "You're doing just fine." The arms she curled around him felt soothing. He realized at that moment he needed her as much as she needed him.

Rachel slithered out of his arms. A smear of red turned her face into one gigantic cherry. "Thanks. I guess it would be wrong to quit. After all, this is the job God gave me when I didn't have any work. Okay, I take back my resignation."

"Good. We'll celebrate. A jog around the block with Spot. Then a stop for a sundae. My treat."

Rachel laughed. "You're on!"

To Brian's amazement, Spot acted the perfect angel as far

as dogs were concerned. He heeled when ordered and walked at a proud pace, never breaking once into a run. "Are you sure this is the same dog?" Brian asked.

"Same dog. He likes you."

"I never had a problem with animals liking me. Just humans."

Rachel eyed him. "Really? But you and Bob are good friends."

"He's it. The one and only. Amazing how we bumped into each other in college. We've stuck it out all these years, too. Now he's this bigwig in computer repair and I'm the peon with my animal store."

"I hardly think someone successful in business is a peon. It takes a lot of planning and know-how to make it in the world of business. I hear that most businesses shut down after only a year. You've had Noah's Ark going how long?"

"Three years. Three years and still kicking."

"Then you've already beaten the odds. That says a lot right there. And besides the fact," she said lowering her eyes to stare at the sidewalk, "you have Stu now. It can only get better."

"I have you and Stu," Brian corrected. The statement sent her dark eyes darting upward to meet his. "Every joint supplies, as the Bible says. In this business, you need everyone helping to make it work."

Rachel sighed. "I just hope I'm doing the right thing by staying on." She paused for a moment. "But I do have a question. My position in the store wouldn't have anything to do with Bob, would it? I mean, I know he helped you buy the place. Are you keeping me on because of him?"

"Well, I. . ." Brian halted, wondering how this came up. "Look, I'm getting hungry. Let's leave pooch, er. . . Spot at home and go get some ice cream."

To Brian's relief, Rachel let the question go and put Spot in the fenced yard. When she returned, they began walking down the sidewalk toward the ice cream shop. To distract her from further questions about Bob, Brian talked about his days with his menagerie at home, along with asking Rachel about her encounters with pets. Only when they reached the doors of the ice cream shop did Rachel bring up the topic.

"You never answered my question, you know."

Brian could feel himself turning red. He looked away. "What question? You mean, how I was able to endure the hostility of my sister with a house full of animals?"

"No. . .if you've kept me on because of Bob."

Brian kicked a stone into a ditch. "Okay, I'll be honest. Yes, I did hire you because of Bob. He asked me to. What was I going to say—'No Bob, even though you did foot the down payment to start the store'? I couldn't do that. Besides, I needed the help. It saved me from interviewing a lot of would-be employees. He came up with the suggestion and I took it."

"And I'll bet you've been regretting the decision ever since," Rachel finished. "Look, I'm a big girl, Brian. You're the boss. You can let me go if you want. I know I've made some big blunders, even though the Bible does talk about forgiving mistakes and going on."

"And that's what I've done." Brian reached out to grab

hold of the door leading to the ice cream shop. Several kids pushed by him, along with their mother. One kid stepped on his foot. Brian cringed at the throbbing pain in his big toe. "Look, are we going in or not?" *Before I get another toe mashed.*

Rachel shrugged her shoulders and went inside. They stood staring at the selections for a long time. Again Brian felt a flush fill his face. He knew what Rachel was thinking—that they were only here for ice cream because of Bob, that everything he did for her was because of Bob. *But those cherry red lips are Rachel's alone,* he told himself, eyeing the picture of a sundae topped with a huge maraschino cherry. *And so is the perfume.*

"What are you having?" Rachel asked.

"Cherries. . . ," he said, "that is, a sundae with cherries on top. I love cherries." He stepped up to the counter and gave his order. Rachel ordered a thick shake made with cookie chunks. She opened her purse to pay, but Brian quickly thrust the bills on the counter. "My treat. And no, it's not because of Bob. I plan to break free from him, starting right now."

Rachel stared at him before her cherry red lips broke open into a smile.

Four

B ob, this is a surprise," Brian exclaimed when Bob appeared in his store one day, dressed in an expensive suit with a briefcase clasped in one hand. Brian glanced nervously at Rachel who was replacing gravel inside an aquarium. He wondered what Bob would think—watching his sister performing menial jobs like cleaning bird cages and siphoning out old aquarium water. He moved to the rear of the store. "Hey, Rachel, would you mind holding down the cash register so I can talk to Bob?"

"Bob's here?" She squealed like a little girl and hastily threw the aquarium cover in the direction of the tank. The cover missed the target and fell to the floor with a clatter. "Oops, sorry."

"Don't worry about it." He swiped up the cover and replaced it on the tank before looking over to find brother and sister engaged in noisy dialogue. No doubt Bob was here for his monthly chat about the store finances, even though he was a week early for such a discussion. The two of them met monthly to discuss operating budgets versus the profits generated by the store, and to pitch new ideas. While waiting for the reunion between the siblings to conclude, Brian generated a few forms from the computer database. Since Stu came on board, the last few weeks had seen the store profits skyrocket. No doubt Bob would be pleased.

The sales ventures had gone well also. Brian sold the Great Dane puppy in just a week for double the price paid. Even now, Brian could hear the faint meow of a kitten they had recently acquired, and the yipping of another puppy—a cocker spaniel. The increased stock included a variety of both fresh and saltwater fish, exotic birds, albino rats, and two ferrets that lounged in the small hammocks Rachel had made for them. Brian took one look at her face, puckered into a smile while the furry friends played on the hammocks, and felt his heart bounce in response. Every day he realized more and more how attracted he was to Rachel. Soon he would have to summon the courage to ask her out on a real, honest-to-goodness date instead of these mad dashes around the block with Spot.

"I need to talk to you, Brian," Bob said.

"Sure, c'mon in. I got the data all ready for you."

Bob took a seat across from Brian and briefly scanned the reports. "Looks like you're turning in a good profit." He exhaled a sharp sigh. "I almost wish you weren't. It would make things a lot easier."

Brian felt his cheerful expression melt. "What do you mean? I think this is great. It's the start of something big. I can feel it."

Bob laid the papers on the corner of Brian's desk, then sat back with his hands folded. "Brian, I'm not sure how to tell you this."

"Look, I know what you're going to say."

Bob raised an eyebrow. "You do? How did you find out?"

"Well, it's pretty obvious. I know you want Rachel doing more than just cleaning up around this place—and I do let her perform a few managerial tasks. I just found out that Stu, my other employee, is a natural at this job. In fact, he's the one that's made the profits for Noah's Ark over the last month. He suggested the ad campaigns, and even getting a dog or two to sell."

Bob coughed a bit and stirred in his seat. "I'm not here to talk about Rachel or your other employee. I know you have treated her as fair as possible, under the circumstances. I'm glad you've hung in there with her. But that's not what I wanted to say."

Brian felt the tension rippling in the air. "Okay."

Bob squirmed in his chair. "Look, I'm in a tough position. You know that Lester Feldon practically owns this whole block. He's going to tear down this section of Main Street and build a huge computer showroom. He wants me to be his right-hand man. Computers are hot items these days. Customers demand the newest and the best. Feldon told me we would be business partners. So. . ." Bob inhaled a deep breath. "I need to get out of this business deal."

Brian stared in bewilderment. "Huh?"

"I need you to pay off my chunk of the loan for the pet store as soon as possible. I need the money so I can go into business with Lester."

"Are you kidding? I don't have the money to pay off your loan and mine too. You know that. We agreed it would take many years to make this work and. . ."

"The contract we signed stipulates that you would pay off half of it in three years, Brian. I haven't seen a stitch of money."

"Bob, you told me not to worry about it, that it was just a formality. It takes years to get a business rolling. We're talking several thousand dollars here." He began to chuckle uncomfortably.

"Look, Brian, the landlord who owns this place has already sold it to Feldon. In a month, this building won't exist anyway."

"What?" Brian began to choke from the phlegm of apprehension clogging his throat. He reached for his coffee cup that stood empty but for a brown stain inside.

"Like I said, this block is being torn up to build the new computer showroom. If you pay off my part of the loan and find another location for the pet store, you're all set. You'll own the whole thing lock, stock, and barrel. Isn't that what you wanted all along?"

"But you know very well I can't pay you, my own loan, plus find another place to boot. That's impossible!"

Bob lowered his head as if he did know.

Brian leaned over the desk and held out his hand. "Bob, this is an important business venture that we went in on together. You can't turn your back on me." He snapped the papers on his desk. "The profits are way up. We're making headway. Even if we have to move down the street, we'll be okay. Don't give up on this place."

"Brian, I'll make a lot more money with Feldon's deal than a pet store could ever get me. To be honest, this place is a real thorn in my wallet. I'm sorry, but I need to get out of it. Noah's Ark may have to go."

Brian choked again. He reached for the coffee carafe containing old coffee brewed that morning, poured out a mugful, and threw the cold liquid down his throat. *Feldon's gonna tear down my pet store. . . . Bob wants money. . .this is a nightmare. How can Bob do this to me? He's my best friend. . .or was my best friend. Now he's after money like everyone else.*

"I know this is tough, Brian, but you'll make it. You're a survivor."

"I can't afford another location on Main Street if I pay you now. I'd have to move to some shack in the wilderness. I'd need another bank loan. . ." *Two loans,* he groaned, picturing himself drowning in a sea of bills.

Bob shrugged his shoulders. "I doubt you could get another loan from the bank, especially since I had to cover one of your loan payments. That kind of thing goes on record, you know."

"What do you mean? I pay it every month, along with the rent. I may have been late one or two times, but I always get it in."

"The payment from three months ago. For some reason, I got the notice about it. Since I didn't want my credit going up in smoke, I paid it along with the late fee. But I made certain the bank knew it was your oversight."

"But I pay all my bills," he continued, whirling back to the computer. "That was before my computer, wasn't it? My ledger. . .I need my ledger to check this out. But I'm sure I paid it."

Bob shook his head. "You never were very organized, Brian. If it hadn't been for this employee of yours showing up when he did, you might have already hit the dirt. Face it. Noah's Ark has been a fun venture for three years, but it's time to move on. We both learned about running a business. I'm sure I can get you a good position in the new computer store. Dream bigger dreams, Brian."

"You mean your dreams," Brian said evenly, "and Lester Feldon's. Not mine."

Bob rose to his feet. "Anyway, I'm gonna need at least half the down payment like our contract stipulates as soon as possible. Maybe that other guy you hired will take over my loan. And you've got a month to get out of here so they can start tearing the place up. Sorry it's come to this."

Bob walked away, leaving Brian with a sense that he just been pushed off a precipice. He slumped his head in his hands. "Oh, God, why? Why, when everything was going so well? Why?"

"Brian, is something the matter?"

Brian looked up to find Rachel standing in the doorway. All at once he saw a vision of Bob beside the grinning face of Lester Feldon, holding up a sign of triumph over the demise of his precious store. Lester and Bob. Bob and Rachel. Every one of them had ruined his life. "Get out!" he yelled. "I don't need your help anymore."

Rachel stared at him wide-eyed. Her lower lip began to quiver. "Brian, please, what happened?"

"You know perfectly well what happened." He pushed papers to the floor in a fit of rage. "You were in on it the whole time. . .making mistakes so I would look like a fool. You probably messed up my ledger too so it looks like I didn't pay the loan that month. You and your brother—conniving swindlers. . .allies of Lester Feldon. Get out!"

Rachel's mouth looked like the entrance to a huge cave. "Brian, I don't know what happened between you and Bob, but I—"

"Sure," he snapped. "Of course you don't know anything. Little Miss Innocent. Well, you're fired! Go work in Bob's new computer showroom with the dazzling lights and hefty paychecks." His head fell once more into his hands. *I've never cried in my life, but my world has been ripped away. Bob, how could you do this to me?*

At that moment, Brian felt soothing hands wrap around his shoulders. He turned and fell into the tender arms. "What am I gonna do?" he moaned. "It's over. Everything. The store is gone. My life is over."

"It's going to be okay," cooed a soft voice, stroking his brown hair with fingers like a mother comforting her child. "Everything's going to be fine." With that, the figure rose and left.

Brian lifted his face and smelled the hint of flowers in the air. "Rachel, oh Rachel," he groaned. "I need you."

Brian spent the next three days calling and e-mailing anyone that might be able to lend him the money so he could pay off Bob without sacrificing his store's inventory.

He even e-mailed Cathy whom he figured would laugh at him outright if the keyboard contained a "laugh" button. Instead she wrote back and said she was sorry, but all her extra money had to go toward paying off college loans. He called Aunt Harriet in California who empathized with his predicament, but had no money like that to spare. In a last ditch effort, Brian again asked Stu if he wanted a partnership in the business. When Stu heard the store would be bulldozed in a month, requiring them to find a new place, he gave Brian his resignation for a new job at a high-paying pet store in the city.

"You should think about a change too, Brian," Stu said. "I know this is a tough break for you, but maybe your business pal is right. Maybe it's time to think about a new direction."

"There's nothing else I can do," Brian mumbled to himself, staring through glazed eyes at the gerbils shuffling wood chips in their cages, the fish swimming peacefully in their aquariums, and the shelves lined with pet products. He imagined the linoleum buckling and store shelves crashing to the ground under the pressure of the bulldozer. Behind the controls of the machine was Lester Feldon, grinning from ear to ear as he smashed Noah's Ark into a pile of rubble.

At that moment, Brian heard the tinkle of a bell and sniffed the fragrance of flowers. His mind had been so intent on finding another person to help with the loan, he had forgotten about Rachel. He had not laid eyes on her since the day he told her to leave his store. Now the powerful scent of her perfume rejuvenated his weary mind.

"Here," she said, plopping several crisp hundred-dollar bills on the counter.

"What's this?"

"Bob told me everything—how he needs you to pay off his loan and how they're going to tear down the store. This is the money I've been saving to get my own apartment and I. . .well, I sold a few things. I don't want you closing Noah's Ark. Maybe at least you can keep the store going somewhere else." She looked away, but not quick enough for him to catch the glimmer of a tear hovering in the corner of her eye.

Brian stood to his feet and went to her. He wrapped his arms around her, inhaling the flowery fragrance that soothed his aching heart. "Thanks so much, Rachel. You don't know what this means to me."

She wiped a hand across her face. "Sorry, I shouldn't be crying. I'm glad to do it."

"Look, keep your money. Unless God gives me an open door soon, I know this place is a goner." He glanced at the dog food aisle that had grown bare since he stopped ordering stock. "I guess everything in this world must die, including pet stores."

Rachel whirled in his arms, her eyes blazing. "Brian, you're not going to lose this store."

"I don't have much choice. It's already a loss, thanks to good ol' Bob."

"Bob and I had a bad argument about it. I wanted to leave the house, but Bob insisted I stay, especially since I had no money to live anywhere else. He's been so busy seeing Lester Feldon that we haven't even seen each other.

I don't know why he is doing this to you, but he is." She shook her head. "He's caught up like everyone else with the idea of making money. I never knew Bob could be this way."

"I thought he understood dreams," Brian said glumly. "Once he did. The pet store was his idea to begin with. But since I loved boarding animals as a kid, I fell into the position of manager. Bob wanted the store, but he didn't want the responsibility. Now he wants out of the whole nine yards." He paused. Rachel's compassionate face stirred up the guilt in him. All the nasty accusations of Rachel being a co-conspirator in Bob's schemes came tumbling back. "You know, I owe you a whopper of an apology."

Large chocolate eyes and cherry lips that made him think of his sundae long ago at the ice cream shop stared back at him. "Brian, it's okay."

"No, it isn't. I said some pretty rotten things to you when Bob came in here and gave his ultimatum. It was wrong." He stared at the bills lying on his desk. "Now you come in here, giving me all the money you have in the world."

"Brian, I want to do this. I want you to keep Noah's Ark."

"Thanks. You're probably the only one in the whole world who does." He sighed. "C'mon, let's close down early and take Spot for a walk. I need a walk tonight." He whirled to check on the aquariums and cages when he heard a small sniffling voice.

"I–I can't."

"Huh? Why not?"

"I–I. . ." She gave a wail and hurried out of the store.

"Rachel? Rachel, wait." He raked a hand through his hair in confusion and scanned the store before turning the sign to CLOSED and locking the door. Outside, a refreshing breeze caressed his face. He glanced up and down the sidewalk in front of the store, looking for the petite young woman with brown hair flying in the wind. "Oh, Rachel, where did you go?"

After scanning Main Street, he jumped into his car and made for her house, cruising around the block in search of her familiar face. At last he found her race-walking along the cement sidewalk, puffing hard from the exercise. He rolled down the window. "Rachel!" She leaned over to catch her breath while Brian parked the car and headed toward her. "Why did you run away like that?"

"S—sorry," she sputtered. "I just had to."

"Look, I hope you're not mad at me for what I said."

"No, it's not that. It's just. . ." She gulped. "I really shouldn't tell you this."

"Tell me what?"

"I don't have Spot anymore. I sold him to a family friend who always thought the world of him. The guy gave me fifty dollars. Pretty generous."

Brian's jaw dropped. He stood there, dumbfounded.

"That's why I took off when you mentioned Spot. I did it—"

"For me and my store," he finished. "I don't know what to say."

Rachel shrugged her shoulders. "It's okay. I wanted to do it and you needed the money. But I—I do miss Spot."

Brian took her in his arms. In the past he wanted to

kiss Rachel for the attractive cherry red lips and pleasing perfume, but at this moment, he kissed her for the feelings welling up in his heart—for the selfless love she had shown and for the love overflowing within him.

"Was that my thank-you?" she asked breathlessly, with a smile on her face.

"I guess it was. I can't believe what you did. I'm still in shock. Now I know what Jesus meant when He talked about the widow who gave more than anyone after she put a coin in the treasury. Bob gave from what he had. You gave from your heart. Spot meant more to you than anything."

Tears glimmered in her eyes. "Maybe. But it was the right thing to do."

Five

For the next few weeks, Brian felt as if he were living in a fog. He held a big sale at the store to liquidate his stock and made enough money to help pay off Bob's loan. After that, no money remained to start up the store in a new location. He roamed the empty aisles that contained a few leftover items. Spilled bottles of dog shampoo created a rainbow effect of yellow and green on the shelf. A few leashes hung from pegs. Several shelves contained lizard supplies. There were bags of instant ocean to create a saltwater environment and boxes of cat litter. A few fish still swam about in two lighted aquariums with bright red tags boasting fifty percent off. Even at a buck a fish, he found no one willing to buy them.

Guess I'll have to start a little pet store at my house, he thought. The mere notion sparked a new set of worries. How would he pay the rent and utilities for the small two-bedroom place where he lived? How would he pay off the remainder of the bank loan for the store? Maybe he should look into work in the city as Stu suggested, but that would mean leaving this small town. Brian shook his head. The weight of everything left him feeling depressed.

He sat down at his desk with a *thud*. His whole world had crashed around him, thanks to Bob in his fancy suit. Lester Feldon always wanted the pet store driven off the face of the earth and he used Bob to do it. Feldon the snake and Bob the two-timing weasel, united together to see his dream cut to pieces.

The tinkle of the store bells interrupted his brooding. He lifted his head to find Rachel carrying two bags. "I brought dinner," she announced.

"I'm not hungry. Besides, you don't have the money. Bob must've tipped you."

She blinked at the remark. "I have money. I'm working at a drugstore. I didn't happen to tell you."

The aroma of Chinese food sent the juices swirling in his mouth. He had to admit he was starved. She opened the bag and took out the container of rice and a box of Mu Shu Pork, his favorite. From another bag she removed bottles of springwater.

"Thanks," he said shortly, wishing he was in a better mood.

Rachel glanced around the near empty store. "I know this is a sad time, Brian, but it will get better." She reached over and took his hand. "Remember how you told me that God starts us off in the lowest positions before promoting us to bigger ones?"

"Yeah, but I thought this was it. Now everything's been ripped away. Where did I go wrong, Rachel? Maybe I was too much into making a buck, like Bob. I used to get so worried about the money you were wasting with your little accidents. Maybe God is punishing me now for it all."

"God isn't punishing you. I think He's getting you ready for something even better. Maybe He had to take away Noah's Ark to get your eyes on something else."

At that moment, Brian's gaze was focused on Rachel. "I don't see anything on the horizon."

Rachel scooped out the Chinese food onto the paper plates she had brought along. "It takes time. I think He will tell you what it is in His timing." She bent her head and prayed over the food while asking God to enlighten Brian with the plan for his life.

Brian absorbed the prayer into his heart. Maybe he had spent too much time and effort in this place rather than focusing his time and effort in God. Maybe God did have to strip away everything he loved to show him that Brian doesn't live by the "bread" of Noah's Ark Pet Store, but by God Himself. And didn't he say a long time ago at the ice cream shop that he wanted a break from Bob? *Okay God, I'm slowly getting the message,* he said quietly in his heart. *I know You sent Rachel here to open my eyes. And I know You're closing Noah's Ark for a reason. But I need to know what You want me to do. Please show me where I go from here.*

The days leading up to the final closing of the store were some of the longest in Brian's life. Each day he stared glumly at the date circled in red on his calendar—the day he would close the doors of Noah's Ark for good. A few customers had graced the doorstep, looking for any last minute deals left from the sale. Along the front windows of the store hung the huge orange signs that read, GOING OUT OF BUSINESS. Brian hated the signs. They were like billboards advertising victory for Lester Feldon. One day he strode over to the windows and tore down the signs. At least he would have some measure of decency in his last days. No more would he advertise his defeat to every person that walked down Main Street.

While he ripped one of the signs into small pieces, the door to the shop opened. The breeze nearly swept him off the small stepladder. He heard a gasp of disbelief.

"Oh no!" came an elderly voice. "What is happening here?"

Brian looked into the startled eyes of Mrs. Wilson. Her cane shook like a tree branch caught in a March wind.

"What are you doing, young man? Where is all the dog food?"

"Sorry, Mrs. Wilson, but I'm closing the pet store."

"Closing! But you can't. You're the only place where I can buy dog food for Sparky! What am I going to do? How is Sparky going to eat?"

Brian shrugged his shoulders as he crushed the remnants of the GOING OUT OF BUSINESS sign into submission. "Guess you'll have to travel to Richmond if you want real dog food from a pet store," he told her glumly.

Mrs. Wilson stared at him and shook her head. "I can't go to Richmond! It's too far away! You have to stay open."

Her insistence nearly caused him to smile. "I wish I

could, Mrs. Wilson. Lester Feldon on the board of super-visors intends to demolish this section of the business district to make way for a new computer store." *And I'll bet a million dollars my store is the first one he bulldozes.*

Mrs. Wilson pointed her cane at him. "That's terrible! He can't close down the only pet store in this community. You know, I'm the president of the Senior Citizens Club. I'll take a few ladies and go right over to his office and complain. We poor widows count on our pets to help us, and we count on you to supply the food. He has no right to interfere."

"You can try, but I think he's pretty much made up his mind."

"Humph. We'll see about that." She squinted at the bare shelves. "Don't you have any dog food left?"

Brian trotted to the rear of the store and picked up the last ten-pound bag of food. "All I've got is this, Mrs. Wilson. I had a big sale last week and got rid of most of my products."

She sighed. "I guess I'll have to take it. Sparky needs food. Only I don't know where I'll buy food for him from now on. He hates that terrible food they sell in the super-markets. I just know he'll starve to death if you don't keep this place open." She opened her purse and counted out the money.

"You gave me too much," Brian said, handing back a few bills. "The food is half price."

Mrs. Wilson peered over her glasses. "Half price? I don't understand. I've never paid half price."

"It's a going-out-of-business sale, so everything is half

price. Can I deliver it to your apartment after work this evening?" In an afterthought he added, "Let me know if there's anything I can do at your place while I'm there."

"That would be fine. Thank you." She stared at him for a moment or two, ready to say something, then nodded. "Thank you again, young man." She turned and ambled out the door, dragging the cane with her.

Later as he was closing up the shop, Rachel arrived from her job at the drugstore. The sight of her and her warm smile renewed his spirits. "It doesn't look like you sold too much more," she noted.

"Just a bag of dog food today."

Rachel tipped her head. "I'll bet it was Mrs. Wilson."

"Good guess."

"And I'll bet she wants you to deliver it."

"Presto. Another good guess." He picked up the bag of food, along with materials to be thrown into the Dumpster behind the store. Out of the corner of his eye, he saw a piece of paper lying on the floor. He swiped it up. "Well, I'll be. The loan payment I forgot to pay that one month when good ol' Bob picked up the tab." He crumpled the bill in his hand, sensing the despair overshadow him once more. Choking back the emotion, he turned to Rachel. "Hey, can you check to make sure the front door is locked? Though I don't know why I bother. There's nothing left to steal. Whatever the burglars want, they can have. It'll take a load off my mind."

Rachel quickly complied before following him to the rear exit, helping him carry out old cardboard boxes and plastic cartons. "Bob said he got your check."

"Mail sure is fast when you don't need it to be," Brian answered, refusing to look at her while he tossed the garbage into the Dumpster. "I remember ordering stuff for my pet store and the mail would take its grand old time. I mailed that thing to Bob only yesterday."

"I can tell you, he's not very happy. He took one look at the money, then plunked himself down and buried his head in his hands. I don't think he likes what's happening, Brian."

"That makes two of us. Look, if you want me to start feeling sorry for him, check back with me in a few months. In fact, make it a year."

"I know it's hard. I wasn't expecting you to feel sorry for him. I just wanted you to know he wasn't waving the check in the air, gloating over the fact he got the money from you."

"Are you two still talking?" he questioned, unlocking the doors to his blue compact.

"Yes. We're civil with each other. He's told me a few things about the plans for the store. Then he picked up his zoology book from college and began thumbing through it."

Brian raised an eyebrow, accompanied by a frown. Why on earth would Bob want to pick up the book that reminded him of the class where they began sharing ideas for a pet store?

"He's really hurting, Brian."

"Bingo. Two of us again."

Rachel settled into the front passenger seat and buckled the seat belt. "Maybe once everything cools down, you and Bob can get together and talk things out."

"That will be a snowy day in July," Brian retorted, maneuvering the car onto busy Main Street. He couldn't think of one nice thing he'd say to Bob, other than calling him a modern day Benedict Arnold. The last few weeks had not been prime time to think of nice things. Brian could only think of his dreams being tossed into a Dumpster and his life a void of emptiness with nothing left to fill it.

They arrived at the Cedar Apartments to be greeted by Mrs. Wilson's dog, Sparky. "Oh, what a sweet dog," Rachel cooed, scratching the mutt behind the ears.

"Thank you for bringing the dog food, young man," Mrs. Wilson said before staring over the tops of her glasses at Rachel. "And who's this? Your girlfriend?"

Brian felt a flush crawl into his cheeks. "Uh. . .Rachel is one of my employees. Or former employee, I should say."

The elderly lady shook her head. "It's so sad about the store. Come in and sit down. I'll get you some lemonade."

Brian sat on the sofa while Rachel wandered into the kitchen to help Mrs. Wilson pour the lemonade. Through the doorway, he could hear the women jabbering about the pleasant weather and how it was perfect for walking dogs. "You must have a dog," Mrs. Wilson said to Rachel.

She looked back at Brian through the kitchen doorway. "Well, I did. A friend has him now."

"I couldn't live without my Sparky, could I, Sweetie?" The dog barked in response, then stood on his hind legs and begged for a treat. "Oh, he wants a cookie. Can you give him one, Dear?" she asked Rachel. "They're over in a tin on the counter."

"Yes, Ma'am." As Rachel began opening the tin, the dog hurried over to her side and stood on his hind legs with a red tongue hanging nearly to the floor. "There you go, Sparky." The dog snatched the treat with skill. "Good boy."

"I'm so glad to be around young people who love animals," Mrs. Wilson mused as they sat together in the living room. "You know, I tried reaching Mr. Feldon's office. The secretary said he was out all day, visiting the architect."

Brian could already picture his beloved Noah's Ark Pet Store overwhelmed by the huge sprawling megalopolis created by Lester Feldon, complete with blinking neon signs.

"I just can't stand the thought of having to buy food for Sparky at one of these supermarkets," Mrs. Wilson continued.

Brian coughed and returned his glass to the table. "Mrs. Wilson, I'd be glad to go find the nearest pet store and get the food for Sparky. You have been a valued customer of Noah's Ark since I opened it for business. It's the least I can do."

Tears began to fill her gray eyes. "That's so nice of you, young man. I—I don't know what to say."

"I'm glad to do it." Brian inhaled a deep breath. "I need to stop moaning about the store and find a new meaning for my life. Noah's Ark is gone for good. Tomorrow I'm going to scan the classifieds for a new job. Maybe I'll even do a little dog-sitting for people when they go on vacation. And I can run errands if needed."

"You can help here, too," said Mrs. Wilson, rising to her feet. "I have my list for you. The toilet seems to be running and I know I'll never get the people in this place to fix it. I have another loose curtain rod from when Sparky pulled off the curtain with his teeth. You know, I had to swat him with my morning newspaper. I hated doing it, but he must learn."

Brian grinned at Rachel who gave him a dazzling smile in return. He then followed Mrs. Wilson into the bathroom where rushing water greeted him. An hour later, they emerged from the apartment with a plate of gingerbread cookies Mrs. Wilson had baked earlier that afternoon.

"What a sweet lady," Rachel mused, "and a sweet dog, too. I can tell she thinks the world of you. Just the way she looked at you when you were explaining to her about the running toilet, why, you could've been her son."

Brian chuckled. "Right. Maybe I should head down to the courthouse and switch my name to Brian Wilson."

"You mean a lot to her," Rachel insisted. "And when she gave you that plate of cookies, I knew she made them just for you. Does she have any family?"

Brian pondered the question while unlocking the car. "I don't really know. She never mentioned having family in the area. Once she talked about her husband Joe. He was a World War II vet. 'Stormed the beaches of Normandy,' she said proudly, 'and got a bullet in his leg for his trouble.' He died ten years ago, I think she said. A heart attack or something. She said it was the most peaceful passing she'd ever seen. He just went to bed one night and never woke up." Brian scratched his head. "But she never mentions children. Maybe she didn't have any."

"What a shame. Anyway, I'm glad you helped her out. And that offer to drive to a pet store just to buy special food for her dog—that was so sweet."

Rachel's voice tinkled like bells in his ears. *You're sweet too*, he thought as they drove away. *I don't know anyone who would've stood by me through all this*. But Rachel had, through the good, the bad, and the ugly. She had stood by him, unwavering, even when he said nasty things to her and booted her out the door. She even sold her dog for him. He had to wonder what motivated her to do all those things.

Brian drove on until he turned onto her street. When he arrived, several large, expensive automobiles were parked in the driveway. Bob's house was lit up like a Christmas tree with light gleaming from every window. Several men in suits stood on the front porch, sipping coffee. Brian inhaled a sharp breath. "Looks like ol' Bob is throwing a 'Death to Noah's Ark' party.'"

"I guess he is." Rachel shrank down in her seat. "Drive on, Brian."

"What?"

"Just drive on. I don't care to be there right now. You can drop me off in the park or something."

"I'm not going to leave you in the park when it's getting dark out." He placed his foot on the accelerator and drove on. After several turns, he ended up at a familiar stomping ground—the ice cream shop. "Guess we can bury our sorrows in ice cream."

"There's nothing better," Rachel said, allowing him to open the door for her.

When she rose to her feet, they stood but inches apart, staring into each other's eyes. He then bent his head over hers and kissed her, oblivious to the horns beeping at them and customers staring as they walked toward the store.

Rachel pulled away and giggled. "Couldn't you have thought of a more private place than the parking lot?"

Brian looked heavenward to find the huge white streetlamp blaring down on them as if they were onstage. "I'm not worried. All I see is you, Rachel. This may sound strange, but the best thing that could've happened to me was Bob."

"Bob turned his back on you."

"Maybe, but without him, I would've never met you." He took up her hand and gave a squeeze. "Even if everything else has fallen apart in life, and the animals have gone to the happy hunting grounds, one person has stood by me through it all. And that person is you. Rachel, will you stand by me for the rest of your life?"

Rachel gasped. "Brian—you can't mean. . . Are you proposing to me? Here?"

A car drove up and parked right beside them. Kids hollered out the open windows.

"Okay, so I'm not very tactful. In fact, I'm as blunt as a dull razor. But I can't help how I feel. God brought you into my life. Even when there was no one left, you were there."

"Excuse me," said the driver, trying to wiggle his way out the door of his car, followed by a group of rowdy kids who pushed and shoved.

Brian took one step to the side but never lost sight of

Rachel. "I used to think that animals were the only ones who cared for me. Can you imagine an iguana caring about me?"

"You mean Charlie? No, I couldn't." She laughed, only to pause when his hand began caressing her cheek.

"Charlie doesn't have soft skin like this. It's more like sandpaper—that is, if you're quick enough to duck his tail."

"Brian, you're something else. There are so many things I love about you."

"Good. You said the magic word. Love. So what do you say we make a commitment to spend the rest of our lives together over a couple of hot fudge and cherry sundaes? I'm sorry I don't have a ring yet. Once I get a job and. . ." He never finished the statement. Rachel had been slowly pulling him toward her during the conversation and now planted a warm kiss on his lips that sent his pulse racing. Forget the sundaes. No cherries and hot fudge could top this moment.

She drew away. "I'll say yes, but only if you promise to hold off on a wedding until we have some financial security. I don't want to have to work when I have kids. I want to stay home with them."

"Sure. Wow, I never thought about kids. Guess they're better than puppies, aren't they?"

"Of course, Silly." Rachel poked him in the ribs as she led the way to the ice cream shop. "Though they do like to play. And sometimes they make a mess."

"At least they don't chew up shoes."

Her warm laughter filled the empty void in his heart until he nearly felt like skipping to the counter to order their sundaes. "This is great. Once I get you that engagement ring, we'll go see my aunt Harriet in California. She'll never believe what I've done."

Rachel gave him a quizzical look. "Why go see an aunt who lives all the way in California?"

He eyed the sundae pushed before him on the counter, dripping with hot fudge, and with a large maraschino cherry parked on top. "She's the only one in my family who ever really cared anything about animals. She used to send me money as a kid to feed my strays. When I called her about the pet store going under, she said she wished she had the money to send me. I want to tell her in person how we met—in my pet store of all things. She'd love it." He glanced back at Rachel, thinking, *I want to show you off to the world. You mean more to me than this crummy ol' world.* He vowed to always remember this day, especially when the time came for his beloved store to meet Feldon's bulldozer head-on. On that day, he would think of Rachel.

After the pet store closed for good, Brian refused to drive down Main Street. The news gave updates on the new computer showroom under construction. Brian found odd jobs and ran errands to the city of Richmond to buy food for Mrs. Wilson's dog. The elderly woman thanked him profusely, called him her angel, and gave him presents—usually baked goods. He saw Rachel nearly every day, and even ventured over to Bob's house once in a while to pay her a visit. Whenever Bob was in the house, he went to his office and closed the door, never materializing once during Brian's visit. Brian thought of knocking on the door and asking Bob how he was doing, but he decided against it. Instead he kept his thoughts focused on Rachel.

Brian returned to his two-bedroom place that night to find newspapers scattered across the living room rug. Daily he searched the papers of neighboring towns, looking for anything that might meet his qualifications as a onetime business owner. Odd jobs wouldn't cut it, especially for a wedding. Except for the high-paying computer jobs offered by Feldon's new business, there was nothing.

"I won't stoop to that," Brian declared when he settled his sights on the day's classified section and an ad for Lester Feldon's business that took up half a page. "I know nothing about computers, anyway. Just the idea of working over the foundation where Noah's Ark once stood— it isn't possible. Oh, God, please, I need a breakthrough."

Just then, the phone rang. Brian lumbered over and swiped it up. "Hello? Yes, this is Brian Davis." Pause. "Sure, I know her very well." His jaw dropped. "Oh no! When did this happen? Yes, okay, thank you. I can come tomorrow if you want. All right, thanks." He replaced the receiver with a *clunk*. "I don't believe it."

"Brian, I don't believe it!" Rachel's shocked voice echoed over the phone line.

"Yeah, the attorney called me. Mrs. Wilson died the day after I delivered Sparky's food to her place. A neighbor found her in bed. She must have passed away in her sleep. Wow, just like her husband. She always thought that was the most peaceful way to go." He paused. "But that isn't all.

Before she died, Mrs. Wilson left specific instructions with her attorney. . .and some of it has to do with me."

"With you? I don't understand."

"Neither do I, but I meet the attorney tomorrow. Can you come with me? I could use the support." His heart warmed when Rachel stated emphatically that she wouldn't do anything less. After he replaced the phone, Brian began thinking about Mrs. Wilson and her dog, Sparky. What had become of Sparky after her death? Brian picked up the phone and began calling around.

At last he discovered Sparky at the SPCA. "Don't you do anything with him," he instructed the woman on the phone. "He belonged to a sweet old lady. I used to feed him all the time. I'm coming right now to get him." Brian flung the phone into the cradle and dashed out the door. When he arrived at the SPCA, a chorus of barking dogs greeted him.

"I'm glad you want him," the lady said when they arrived at Sparky's kennel. "I'm grateful when people come to adopt the animals here."

Brian looked down at the dog who lay on the floor of his cage with his head resting in his paws, looking forever like a mournful pup grieving the loss of his mistress. "Poor guy," Brian said softly, scratching the dog's ears. "Bet you don't have any idea what's happened, do you? All you know is that you woke up one morning in this place." He thanked the lady profusely, informing her that he would now be a lifetime contributor to the efforts of the SPCA, before leading Sparky out with a piece of rope he found in his car. The dog seemed to remember him and ambled along by Brian's side.

"Wow, I just thought of something, Sparky," Brian said out loud. "I've got to get you some food, don't I? Can you believe I was once a pet store owner but I don't have a morsel of dog food in my house?" He glanced toward the shopping plaza across the street before recalling how much Mrs. Wilson detested supermarket brands. "C'mon, Sparky. We've got a long road trip ahead of us. I just hope I can make it to the pet store in Richmond before they close."

The next day dawned bright and sunny. Sparky had spent a peaceful night at the foot of Brian's bed, and now Brian was jogging with him down the block for a bit of exercise. The dog bounced beside him with his ears flopping, wearing a huge smile as if delighted with this new arrangement. When they arrived home, Brian barely had enough time to shower and dress for the attorney's appointment. "Okay, Sparky, I expect you to be on your best behavior," he informed the canine, checking to see that the new stainless steel bowls contained fresh water and kibbles. The dog stood there, politely wagging his tail. Brian dashed out of the house and into his car, arriving at Rachel's house with a few minutes to spare. He laid on the horn for Rachel to appear, only to find Bob stepping out the front door.

"Oh no," Brian mumbled when Bob approached the car, holding a cup of coffee in his hand.

"Lookin' pretty spiffy there, Brian. Where are you off to?"

"The lawyer's office."

Bob raised an eyebrow. "So you got a lawyer, eh? Guess you won't tell me why, will you?"

"You guessed it."

"Well look, I know you don't like what I did to you and the pet store. You probably think I'm enemy number one."

"Actually, Bob, you did me a huge favor."

"Huh?"

"You got my eyes off my store and onto more important things." He smiled big time when Rachel emerged in a rose print dress, looking like a garden of colorful flowers in the warm sunshine. "If you'll excuse us." He rose out of his seat and opened the passenger door for her. Bob stood there, staring blankly, as Brian hurried to the driver's side and drove away.

"Boy, have I got a surprise for you!" Brian sang. "But I'll tell you point-blank, it isn't an engagement ring. . .at least not yet."

"It's not? Well then, maybe I won't want it."

"Oh, you'll want this all right. Trust me." He turned onto Main Street and for the first time, saw the huge brick complex now occupying the place where a strip of small businesses once thrived. Brian slowed the car before the spot that used to be Noah's Ark Pet Store. Now it was the main entrance to the new computer showroom.

"Brian, don't do this to yourself," Rachel said softly.

He swallowed hard. "I'm okay," he managed to choke out. "I just wanted to see it one time, or at least the place where it once stood." Memories flooded him, of the first time he used the shiny silver key to unlock the front door, his excitement at the first shipment of tropical fish, and then Rachel, smiling with her set of cherry red lips while holding a squirming ferret she had named Jacob. He shook his head, wishing he had captured all those moments on film. Now all he had were memories.

Brian turned the car around and sped off, stopping when he reached the lawyer's office. Once inside the plush waiting area lined with leather chairs and huge murals of modern art, he felt his throat tighten. *Why on earth am I here?* He felt the reassurance of Rachel's hand on his. They entered the office of the lawyer to find a large man in a tight suit, sitting behind a desk. When they occupied their seats, the man rattled off a bunch of legal jargon, telling them that he was Mrs. Wilson's attorney and how he had found Brian's name listed in her will.

"So here it is," the lawyer said, shoving a piece of paper across the desk.

Brian blinked in confusion. "Did I miss something?"

"This is a deed Mrs. Wilson signed over in your name before she died." He smacked the paper with his fingers. "If you want to sell it, it should bring you a healthy profit. Land is going like hotcakes down there, with many of the elderly buying up parcels to build winter homes. In fact, my own mother lives there practically the whole year-round. Winters up north aggravate her arthritis."

Brian picked up the paper with a shaky hand.

"What does it say?" Rachel asked.

"Mrs. Wilson owned some land in Florida," he said slowly. "She inherited the land after her late husband died. Sh—she willed it to me."

"What?" Rachel nearly ripped the paper out of his

hand. Together, they held onto each corner while reading the contents. "I don't believe it!"

"I can handle all the legal aspects of it," the lawyer said, straightening his tie. "Saves you the trouble of hiring your own attorney. Of course, a percentage of the sales will need to pay a small legal fee, but that's of little concern at this point. However, I think you could easily walk away with a good fifteen to twenty thousand dollars, considering the location and all. It's prime real estate."

Brian gulped. His hand began to visibly shake. "F–fifteen to twenty thousand dollars?" He left the office, reeling from what had happened. "Fifteen to twenty thousand. . ." He drew a breath. "Dollars."

"Oh, Brian, this is so wonderful!" Rachel exclaimed, throwing her arms around him.

"I don't believe this," he murmured as they drove off. "Rachel, do you know what this means?"

"I think I can guess," she said, leaning her head on his shoulder. "God just gave you back Noah's Ark."

"Even better. It means we can get married."

Rachel jerked her head upright. "But Brian, God gave you back your money. Now you can start your pet store over again, in a new location. It will be better than ever. Noah's Ark Pet Store II."

"Maybe one day. But right now, I'm just glad we'll have the money to get married. That's all that matters." He turned into the driveway of his home. When they emerged from the car, a round of barking greeted them.

Rachel crinkled her forehead in confusion. "Brian, what's that noise?"

"Come see." When Brian unlocked the door, Sparky ran to greet them with a slobbery lick to their hands. "Remember Sparky, Mrs. Wilson's dog? I rescued him from the SPCA."

"Oh, Brian!" Rachel stooped to scratch the dog around the ears. "I can't believe this. First the money, and now a dog. God has restored everything that was lost!"

Brian nodded. "He sure has. It's amazing. When we get our eyes off ourselves and onto others, that's when things really start to happen."

Rachel rose to her feet with tears swimming in her eyes. In that face, Brian did not see chocolate syrup and cherries, but love and a hope for the future. The kiss they shared topped the best ice cream sundae he had ever eaten.

LAURALEE BLISS

Lauralee is a prolific writer of inspirational fiction who divides her time between writing, homeschooling, church activities, gardening, and caring for the pets. She lives in Virginia with her husband, son, a coonhound, and two cages of gerbils. Her other published works include two novels for **Heartsong Presents**—*Mountaintop* and *Behind the Mask,* a novella, "Island Sunrise," in the *Rescue* collection by Barbour Publishing, and an inspirational romance, *Blackberry Hollow,* from MountainView Publishing. Lauralee welcomes you to visit her website: http://lauraleebliss.homestead.com/lrbweb.html

Walk, Don't Run

by Pamela Griffin

Dedication

Special thanks to my faithful "critters"—Tracey B., Tamela H. M., Paige W. D., and Mom.

Also with abundant gratitude to my Savior, Jesus Christ, Who has endured my foolishness more times than I can count and has gotten me out of more scrapes than I care to remember. As always, I give You the glory for every good thing in my life.

My dear brothers, take note of this: Everyone should be quick to listen, slow to speak and slow to become angry.
JAMES 1:19

One

T his isn't happening to me," Kerry Bradford
mumbled. She put her forehead to the sliding
door, cupped her hands around her mouth, and
tried to make her nineteen-month-old niece understand
her. "Come on, Ashley, Honey. Unlock the door for Aunt
Kerry."

In response the toddler waved her hands, letting loose
a stream of garbled words Kerry could barely hear—
thanks to the thick pane of glass separating them—then
fell to her bottom.

With dismay, Kerry realized Ashley's wet bathing suit
would stain the cream-colored carpet, since the child had
plopped down in the flower bed before Kerry managed to
get her inside. And if there was one thing Kerry's sister
was fanatical about, it was the cleanliness of her home.

Kerry again tugged the handle, but the door remained
stuck. Why did things like this always happen to her?

Seeing Ashley would be no help, Kerry looked over
the rail of the second-story apartment balcony, the heat
of the Texas sun searing her already punished skin. She

supposed she could climb over, jump to the ground and try to avoid the prickly shrubbery directly beneath.

She put a leg over the rail then changed her mind. What good would that do? She had locked the front door when they returned from the pool. Then, too, she didn't want to let Ashley out of her sight. And those man-eating bushes looked as if they'd inflict even more damage to her roasted skin. But she couldn't wait out here all day!

Kerry blew out a frustrated breath, setting her sparse, honey-colored bangs to flight. She supposed she could use a neighbor's phone and call a locksmith, then force herself to eat humble pie when Dani found out. Shaking her head, Kerry could almost hear the caustic comments her sister would hurl her way.

Wait a minute. Wasn't maintenance equipped to handle situations like this? And they could get here before a locksmith, nullifying the possibility of Dani ever finding out.

Positive she'd arrived at the best solution, Kerry debated a safe way to drop to the ground, when a young boy wearing a pair of bright yellow swim trunks ran past.

"Hey! Hold on a second," she called after him.

He stopped, looked behind him, then his gaze lifted to Kerry. "Yeah?" he asked a bit on the irate side, obviously upset about his delay with the cool water.

Kerry put on her most winning smile. "I need your help. I've locked myself out of the apartment and there's a baby inside. I need you to find maintenance and tell them apartment 236 needs a key." Seeing irritation cloud his face, she coaxed, "There's a tall iced lemonade in it for you, if you help me."

The boy, who looked thirteen—though the hair shaved on both sides of his head was probably an attempt to make him look older—scrunched up his freckled face. "You're locked out, huh? No kiddin'? Did you try jigglin' the handle?"

Great. Of all the people in the apartment complex she had to wind up with a miniature Bob Vila. "Yes. Look, please hurry, will you? I've been out here close to fifteen minutes now."

"Okay, Lady, okay. Don't blow a gasket or anything." Turning, he slowly ambled toward the office.

Kerry let out a sigh of relief mixed with frustration. Kids today! She moved back into the shade by the door and smiled at her niece. "I'll be there soon, Honey."

"Ashy go poo-ee."

The faint words struck a chord of sheer terror in Kerry's heart. "Ashley, no! Go to the potty chair in the bathroom like a good girl. Go on, Honey! Hurry!"

A relieved look crossed the toddler's features, and with a sinking realization, Kerry knew it was too late. She closed her eyes and remembered a greeting card she'd recently designed.

On the front was a drawing of a bedraggled woman who stood under a broken umbrella, rain soaking her, a bag of soggy groceries clutched in one arm—several items having fallen into the many puddles surrounding her—and a tiny dog viciously tugging at one of her rubber galoshes. Above were the words "Having one of those days?" And on the inside "Into each life a little rain must fall, but don't give up. The Son will soon shine for you again."

It was how Kerry, or "Hannah Kerry," as she signed her artwork, designed her cards. Something humorous on the front—laughter was often the best medicine—with something inspiring on the inside to encourage and a Bible verse relating to the theme underneath.

Maybe one day I'll design a card relating to this, Kerry thought. *That is, if I live that long. If Dani gets home early and takes a look at her carpet before maintenance gets here, I'll be pushing up daisies.* What was taking so long?

She moved to the balcony, again eyeing the evil-looking shrubbery beneath her. Or was it some kind of cactus? Whatever it was, it didn't look like something she wanted to tangle with.

A beautiful collie trotted by on the sidewalk. Recognizing the dog as belonging to Sarah, the apartment manager, Kerry leaned over the rail with relief. She'd never met Sarah, but had seen her walk her dog from a distance and had heard about his strong penchant for car rides. "Here, Prince! Here, Boy!"

Tail wagging, the collie stopped and stared up at Kerry with soft brown eyes, tongue lolling.

"Good dog!" Kerry's heart soared. "Go get help, Prince. Get Sarah."

He plunked his hind end down on the cement and scratched behind a pointed ear with his hind leg.

"No, Prince. Get help. Go on, Boy!"

Yawning, the collie took a few steps her way, stretching his forepaws out, and then flopped to his stomach.

"Stupid dog," Kerry muttered. "You're sure no kin to Lassie."

Prince rolled on his back and wriggled in the short grass.

"Go on, Prince. Get maintenance. Get Sarah. Emergency! Fire!" Kerry thought a moment then smiled. "Go bye-bye!"

The dog rolled over as if someone had set fire beneath him. He shot up and ran toward the office, barking with enough frenzy to alert the entire neighborhood.

The smile faded from Kerry's face. What good had that done? Prince probably wouldn't come back, much less lead someone here. More than likely he'd jumped through the rolled-down window of Sarah's car, waiting to "go bye-bye."

Jake Hartwell swam one last lap, planted his hands on the hot cement bordering the pool and hoisted himself from the cool water. Not bothering to towel off, he sauntered to a lounge chair and lowered himself to it. Eyes closed, he swept one hand over the pavement beside his chair until his fingers connected with his sunglasses. Snatching them up, he put them on.

Ahhhhh. . .this was the life. Sarah was right. He had needed a vacation. . . .

Frantic barking interrupted his peaceful slumber, and groggily he opened one eye. Through the black rails of the pool fence he could see Sarah's collie bounding past, white and golden brown fur flying. Jake forced himself to sit up and leaned on his elbows.

"Prince! What's wrong?"

At Jake's shout, the dog stopped his mad trek toward the office and faced Jake, still barking.

"Stop that, Prince!"

The dog took off in the direction from which he'd come, then whipped around and barked again.

Prince's strange behavior alerted Jake to trouble. He rocketed up, grabbed his T-shirt, and hurried to the gate. It wasn't like Prince to disobey a direct command.

"Okay, Boy, show me what's up."

The collie took off running and Jake followed.

After several minutes passed with no sign of help, Kerry decided none was coming. She'd have to take matters into her own hands and pray the bush didn't slice her to smithereens.

Muttering, she cast off her flip-flops and threw one leg over the rail, holding the hot banister in a death grip as she straddled the bar. Carefully she brought her other leg around and over the banister. Now facing Ashley, she forced a bright smile in the toddler's direction. Ashley pressed her palms and face to the glass, blue eyes wide, as though she questioned her aunt's sanity.

Kerry was beginning to do the same.

Biting her upper lip, she took one bare foot off the solid and secure edge of the wooden balcony, lowering it at an angle while bending her other leg, trying to escape the sharp claws of the monster bush. A needlelike prick bit the sole of her foot.

"Ouch!"

Hurriedly she pulled her leg up and looked over her shoulder and down. Maybe if she scooted over and tried with her other foot. . .

She inched over a few feet and lowered her left leg at an even greater angle, relieved when she touched only air. . . But, come to think of it, what good would that do? She couldn't jump backward in an arc, could she? She was no gymnast. Maybe if she turned around, with the rail to her back, and jumped forward as far as she could. The worst she could do was sprain an ankle. At least she hoped that was the worst she could do. . . .

"Hey! What are you doing up there?"

The abrupt masculine shout startled Kerry, and she almost let go of the rail, which had grown slippery. She brought her leg back up and turned her head to look over her shoulder.

A part of her mind quickly assimilated that the bronzed face turned upward was attractive, the hair dark and wavy, and though she couldn't see the eyes because of the sunglasses he wore, she imagined them to be brown. Deep brown.

"Just stop right there and don't move," he drawled.

Don't move? What did he think she was going to do—a jig on the edge of the balcony, with the rail for her partner? And then it hit Kerry. He thought she was trying to break into the apartment! Well, if she were a felon, she'd sure have more sense than to take a flying leap over a cactus with bare feet in broad daylight, wearing only her yellow maillot and cover-up. Couldn't he figure that out?

Swallowing her irritation, she forced herself to remain

calm. "Could you please help me? There's a baby inside. And both doors are locked."

"A baby?" He frowned as he studied her. "I'll have to get the spare key."

He loped off, Prince running after him, and Kerry took the welcome opportunity to climb back over the rail and assume a more dignified position. The dog must have alerted someone in the office after all. Or had the young boy been the one to locate maintenance? No matter, help had come.

"Won't be long now, Sweetie." Kerry smiled at Ashley and talked nonsense with her through the glass while she waited.

The man from maintenance was back within minutes, taking the outside stairs leading to Dani's front door. Kerry heard him mumble something about ditzy blonds, and how people shouldn't leave small children alone.

His words stung and added to her already bad afternoon. *He acts as if I left Ashley there on purpose!*

After he let himself into the apartment and opened the sliding glass door, Kerry lit into him. "If it hadn't been for that stupid door, this wouldn't have happened! The lock slips, and when I came outside to put the beach ball in the storage shed, Ashley closed the door on me. The door *you* were supposed to have fixed three weeks ago!"

His mouth tightened into a narrow line, but his voice came level. "You reported this three weeks ago?"

"As if that's news to you," Kerry huffed as she stepped inside. "I happen to know it was called in at least four times! But each time they say the same thing—'There are other work orders, and they are taken in the order they're received.' "

For the first time she noticed his dark hair was beaded with drops of water. Her gaze traveled to the damp T-shirt covering a muscular chest, a pair of wet neon swimming trunks underneath, then to his bronzed legs and thonged feet.

"Oh, yes, I can see you maintenance men are kept quite busy," she murmured with a saccharine-sharp twist. "Well, if you can spare me a few minutes, would you mind taking a look at the door? I have to take care of the baby."

Turning away before she said something she'd really regret later, Kerry scooped up her niece from the soiled carpet. She stopped short when she noticed a strange man in faded denim coveralls at the open front door. "Can I help you?"

"You send for maintenance?"

"Yes, but your partner's already here."

He lifted a thick dark eyebrow and looked beyond her to the man in swimming trunks jiggling the door handle.

"Give me a Phillips," Kerry heard the first man order tersely from behind her.

Anxiety covered the newcomer's face, but he lifted the requested tool from his tool belt, walked to the porch, and handed it to the other man.

Kerry headed for the baby's room; she couldn't put off what needed done any longer. "I have to get her into some dry clothes," she threw over her shoulder. "I'll be back in a minute."

She knew she shouldn't leave two strangers unsupervised in her sister's apartment—even if they were from maintenance—but she didn't know what else to do.

She divested Ashley of her swimsuit, powdered her, stuck her in a pair of training pants, and snapped her into a pink sunsuit in record time. Cradling her niece on her hip, Kerry hurried for the front room.

Both men had gone.

Two

K erry stopped scrubbing the stain on the carpet. Sitting back on her heels, she eyed the chic woman holding Ashley in her lap. "What have you done with my sister?" she said, only half joking.

Ten minutes earlier Dani had come home, and after hearing a short version of Kerry's eventful afternoon, had offered the response, "I'm sorry you had a bad time." No tongue-lashing. No cruel jibes about Kerry's clumsiness. Nothing.

Dani grinned. "I had a good day, that's all." She kissed the top of Ashley's blond head and lowered her to the carpet. "I'm glad Joe finally fixed the door. But, to be fair, he is kept pretty busy."

"He didn't look too busy to me." Rekindled anger at the easygoing maintenance man put a bite to Kerry's words. "Unless, of course, he was saving a drowning victim—a marvelous coincidence he just happened to be wearing swim trunks at the time."

Dani looked in Kerry's direction. "Swim trunks? Really? I've never seen Joe in anything but a faded pair of coveralls—even on the hottest days."

A niggling dread sprouted inside Kerry. "It must have been his partner then. The man you described came later."

"His partner? You mean there were two of them?" Surprise lit Dani's blue eyes as she leaned forward.

The dread began to crawl upward and grow vines. "Yeah, of course that's what I meant," Kerry said with forced casualness, sponging the stain again. "Both maintenance men came to the apartment. One right after the other."

"Kerry," Dani explained softly, as though she were speaking to a child, "Joe works alone. He's been alone since Phil quit two months ago."

"Well, maybe this man was his new partner."

"Swimming during working hours?"

Kerry stopped furiously dabbing at the carpet. "Oh, Dani, what have I done?"

"You tell me."

"Well, I didn't exactly lop off his head, but I *was* pretty hard on him," Kerry admitted. "You don't think he was a Good Samaritan answering the call of a woman in distress, do you? Maybe a tenant?"

Dani shrugged, her brows drawn together. "One thing still puzzles me. How was he able to get a key? If Sarah had been there, she wouldn't have given it to just anyone."

Kerry groaned. "What if he was the assistant manager?"

"No, I don't think so. From what I've seen, Sarah works alone—except for when Tina comes on weekends. I know them both well from the times I've had to go plead for more time to pay rent."

"Oh." Brow creased in puzzlement, Kerry idly sponged the stain again. Just who was Mystery Man?

"But hey—I just thought of something," Dani said. "As glad as I am to see you, why did you come? You usually don't pop over without calling first. And what happened to the baby-sitter?"

"I sent her home after I got here. And I came because I want you to join me in a celebration dinner."

"Celebration? What are you talking about?" Dani's voice grew impatient. "Will you stop scrubbing that silly stain and come talk to me? I'll rent a steam cleaner to take care of the carpet later."

Smiling at the alien words coming from her super-neat sister, Kerry joined her on the couch. "Mike called this morning. He said a few stores outside the area are interested in carrying my line. Customers have been asking for my cards."

"Oh, Hon, that's great!" Dani hugged her. "Didn't I tell you it would happen one day?"

"Yes." Kerry winced at the contact with her burnt skin and pulled away.

"You don't have to be a Rembrandt or Monet to touch people, Kerry. I just wish you'd see the difference you make—and stop being so down on yourself all the time."

A half smile crooked Kerry's lips. "I guess. Well, anyway, I want to take you and Ashley out to dinner, to celebrate."

"That sounds great, since I have tomorrow off. Just let me change into something more casual."

"Huh-uh," Kerry said, her smile growing. "No fast food for us. Tonight we eat in style."

Dani cast a doubtful look at her daughter, who had pulled the kitchen rug over herself and was rolling around on the tile floor. "I don't know, Kerry. Ashley's a little young for one of those ritzy places, don't you think?"

"Hey, they have high chairs in the nice restaurants, too. At least I know they do at the one I plan to take you to. Come on, it'll be fun—a change from hamburgers and fries anyway."

"I haven't been to a nice restaurant since Bruce and I split up. . ." Dani's voice dwindled, a wistful expression covering her face. Kerry felt a stab of anger at her absent brother-in-law. Dani made an obvious effort to cheer up, and Kerry could have applauded her sister.

Dani lifted her shoulders and offered a wavery smile. "So, when do we eat?"

Forty minutes later they walked across the expanse of wine red carpet, following the waitress to a far booth in the nonsmoking section. Though the Thursday night crowd consisted mainly of couples, young and old alike, Kerry saw a family with a child close to Ashley's age and noted Dani's obvious relief.

Dani settled Ashley in a high chair and took a seat across from Kerry in the last booth, facing the glossy paneled wall. Kerry took her seat, giving her a wide view of the classic, dimly lit restaurant. The waitress returned, bringing tall glasses of ice water. After scanning the menus, Kerry and Dani made their selections and nibbled on buttered rolls the waitress had set before them.

"Mmm," Kerry murmured as she pulled apart the

warm crust and popped it into her mouth, chewing with delight. "Nothing like fresh baked bread." Her eyes cut to the other side of the restaurant and she choked.

"Kerry, what's wrong?"

She shook her head, reaching for the water glass. In her haste, she knocked it over, spilling ice and cold water onto the table and carpet. Ashley banged her roll on the table and squealed with glee. Dani righted the glass, then took her cloth napkin and sopped up the spill as best she could.

"What's wrong with you? You look like you've seen a ghost. Hey—that's my water!"

Kerry batted the air with one hand, trying to hush her sister while taking several gulps from Dani's glass to clear her throat. "It's him—I'm sure of it," she croaked when she could speak coherently. "No! Don't look! Just keep talking to me and pretend like nothing's wrong."

"What are you talking about? We have Niagara Falls running off our table and you want me to pretend nothing's wrong? I need to get more napkins to clean up this mess." Disgusted, Dani made as if to rise, but Kerry reached across the table and clutched her sister's forearm in a death grip.

"Don't move, Dani. It's him, I tell you."

"Him who? Stop acting like we're in some kind of spy movie and make some sense, please!"

Kerry took a calming breath. "Mystery Man. You know, the Good Samaritan who fixed your sliding door."

Dani's eyes took on a look of interest. "He's here? Alone?"

"No, he has a woman with him."

"Really? Where?" Dani started to turn her head, but Kerry dug her nails deep into her skin. "Ow! Watch it with those things—they're lethal weapons!" Seeing Kerry wasn't going to back down, Dani relented. "Okay, listen. I'll head to the waitress's station and get more napkins. On my way I'll casually take a look and see if I recognize him. Okay?"

"Do I have a choice?"

"Well, we could wade through dinner, but I'm not really dressed for it," Dani said with a deadpan expression, motioning to her beige silk shirtwaist.

"Okay, okay. But try not to draw attention to yourself."

Dani's brow sailed upward. "Me draw attention to myself? Listen to who's talking! I didn't spill *my* water on the carpet."

"Just go," Kerry muttered. "He's sitting two booths down, across from us, next to the large hanging plant with dark purple flowers."

She watched as Dani gracefully stood and glided past. The man didn't look up once; his gaze seemed permanently fixed on the stunning brunette across from him. Kerry felt something clutch her chest when she noted how the woman laughed at something the man said and he smiled in return. He was obviously enamored with his companion.

Dani soon returned, a strange look on her face. Kerry clenched her hands while Dani sopped up the rest of the spill. "Okay, tell me. I'm prepared for the worst," Kerry mumbled.

"I have no idea who he is, but the woman with him is Sarah, my apartment manager," Dani said under her breath. "I can see why you're so nervous, though. He's a hunk, isn't he?"

"Your apartment manager?" Kerry furrowed her brow, ignoring Dani's observation. Great. She'd told off the boyfriend of her sister's apartment manager. Now what should she do? Go apologize? Run for cover? Forget the whole thing and hope he would, too? The best solution would probably be to eat fast and leave before her presence was discovered, since she and Dani had each taken their own car. How embarrassing this day had turned out!

The waitress arrived at that moment with their entrées, and Kerry lit into her meal as if it were her last. After shoveling the second bite into her mouth, she sheepishly realized she'd forgotten to pray. Quickly she offered a silent prayer asking God for guidance to get her out of the mess she'd made, as well as asking Him to bless the food.

Ashley loudly claimed she had to "go poo-ee," and Dani plucked her out of the high chair and hurried to the ladies' room.

Jake looked away from his dinner companion and across the room—into a pair of startled sky blue eyes staring at him from a sunburned face. A few electric seconds passed before the blond lowered her gaze. She snatched up the glass from the place setting across from her, took a huge drink, then put it down and became extremely interested in salting and peppering her baked potato. He winced at the exorbitant amount she used. She seemed agitated, and Jake couldn't help but feel there was something familiar about her. . . .

"Jake? Are you listening?"

With difficulty, he brought his attention back to Sarah. He took a bite of his crème de menthe chocolate pie, "uh-huhing" and "huh-uhing" at the appropriate times.

Loud coughing from the blond's booth brought his gaze back her way. She waved her hand in front of her mouth, took another long drink of water, then brought her napkin to her lips and coughed into it. Her gaze swung to his. Embarrassed to be caught staring, this time he looked away and concentrated on draining his coffee.

After the waiter had given him his second refill of decaf, a loud clatter came from the front of the restaurant. Jake swung his head to look, as did the other diners.

The same blond crouched on the carpet, helping to retrieve spilled dishes from a waiter's tray. She profusely apologized to the young man, who gave a stiff nod and hurried off once the wrapped silverware and glasses had been returned to their place.

Jake watched the petite woman straighten to a standing position and smooth the skirt of her blue sundress. She turned her head, her eyes widening when she met Jake's. Quickly she averted her gaze. Like the shutter of a camera capturing a still shot, memory clicked inside his brain.

"Jake, you're not listening to me," Sarah complained. "And don't say 'uh-huh' again or I'll deck you."

"Sarah, do you know that girl over there by the entrance—the blond with the bad sunburn?"

"Hmm. . .it's too dark in here to tell for sure, but it looks like Danielle Amberton, one of my tenants. Why?"

"We had a little run-in earlier today," he mused.

"She's married and has a daughter named Ashley," Sarah said in a warning tone. "Dani's had it rough, but I've tried to help when I can by extending her rent." Sarah pinched his arm. "Hey there—Earth to Jake. Did you hear me? She's a married woman."

"I heard you." Jake moved his arm out of Sarah's reach, his eyes never wavering from the blond. Curious, he watched her dig through her shoulder bag for her wallet, pay the cashier, then grab her keys and hurry out the restaurant's leaded glass door. He wondered where her husband was, remembering he'd seen two place settings at her table, as well as a high chair. Her spouse was probably tending to Ashley and giving his wife a chance to eat in peace. How well Jake remembered those days. . . .

He dragged his gaze from the door and concentrated on finishing his meal.

"So, Jake," Sarah said, a hint of impatience in her voice. "Just when are you planning to visit Ruth? I know you've been busy, but don't you think you should at least call her? It's been two months."

He grimaced, her words slicing him to the raw. "Drop it, Sarah. I don't want to talk about it right now."

She sighed. "That's the problem. You never do. . . ."

Guilt wrapped sharp talons around Jake, and he called himself a fool and a coward. But he just wasn't ready to deal with personal issues yet, especially those concerning Ruth.

Green. Not brown. They'd been green. A light, vibrant green that could be seen even in a dimly lit room, two tables away. Kerry sighed, remembering those eternal seconds she'd looked into Mystery Man's eyes. They'd stared at one another, across the crowded room, as if they were the only people there. . . .

"With his date sitting in the booth across from him," Kerry wryly added aloud. "What's wrong with me?" She shook herself out of the mental trance she'd been in for the past five minutes, grabbed her mug, and took another sip of cappuccino.

She hoped Dani wasn't too terribly upset to return to their booth and find Kerry gone. At least she'd obtained the presence of mind to pay for their meals first. But there was no way Kerry could have remained with Mystery Man in full view and aware of her presence—not after the way she'd let him have it earlier today.

"Some celebration dinner," she muttered.

Sitting at her drawing table, Kerry tried to concentrate on her latest project, but tonight was hopeless. Her gaze went to a small figurine of a dachshund wearing a straw hat that she kept nearby. Her great-aunt Harriet had made it for her years ago, and Dani had received a squirrel in an old-fashioned bonnet.

Kerry's lips turned up a fraction. Good ole Aunt Harriet. Her boundless energy and "Go get 'em!" attitude never ceased to amaze. The woman was nearing seventy, yet she still dabbled in all sorts of crafts, as well as being an active member of the SPCA.

Kerry continued to stare at the ceramic dog with the soulful brown eyes. If only there were something she could do to apologize. . . .

A crazy idea struck. Her smile growing wider, she put a fresh piece of paper on the table, picked up her drawing pencil and set to work.

Bleary-eyed, Kerry tumbled out of bed the next morning, wincing. She slathered a large amount of the aloe vera lotion Dani had lent her over her pink legs and arms, then headed for the kitchen.

She'd labored most of the night on her personal project, though she knew she might never get the opportunity to deliver her work. Chances were she'd never see Mystery Man again. But at least she'd made an effort to apologize, and that gave her immense satisfaction.

Kerry fixed a mug of French vanilla cappuccino and trudged to her small breakfast niche, grabbing a sack of store-bought donuts on her way. She opened the package and frowned. Stale.

Sighing, she dunked the rock-hard frosted ring into her mug. The phone insistently jangled, sounding louder than usual in the still apartment. Startled, she glanced at her wall clock. Eight-forty—too early for phone calls. It was probably just an overeager telemarketer or a wrong number. She listened as her recorded voice gave the usual message. A beep, then, "Kerry? Are you there?"

Kerry let the donut sink and snatched up the phone. "Dani? You sound terrible. Is something wrong with Ashley?"

"No. . .she's fine. Oh, Kerry!" Dani broke down cry-ing—a characteristic totally alien to the persona of the cool businesswoman she showed the world, even those closest to her.

"Dani, I'll be over in ten minutes. Just hang tight. Whatever it is, it can't be that bad."

Kerry replaced the phone without waiting for her sis-ter's response and sprinted for her room. She changed into a T-shirt and a pair of cut-off jeans that ended above the knees, frayed threads at the bottom. Sliding her feet into her flip-flops, she grabbed her purse and headed for the door, praying all the while her last words to Dani proved true.

Three

O h, Kerry, what am I going to do? I'd so hoped. . ." Dani's words broke off, and she dazedly shook her head.

As a Christian, Kerry knew she was supposed to exhibit God's love and mercy to the unlovable. But when she thought about the creep she had for a brother-in-law, that truth fled her mind.

Frowning, she studied her sister's pale face and watched her smooth the letter in her lap with an odd, detached movement. It was the first communication Dani had received from Bruce in months. How like Bruce to turn the tables and place all the blame on Dani.

Kerry struggled for words of comfort. What did one say to a person who'd just had her world turned upside down and been tossed aside like yesterday's garbage? "Dani, I know this is hard, but maybe it's for the best—"

"Don't." Dani put up a staying hand, her eyes sparking with confused pain and anger. "Don't give me one of your pat Christian sayings, telling me how much God cares about me and all that tripe. Save it for your greeting cards.

I didn't believe it six months ago when Bruce walked out that door, and I certainly don't believe it now when he's filing for divorce. Is it God's will that Ashley no longer has a father in her life?"

"Has she really ever had one?" Kerry asked softly. Dani seemed to wilt before her eyes, and Kerry cringed, realizing she'd just made things worse. "Oh, Dani, I'm sorry. I just don't know what to say. I'm better at writing words of encouragement than speaking them, I guess. But I do know one thing. God hurts for you. I know you don't want to hear it, but He understands how you feel. Those closest to Him betrayed Him, too. If you'd only turn to God and let Him help—"

"That's nice, but no thanks. And I don't want to hear any more about God." Dani woodenly rose from the sofa and walked to the sliding door, her features frozen into a hard mask.

Kerry bit her tongue, stilling the words she wanted to say. The Holy Spirit needed fertile ground in which to work, and Dani was anything but that. As she did every day, Kerry silently prayed her sister's heart of stone would turn to flesh, yielding and receiving God's Word and God Himself.

"What say I get breakfast?" Kerry grabbed Ashley from the playpen. "I'll take this little angel and we'll go get a dozen glazed donuts. Why don't you go jump in the shower or something and relax while we're gone?"

"Is that a nice way of telling me to go jump in the lake?"

"Dani! You know I didn't mean anything like that—"

"I know, I know." Dani let out a weary sigh and turned from looking outside. "I also know I've been horrible lately. I don't see how you could stand me. Bruce was right when he said—"

"Bruce was not right!" Kerry interrupted, fuming when she remembered the insensitive words her brother-in-law had scrawled. "About anything. You are sweet and fun to be with and one of the best mothers I've known! So don't you believe one word that jerk said!"

Dani gave a wisp of a smile. "You never did like him much, did you—since that first day I brought him home to meet Mom and Dad? Well, I guess you were right. . . Okay, Mother. Thanks for the pep talk. Now go get the donuts—and make mine chocolate with chocolate sprinkles. And throw a few bear claws in, too. I feel the need to indulge." Turning, she headed for her bedroom.

Kerry's anxious gaze followed until the door softly clicked shut. Conflicting emotions warred within her. She didn't want to leave, though she knew her sister wasn't the type to do anything rash. Yet Kerry knew Dani needed time alone to vent. Kerry had seen how hard Dani tried to hold it in, not wanting to break down in front of her daughter.

Forcing a smile to her face, she looked to the toddler in her arms. "Ready to go with Aunt Kerry and get some donuts, Precious?"

"Do-na." Ashley smiled and clapped her hands.

Crrrrunch!
The sickening noise and sudden jarring sensation

made Kerry's stomach somersault. Ashley squealed, thinking it a game. Hands shaking, Kerry put the car in "drive" and inched forward, returning to the curb. She shut the motor off and closed her eyes, wishing she could sink into the dark upholstery and disappear. The feeling intensified when she opened her eyes and looked in the rearview mirror—spotting the owner of the sleek blue sports car she'd just backed into. Her gaze whipped to the windshield.

"Oh no," she mumbled. "God, what did I ever do to deserve this day? Can't we go back and start all over again? Is this some kind of penance I'm destined to serve?"

Seconds later she heard a tapping on her window. She clenched her teeth. "Well then, Lord, please help me through this."

Turning in the seat, she looked over her shoulder, not facing the driver's window. "Be right back, Ashley," she said cheerfully to the toddler in the car seat. Ashley clapped her hands, her eyes sparkling. At least the baby wasn't harmed.

Mustering courage, Kerry unbuckled her seat belt, opened the car door, and stepped outside.

"You!" Mystery Man's eyes widened in recognition. "Tell me, Lady," he drawled, "is your middle name 'dangerous'?" He motioned to his dented car. "Or is this in retaliation for failing to fix your sliding door on time?"

"I'm sorry about your car, but I do have insurance," she said, trying to remain calm and levelheaded. "I don't have anything to write on, but if you get something, I'll jot down the phone number of the agency and any other information you need."

He casually leaned against her silver compact, crossing his arms as if he had all the time in the world. "A pen will do."

Puzzled, her mind visiting several places at once, Kerry retrieved her shoulder bag and absentmindedly pulled out a pack of gum, offering it to him.

His brow lifted. "I think a pen might work better."

"Oh! Sorry," she mumbled, her face heating as she pulled out the desired item and handed it to him.

He uncapped the pen and held his hand out in front of him. "Now, the name and phone number of your insurance agency for starters," he said, pen poised above his large palm.

Kerry gave it to him, the absurdity of the situation almost making her laugh. Here she stood, alone in the parking lot with the attractive mystery man whose passenger door she'd just smashed, rattling off information—which he then wrote onto his open hand with a leaky pen. But this was anything but funny.

Afraid to look but knowing she should, Kerry cast a hesitant sideways glance to assess the damage to his vehicle. A monstrous, black-edged silver dent marred the blue paint. *Oh, Lord, how much is this going to cost me. . .?*

"And your phone number?" he asked.

Kerry stiffened. "Is that absolutely necessary?"

"I think so." His clear green eyes didn't give an inch. Green eyes with even lighter green flecks in them, she noticed. She quickly looked down and gave him the number. He handed her back the pen and nodded. "I'll be in touch." Before he walked away, he bent over, looked into the backseat of her car and smiled. "Bye, Ashley."

"Bye-bye." Ashley flapped her hand.

He made it all the way to his car before something occurred to Kerry. "Wait! Don't you need my name?"

He looked at her, his expression unreadable. "Not necessary. I already have that information." He slid behind the wheel and started his car. She watched as he drove away.

Alarm seeped through Kerry. How and why had he gotten her name? And how had he known Ashley's? Dani had said she didn't know him.

Telling herself she was being overly dramatic, Kerry put the car in reverse, this time carefully looking behind her, and headed for the donut shop. At least the incident had helped her forget her brother-in-law, about whom she'd been fuming when she'd backed into Mystery Man's car.

Memory of the little project she'd stayed up almost all night to finish flashed across Kerry's mind. Her hard work was still tucked snugly inside her canvas shoulder bag. Well, this hadn't exactly been an opportune time to deliver it. She should probably add more after today's mishap. Her eyes widened as she glanced in the rearview mirror at her niece.

"Ashley! I just realized—I still don't know Mystery Man's name. But he knows yours and mine. . .strange. He doesn't look like a deranged psychopath or stalker, though looks can be deceiving. . . . But actually he seemed kind of nice, considering. What do you think?"

Ashley squealed, and Kerry smiled.

"My thoughts exactly."

Jake slammed the door of the office and stormed down the sidewalk to his car. Sarah didn't understand—no one did! He didn't want to cause Ruth more problems, and at this point in his life, he was certain to do just that. Besides, he was moving soon. There was still a lot to do.

As he hurried past Danielle's apartment, his gaze lifted to the empty balcony. Unwittingly his mind formed a picture of the tiny but feisty blond he'd rescued. His first sight of her—short pink legs awkwardly groping beneath her while she clutched the rail—had been followed by a glimpse of her face. Her honey-colored hair had been swept back in a ponytail, her blue eyes blazing at him in anger and pale as a Texas summer sky. And the sprinkling of freckles over her sunburned, peeling nose had made her look like a teenager.

Another picture formed of the same blond in the restaurant—this one markedly different. A slim, womanly figure outfitted in a flattering blue dress, the dim light making her thick cascade of hair shimmer like spun gold over her pink shoulders, her eyes wide as she stared at him in recognition.

And the final picture—this one two hours ago when she'd smashed into his car. She'd looked hastily put together—her T-shirt inside out, though he doubted she realized it. Her hair had been uncombed, her bangs falling into those impossibly huge eyes.

Just who was the real Danielle Amberton? The feisty girl from yesterday? The awkward beauty from last night? Or the absentminded woman of today?

"And why can't I stop thinking about her?" Jake muttered. "She's a married woman." Of course, she'd been constantly thrown into his path since the moment they'd met, making forgetting an impossible feat.

Shaking his head, he snapped his keys against his leg. He reached his car and slid behind the wheel, hoping to put his troubled thoughts to rest with several quick laps across the pool at his apartment. A rectangle of white sat underneath his windshield wiper.

Puzzled, he reached out the open window to pluck the mysterious article off his car. He opened the envelope and pulled out a card. A smile tugged at the corners of his mouth.

The caricature of the woman in the drawing bore an amazing likeness to Danielle. So much so, Jake wondered how she'd managed to find such a perfect card. The woman was propped on hands and knees inside a doghouse, a sad puppy-dog expression on her face. Inside, the card read, "I'm sorry. Won't you please let me out of the doghouse? And if you can't forgive me 490 times, could you at least forgive me once?" She had crossed out the "once" and written "twice" above it. Underneath, a Scripture verse stated, "I tell you the truth. Forgive your neighbor not seven times, but seventy times seven." And to the side, she'd written, "Sorry I mistook you for the maintenance man and let you have it. And thanks for fixing the door." Then a postscript underneath—"Sorry about your smashed car door, too. If you need to talk to me further, you have my number or you can reach me through my sister, Danielle. You already know her apartment number."

It was signed "Kerry Bradford."

Jake let out a whoop, startling a middle-aged woman, who'd just parked next to him and was removing several small plastic sacks from her backseat.

"Sorry." He smiled at her and revved up his motor. Feeling much better, he drove out of the parking lot and headed for the interstate.

Kerry stroked shimmering beige polish over her last nail. The phone emitted a shrill ring near her ear, and she jumped, knocking over the bottle. "Great," she muttered, tearing off a paper towel to wipe away the spill. She almost tipped the bottle over again when a deep masculine voice filled her kitchen.

"Hello. I'm trying to reach Kerry Bradford. . ."

Recognizing the voice of Mystery Man, Kerry snatched up the phone. "Hello?" she squeaked, her throat tightening from a sudden fit of nerves.

He paused. "Is this Kerry Bradford?" He sounded uncertain.

"Yes—yes it's me," she said in a rush, then stopped and cleared her throat. "I mean, I'm Kerry Bradford," she said more clearly.

"You have no idea how glad I am to hear that."

"Pardon?" She wrinkled her brow.

"Never mind. Listen; is there a chance we can get together this afternoon? This is Jake—the guy whose car you backed into."

Kerry swallowed hard. "Um, I don't know. I mean I don't know anything about you—except that you're good at fixing doors." *How banal can I sound?* she thought with a wince.

He gave a low chuckle, and tingles raced down her spine.

"No, I guess you don't know much about me. Okay, here's the short version. I like all water sports, I cook a mean filet mignon, and I promise I'm perfectly harmless—someone you'd trust with your elderly grandmother. How about it, Kerry?"

A smile tipped the corners of her mouth. Her name on his tongue sounded wonderful, like warm, rich cream. Instantly the memory that he was another woman's boyfriend crowded her mind. "I'm really sorry. I don't think I can—"

"I need to talk to you about the car," he interrupted.

"Oh. Well, I guess. . ."

"There's a pancake house down the street from your sister's apartment. Know the place?"

"Yes."

"Meet me there in fifteen minutes. Okay?"

"Uh. . .okay. Bye." After hanging up the phone, Kerry stared at it stupidly. Why had she agreed to meet him? If he had something to say, couldn't he just as easily have said it over the phone? Her eyes went wide.

Fifteen minutes! She only had fifteen minutes to get ready and meet Jake! Rushing to her room, she rifled through her closet, trying to find something nice to wear. Something that wouldn't say "I dressed up especially for you," but something besides her casual T-shirt and cut-offs. And it had to be something Jake would think she'd been wearing when he called.

Jake. . .what a nice name. And it fit him.

Kerry lowered the butter yellow sundress she'd selected and stared at the wall. "Why should I care what he thinks of me?" she muttered to the white plaster. "He belongs to another woman." Disgusted with herself, she hung the dress back on the rack and headed for the bathroom to wash her face.

Four

"Y ou look great," Jake said when Kerry slid into the booth across from him. "That color looks nice on you."

"Thanks." Kerry lowered her gaze to the silver urns of flavored pancake syrup, heat flaming her cheeks. She'd told herself when she changed into the yellow sundress that she was doing so only because the restaurant might not let her in with cutoffs and flip-flops. And she'd touched her face lightly with makeup and attached gold hoops to her ears only because the dress needed that extra something. But after seeing the admiration shine from Jake's eyes, Kerry silently admitted she'd done it for other reasons, too. How vain—and foolish—could she get?

"The days sure are getting hot, aren't they?" Unease made Kerry spout the first thing that came to mind.

"Yeah. Looks like we're in for another long Texas summer. At least the storm we had a few days ago cooled things down for awhile."

"Yes. That was refreshing while it lasted."

Fortunately, a waitress came and took their order,

putting an end to the trite conversation. After she left, Jake sent a smile Kerry's way, sending a funny feeling straight to the pit of her stomach.

"You wanted to talk about the car?" she asked in a rush of words.

The smile faded from Jake's face, and he nodded. "About the car. Right. We were so intent on mine, I never noticed if yours was damaged."

"I have a broken taillight, but I have insurance to cover it, and my liability will cover the damage to your car." Nervously she ran her fingers up and down the condensation on her water glass, making runny trails.

"Kerry, relax. I'm not mad," he said in that deep drawl of his. "In fact, I'd like to take you out sometime."

Kerry's hand jerked against her glass. This time, thankfully, she didn't knock it over. She put her hands in her lap, clasping them tightly to avoid any possible accidents. "I don't think that would be a very good idea, considering."

He looked at her, clearly puzzled. "I'll admit we didn't get off to a flying start, but we're getting along great now." His brows drew down in a frown. "You're not married, are you?"

Her head shot up. "No!"

"Divorced?"

"No way."

"Jealous boyfriend waiting outside?"

His casual question irked her, and she seriously considered dumping one of the syrup tureens over his head. "You're one to talk," she bit out, her tone frosty.

"Excuse me?"

"Nothing." She averted her gaze.

"What did you mean by that?" he insisted.

She exhaled a loud burst of air. "I mean I don't think it would be a good idea to go out with the boyfriend of my sister's apartment manager. I wouldn't want to cause trouble for Dani. She has to live there. And besides that, I don't steal other women's boyfriends."

His mouth dropped partway open and he stared at her as if she'd grown another head. "Where'd you get a crazy idea like that?"

"Like what?" Kerry grew more uncomfortable with each passing moment. She wished the waitress would come back soon.

"That Sarah is my girlfriend?"

"I saw the two of you at the restaurant last night. Okay?"

"Oh, I see." He settled back and crossed his arms over his chest, his steady gaze never leaving her flushed face. "And so you just naturally assumed Sarah and I were a couple?"

"You were acting awfully chummy," she shot back. *This is ridiculous. I sound like I'm jealous, which couldn't be further from the truth.*

Quickly she backpedaled. "Look, if I was wrong, I'm sorry. Even if I was right, I'm sorry. It's no crime for you to date whomever you want to. Actually this whole conversation is pretty silly when you think about it. I've told you why I don't feel comfortable dating you. So that's that."

"Is that the only reason?"

"It's reason enough for me."

"So you'd go out with me if it wasn't for that?"

She raised her chin a notch. "Don't drop your girlfriend on my account, Jake."

"Kerry," he said softly, his twinkling eyes never leaving hers as he leaned closer, put his forearms on the table, and laid his hands down flat. "Sarah is my sister."

"Your sister?" She blinked, feeling as if she'd been mentally knocked off her feet.

"Uh-huh. My name is Jake *Hartwell*. Sarah Hartwell is my sister," he repeated slowly, giving Kerry time to absorb it.

A groan tumbled out of her mouth, followed by an uncertain smile. "It seems I'm always telling you I'm sorry. Dani says I have a habit of running off the deep end and I need to learn to tread carefully. Will you forgive me for jumping to conclusions yet again?"

A slow smile lit his face. "Depends."

"On what?"

"On whether you'll go out with me tomorrow night."

The waitress picked that moment to arrive with their food, much to Jake's obvious frustration. She set the steaming plates of pancakes in front of them, then more tureens of syrup. "Anything else I can get you folks?"

"That'll be all, thanks," Jake said somewhat stiffly.

Kerry felt his unwavering gaze the whole time she poured blueberry syrup over her mound of blueberry pancakes with the blueberry compote and whipped topping.

"How about it, Kerry?" he asked, a hint of impatience in his voice when some time had elapsed with silence between them. "Will you go out with me? To seal the apology and hopefully make a move toward friendship?"

A teasing grin lifted her mouth. "I can think of worse penance." At his raised eyebrows, she laughed and added, "Nothing, just a private joke. Yes, Jake. I think I'd like to go out with you very much."

"Ready for the latest news flash?"

Kerry managed to hold the receiver between her ear and shoulder and slip her arm into the short sleeve of her tawny knit top while emitting a barely discernable, "Sure."

Dani paused. "Is this a bad time?"

"No," Kerry said, before switching the phone to her other ear so she could do the same with the other sleeve. Realizing she was stuck, unless she wanted to wear the phone tonight, she gave a quick, "Dani, hold on a sec," and set the receiver on the table. She pulled the top over her head, smoothed it over her cocoa brown pants, and retrieved the phone. "Okay, I'm back."

"What are you doing over there?"

"Just getting dressed." Kerry popped the cover off her salmon-colored frosty lipstick. Looking in the mirror, she applied it in three quick strokes and compressed her lips. "Did you have something you wanted to tell me?"

"You better believe it. Get this—your mystery man is Sarah's brother. His name is Jake Hartwell." When Kerry didn't reply, Dani insisted, "Kerry, did you hear me?"

Kerry finished smoothing brown mascara over her lashes. "I heard you, Dani, but your news is old." She screwed the top back on. "I already knew."

"How could you?" Dani asked incredulously. "I just found out when I went to pay rent twenty minutes ago. He was sitting in the office, talking to Sarah—"

"He was there?" Kerry asked, suddenly very interested. "Tell me, Dani, what was he wearing?"

"What was he— *What was he wearing?*" Dani said louder as if they had a bad connection. "Why do you care what he was wearing?"

"Just answer the question."

"Oh, I don't know. A gray sport shirt and dark slacks, I think. . . ."

Kerry looked with approval at her casual outfit. Good. And their colors wouldn't clash either.

"But why—"

The doorbell rang, and her heart fluttered. "I can't talk right now. Jake's at the door. We have a date. I'll tell you all about it later." Kerry hung up the phone, silencing Dani's shocked sputtering. Smoothing a hand over her hair, she hurried to the front room and opened the door. Her heart did another somersault when she saw Jake's handsome form on her doorstep.

"Come on in," she said shyly. "I'm almost ready."

With a mysterious grin, he brought his hands from behind his back, presenting Kerry with a brown paper sack. Her brows flew upward in surprise, and he suddenly seemed embarrassed.

"I didn't want to go the usual route with flowers or candy, so I opted for something different. Something perfect for you."

Curious, Kerry opened the small sack and peered

inside. "Blueberries!" she exclaimed with a squeal. "My favorite! Why there's enough here to make two pies!"

"I stopped at a roadside farmers' market on the way over."

She smiled, touched by the kind gesture. "Thanks, Jake. It was thoughtful of you." Her face grew warm as he continued to look at her, his eyes soft. "Well, I'll just go put these in the refrigerator and finish getting ready. I promise it won't take long. Just make yourself at home while you wait. Oh, would you like something cold to drink? I have pink lemonade, or tea, if you'd prefer it, and of course water." At the negative shake of his head, she hurried from the room.

Jake studied the cozy nutmeg and gold apartment. Gold-framed prints of yellow and white daisies brightened the dull walls and matched the thin stripes in the brown plaid couch. A blue vase of sunflowers sat on the cherry wood coffee table, and a hanging plant with small yellow flowers hung from the ceiling.

The apartment reminded him of Kerry. Soft and bright—like spring sunshine. Feisty, yet shy—a real country girl at heart. Yet Kerry also held a womanly allure that set Jake's heart racing. Strange. He'd thought he could never feel that way about a woman again.

Forcing his mind off the past, determined to enjoy the present, Jake moved toward an open door. It obviously wasn't a bedroom, and he didn't think Kerry would mind if he took a quick peek inside. The sunny room looked inviting.

He walked across the shag carpet, past the computer in the corner, to where a table stood beside a sliding glass door. A chipped soup mug, with a wide array of pencils, pens, and other drawing implements, sat on a smaller round table, as did a figurine of a ceramic dog in a flowered hat.

Rays of sunlight highlighted the half-finished project on the larger table's surface. A drawing of a teenager with hair shaved on both sides of his head, his hands up in a questioning pose, his shoulders lifted in a shrug, covered the front. Gold loops studded both ears, and at the top were the words, "Ever wonder what life's all about?" Curious, Jake opened the card. The inside was blank.

His eyes strayed upward to framed collages of similar cards covering the walls, and with surprise he recognized a couple of them. At the same time he realized whose studio this was.

When Kerry came to the door a short time later, he stared at her, still feeling the shock. "You're Hannah Kerry."

She blushed. "I usually keep this door closed. Guess I forgot."

"I shouldn't have barged in. Now it's my turn to apologize." Something occurred to him. "I never did thank you for the card you left on my car. It means even more to me now that I know you personally designed it." He walked to where she stood nervously running her fingers along the keyboard of her computer. "I've received a number of your cards this past year from Sarah—she's a real fan of yours. She likes to try to find your name hidden in the drawings."

Kerry shrugged, clearly embarrassed. "Instead of signing my work at the bottom, I thought it would be fun to hide my name in the drawings, though sometimes I use my initials. It's sort of my trademark, I guess."

"Did you sign the one on the table yet?"

"Yes. But that's just a rough draft. Not the final."

He lifted his brows hopefully. "Could you show me?"

Kerry laughed, relaxing. "You'll have to search for it like everyone else."

A sense of mischief made him move back to the table and sit on the stool, getting comfortable, as if he'd be there a while. "Well, okay. If you're not that hungry, and don't mind the wait—"

"I'll give you a hint," she quickly interjected. "Look at the upper half of the drawing."

Jake studied the paper, finally finding the initials HK in squiggles among the boy's faddish hair. "Hey, that's good. I don't think I'd have found it if you hadn't directed me."

"Yeah, great talent," she rejoined, a hint of sarcasm in her voice. "You want to see real talent? Come with me." She crooked a finger.

His curiosity aroused, he followed her into the hall. On the wall hung a colorful painting of a rain-drenched English cottage and garden after a storm, the sun peeking from the clouds and casting a rosy glow over the countryside. The oil was a wonderful example of light and color, and even though Jake was no artist he could appreciate the peacefulness the painting evoked.

"Now there's a real artist," she murmured.

"Yeah, the guy has talent. But so do you, Kerry," Jake

insisted. His gaze returned to her face. "Your cards bring encouragement. I should know. Like I told you, I received quite a few of them this past year. They helped me get over some rough spots and learn how to smile again. They reminded me there is a God up there Who cares." His voice was in danger of cracking, and he turned back to the painting before he made a fool of himself.

There was a long, uncomfortable pause.

"Thanks for telling me," she said softly. "I'm glad my cards helped you. . . . Well, I'm hungry. Ready to go eat?"

"One more question." He looked at her. "Why don't you go by the name Hannah? It's a pretty name, though Kerry's nice, too."

She sighed. "You really want to know?"

"Yes."

"Okay. You've got to promise, though—no wisecracks." Puzzled, he nodded.

"All right." She bit her lower lip, as though still undecided, then blew out a resigned breath and walked into the next room. Soon she returned with a small wooden plaque and handed it to him. Curious, he looked at it. The name "Hannah" was scrawled in calligraphy at the top, followed by the definition: "Graceful one."

A smile tugged at the corners of his mouth, and he desperately tried to avoid her searching eyes. "You asked," she finally said in disgust, snatching back the plaque. "Dani gave it to me for Christmas one year. She must have meant it as a joke."

He sobered at her words. "No, I don't think so. Actually, the name *does* fit you." At her skeptical look, he continued, "Grace isn't only about outside characteristics, Kerry. It has to do with the heart, too—what makes a person tick. The grace to forgive and the grace to say you're sorry. The grace to lift others when they need a boost—like you do with your greeting cards. The grace to take things in stride when you get yourself into jams and feel like the whole world is caving in. . ."

"Yeah, I did a great job of that the other day," she inserted wryly.

"The grace to take a compliment when one is given." He winked.

Deep flags of red sailed into her sunburned cheeks.

"Everyone has bad days," he continued. "But even when we're at our lowest and strike out, God is ready to forgive and show us mercy. So stop hitting yourself over the head for your mistakes."

Her eyes lit up. "Then you are a Christian! I suspected it, but wasn't sure."

"Yes, although I haven't been going to church as much as I should. I plan to go next Sunday, though. Want to join me? Or would you rather we went to your church?" He said the words as though it were a given she would go with him, and her smile widened.

"You know what, Jake Hartwell? I think I could get to like you."

Grinning, he took her hand. "Ready for that pizza?"

"More than!" An impish gleam lit her eyes. "In fact, I was trying to figure a way to *gracefully* stick that subject back into the conversation."

Jake let out a theatric moan, and she laughed as they

headed for the front door.

They shared a combination pizza then decided to catch a movie. Since Kerry had chosen where they would eat, it was determined Jake would pick the film. She liked it that Jake wasn't the type who had to have his way all the time and that each of them had made decisions on the date.

The sun reached its final descent turning fireball red. A lull entered the conversation, and Kerry stared out the window of the rental car Jake was driving until his was out of the shop. Her mind went to the man beside her. Earlier at her apartment when he'd spoken of how her cards had helped him through "rough spots" in his life, his eyes had been so sad, and she'd wanted to give him a comforting hug. But she was afraid her action would have been misconstrued, so she had resisted. Whatever hurts Jake had carried, she wondered if he'd fully gotten over them yet. . . .

"You're awfully quiet all of a sudden."

At his soft words, Kerry turned to look at him. She liked the smooth, clean-cut angles and hollows of his suntanned features. Dani was right. He was a hunk. "Just thinking."

He cast a curious glance her way, but to Kerry's relief didn't question. "So tell me how you got started in the greeting card business," he said finally.

Kerry shrugged. "It was a fluke. Ever since I was a kid I have preferred making cards to buying them. A friend of mine who manages a Christian bookstore had surgery three years ago, and I made her a card. She liked it, took it to a booksellers' convention along with several others, and found someone there who knew someone who might be interested in representing me."

Jake nodded, and Kerry shifted on the seat so she could see him better. "Turned out there was a struggling new company in Dallas that not only liked my verses, but my drawings, too. They wanted to launch their company by doing something different—focusing on different designers for both prose and artwork. It was a gamble, but it seems to have paid off."

"Are your cards sold nationwide?"

"No, only in Dallas and Tarrant County. But my agent is hopeful. I am, too. The candle shop where I worked up until last month had a change of ownership and all the old employees were dismissed, including me. I'm not kidding myself. I know I'll need to find another job before long. But at least the rent's paid for the next two months."

"I have a feeling your rise to fame won't be long in coming." Jake glanced Kerry's way and sent her a smile that put her head into orbit. "You're good, and your cards encourage. Two pluses."

"Thanks." Thoroughly embarrassed, she decided it was past time to change the subject. "So tell me about Jake Hartwell."

He stared ahead, his expression thoughtful. "What do you want to know?"

"Oh, everything. From what your mother jotted down in your baby book to present day."

He chuckled. "Mom didn't keep records. She was too

busy chasing after me and keeping me out of trouble." He didn't offer further information.

"So you're going to be a tough nut to crack, eh?" Kerry said in her best detective voice, crossing her arms. "All right. I've got plenty of time. First question: Where do you live?"

His mouth tipped at the corner. "On the other side of Dallas, though I'm moving to this area soon."

Kerry's heart skipped a beat. He was moving here. "And what do you do for a living?"

Her question was answered by the sound of "Dixie" electronically bleeping from his shirt. Jake threw her an apologetic look. "Excuse me." He plucked his cell phone from his pocket and flipped it open and on. "Hello. . . Oh, hi. What's up?"

Kerry watched furrows of worry crease his brow. "How'd it happen?" He briefly closed his eyes and his jaw went rigid. "Where are you now. . .? Okay, I'll be there as soon as I can."

He pressed a button, flipped the phone closed, and stuck it back in his pocket. "I'm sorry, Kerry, but I'll have to cut our date short."

"Bad news?"

He hesitated. "Family problems."

"Oh." She fished for something to say. "I hope it's nothing major." When he only nodded, she lapsed into silence.

He pulled into the parking space in front of her apartment ten minutes later. "I hate to just let you off like this, but I really have to run."

"I understand. Well, I had a good time."

"So did I. Bye." His words came distracted.

Kerry watched the rental car rocket from the parking lot onto the main road. She knew she was being silly, but she couldn't help feel the call had been prearranged by Jake and a friend—an out for him in case he was having a bad time on their date. Like some of her former classmates had done in high school. Jake hadn't said anything about future dates before he'd sped away.

"I'm becoming a paranoid idiot," Kerry muttered, disgusted with her selfish thoughts. Remembering how troubled Jake looked before he'd left, Kerry prayed everything was okay.

Five

J ake zipped into the first available parking space and narrowly missed taking the paint off a red truck. He turned the motor off and shot from the car. Hurrying through the automatic doors, he turned right, the antiseptic smell of the well-lit emergency room hitting his senses.

Grimacing, he scanned the full waiting room, at last spotting a white-haired man sitting on a vinyl chair in the corner. Jake sidestepped a woman in a wheelchair and strode his way.

"Where is she?" he asked, not bothering with a greeting. He ignored the curious stares directed at him from that part of the room.

His father-in-law looked up from his magazine, accusation still evident in his eyes. "Oh, hello, Jake. Nice of you to finally show."

Jake bit back a retort. He deserved this man's censure. Robert Lakely had never forgiven him for his daughter's death. . .and probably never would.

"The nurse took her to a room," Robert said, his gaze

going back to the magazine. "Emma's with her."

Jake went to the desk, explained who he was to the receptionist and was escorted down a corridor to a closed door. The woman gave a short knock. Hearing a weak "yes?" she opened the door.

"Daddy!"

Jake held out his arms to the dark-haired, nine year old who hopped off the examining table, her swollen arm in an ice pack, carefully cradled to her chest.

"Ruthie, watch that arm, Dear," Jake's mother-in-law admonished from her chair against the wall. "Hello, Jake," she said with a diminutive smile. At least her eyes didn't accuse. But she'd made it clear from the start that she didn't blame him for what happened to Anna.

"Hello, Emma," he returned while gathering his daughter close, being careful of her arm. "So, my little tomboy hasn't had enough of climbing trees yet, huh?"

"I was trying to get a really big apple," Ruth explained, moisture filling her eyes and following the dried track of previous tears. "I slipped and fell. Grammy says I might have to wear a cast." Brown eyes—wide and trusting—sought Jake's. "Will you take me home now, Daddy? I want to go with you."

Uneasy, he glanced at the CPR chart on the wall, though he kept his arms around her. "Ruth, you know we decided it'd be best for you to stay on the farm until I find us a place. Besides, you wanted to spend the summer with your grandparents. Remember?"

"But why haven't you come to see me?"

Jake fidgeted. He couldn't tell her the truth. That

looking into her beautiful brown eyes reminded him every day how he'd robbed her of a mother.

He was saved a reply when the door opened and a thickset man in a white uniform coat strode in, a clipboard in hand. He looked with some curiosity at Jake then directed his statement to Emma. "X-rays show a fracture. We'll need to put the arm in a cast."

Ruth began to cry, and Jake softly patted her back. He stayed with her throughout the entire procedure and treated her to a strawberry ice cream bar in the hospital cafeteria afterward, while Emma ran to get the prescription filled at a nearby drugstore. Buckling Ruth in the backseat of Robert and Emma's car thirty minutes later, Jake deposited a kiss on her cheek and smoothed back her short hair. Her eyes were full of questions.

"Honey, I promise we'll be together again soon. Daddy just needs time to work things out first. Okay?"

She gave a weary nod, her eyes sliding shut. The medication must have started working. "I love you, Daddy," she said sleepily, then yawned.

Jake's heart lurched at her easy acceptance and forgiveness. Of all the people in his life, he'd probably hurt her the most. "I love you, too, Honey," he said, emotion catching his throat.

Later, inside his apartment, Jake stared into space, his thoughts in turmoil over Ruth. And the past.

It had been one full year since Anna's death. Things had gone from bad to worse in the months before her accident; she'd grown dissatisfied with life, always complaining. Feeling defensive, as if she were casting blame on him,

Jake sometimes yelled at her during their fights then stormed outside to cool off. That last time he'd complained of the house being a wreck and had snidely commented that instead of filling her days watching game shows and soaps, she should do something about it. Oh, how he wished he could take back those words!

He'd returned hours later to find her prone on the bathroom floor, a damp sponge in hand—the lethal fumes from the mixture of cleaning agents she'd used filling the room. Shaken, he'd hurried with her outdoors, into the fresh air. But it was too late.

Sarah told him from the beginning it wasn't his fault, that Anna should have known better than to mix ammonia with chlorine bleach. But Jake hadn't listened. Deep down he knew he was to blame.

It was only in recent months he'd started dating again. The need for companionship had spurred that on, a need Jake often felt guilty about. Kerry had been the second girl he'd taken out. And though she was a walking minefield, promising trouble wherever she went, she made his heart lighter in a way no other woman ever had—both with her cards and her crazy antics. Still, Jake knew it was probably best if he didn't see her again. He didn't want to be responsible for ruining her life, too. Besides, it was high time to pick up the broken shards of his own life and piece them back together with the superglue of determination and hard work. Ruth was his first concern.

His gaze went to the church directory lying on the coffee table. An enormous amount of help from above would be needed if he were to succeed. He decided to take

Sarah's frequent advice to call Pastor Mark and schedule an appointment for counseling.

Kerry picked up the phone on the second ring. "Hello?"

"Hi, Kerry. It's Jake."

His low words tickled her ear and sent tingles to her toes. She wound the cord nervously around her index finger and tried to act nonchalant. "Jake? How nice to hear from you again. And to what do I owe the pleasure of your call?"

"I couldn't stay away."

Kerry didn't laugh; it had been three weeks since he'd dropped her off at her apartment. Except for church on Sundays, she hadn't seen him since. It had been a shock to discover they shared the same church, though with over five thousand members Kerry wasn't surprised to have missed him earlier. Yet it was ironic that now she saw him every Sunday. At church he'd practically ignored her, only directing a brief nod her way or raising his hand in a wave when their eyes did meet. He'd never once sought her out to talk after services were over.

"I'd like to take you out again," he said softly when she didn't respond. "Just name the time and place."

Kerry's foolish heart lurched. Well, why not? She needed to do some research, and the best place to start would be where teens liked to go. Besides, it didn't mean anything. It would just be a harmless outing.

"Okay. Six Flags. Saturday morning."

There was a pause. "You mean the amusement park? In Arlington?"

139

"That's the one."

He let out a low chuckle, and Kerry's heart did another somersault. "Okay, Six Flags it is. I'll pick you up Saturday morning at nine-thirty. See you then."

"Yeah, see you," Kerry murmured and hung up the phone. She stared at it in confusion. Okay, so Jake hadn't written her off as a bad date as she'd thought. Kerry hadn't been able to get him out of her mind—and she wasn't sure that was such a good thing. She couldn't help but feel he was hiding something from her; she just wished she had the guts to ask him what it was.

Myriad souvenir shops, food stands, and thrilling rides beckoned to Jake and Kerry at every turn. Stores of pink stucco lined the walks, and festive mariachi music played over speakers hidden in lush shrubbery and colorful flowering plants bordering the wide walks.

"Getting too hot? We could duck into a restaurant for a cold drink, if you want." Jake stuck a finger under the neck of his T-shirt and pulled it away.

Kerry shook her head, laughing. "We just got here! It's not even ten-thirty yet." She tugged her flowered ball cap further down over her head, blocking the rays of the sun. Even this early in the day, the temperature soared in the high eighties, promising a sizzling afternoon ahead.

"Well then, what would you like to do first?"

"Shall we flirt with danger and ride the fastest coaster here?" she asked, feeling like a daredevil for suggesting it.

"You're on!" he said with a wink.

Over thirty minutes later, as the coaster moved up the

rails, Jake covered her clenched hand with his. They climbed to an unbelievable height then rocketed through space, Kerry screaming all the while. Once they returned to the ground, she had the strangest urge to kiss the blacktop walk.

"Wanna take another whirl?" Jake asked, a boyish gleam in his eye. "Or are you ready to tackle a different one?"

"Uh, I think I've had enough roller coasters for a while," she managed. "Let's try something else."

They enjoyed the scenic view from the top of the red oil derrick tower, had a hilarious time driving the antique cars, and grabbed a frozen yogurt before taking their places in line to ride what promised to be a wet one. Ignoring the half-inch or so of water on the floor of the log flume, Kerry claimed the spot on the upholstered bench in front, Jake behind her, and three kids behind him. Once the ride ended, with the usual squeals piercing the air, they were drenched from head to foot. Kerry wrung out her tank top as best she could, but soon the scorching sun sizzled her dry, and she wished for the dampness again. She wondered if she should suggest they ride the flume a second time.

Jake wiped a hand over his sweaty brow. "What say we break for something to eat?"

Kerry quickly agreed, opting for shade instead of wet.

At a nearby restaurant, Jake ordered several tacos and an enchilada dinner. Kerry chose a chicken fajita salad. Afterward he bought snow cones, and she felt refreshed as the fruity ice slid down her throat.

Renewed, they shopped at a souvenir store, and Kerry

bought an adorable Indian doll for Ashley, who would be having a birthday in November. Jake purchased a comic book featuring the Old West. Kerry wondered who it was for, but didn't ask.

Stopping in front of the courthouse, they were disappointed to see an old-time placard on the door with news that the Wild West show wouldn't start for another hour.

"We could ride the train," Jake suggested.

Kerry smiled. "I'm game."

Soon they were seated in an empty section of the antique Jefferson Patton steam engine, chugging their way to the other side of the park. The warm breeze carried the sweet scent of flowers mixed with the mouthwatering aromas of food from all over the area. Screams, laughter, and the grinding and clicking sound of machinery filled the air, depending on which ride they passed.

For the first time Kerry noticed her cheeks and shoulders had grown tight. She pulled a tube of sunscreen from her shoulder bag and applied it over her face and arms. At Jake's quiet insistence, she turned, and he slathered the warm cream over her exposed back and shoulders. His fingers on her skin defeated the purpose of the sunblock—to protect her from burning. Kerry felt as if her skin was on fire where he touched. How could a man have such an effect on her. . .?

"You're getting a little more red than you were the other day," Jake said, concern in his voice. "Maybe we should stick to indoor activities until it cools down."

"Okay by me," she said flippantly, trying to remain cool—on the inside anyway—and rein in her chaotic feelings. She turned her attention to the opening of the train, doing her best to pretend she didn't notice when Jake slid his arm along the back of the bench behind her. His fingertips grazed her shoulder, and her heart did a nosedive like the fourteen-story roller coaster they passed.

She'd never been serious about anyone, but Kerry knew she was falling for this man entirely too fast. She didn't want that. She wanted to walk into love with her eyes wide open—not run haphazardly into a relationship like Dani had.

A tendril of her hair blew into her mouth as the train rounded a corner. Jake's fingers brushed her cheek and gently pulled the strand away. Her heart skipped a beat, and startled, she turned to face him.

His eyes glowed with intensity, searching hers, robbing her of the ability to draw breath. His gaze dropped to her mouth.

"Kerry," he whispered and dipped his head, his lips touching hers.

The kiss was sweet, gentle, and all too brief.

When he lifted his head and gave her a soft smile, Kerry realized by the hammering of her heart that it was already too late. She was on the ride of her life and past the no return point to falling in love.

Twenty minutes after they'd exited the train and ridden two other rides, Kerry halted midstep. Her eyes going wide, she pulled her hand from Jake's.

"Kerry?" Jake said in confusion. "What's wrong?"

"The doll!" She whirled around, running smack into

the man behind her.

"Hey!" he growled in surprise as his jumbo cola smashed against him and splashed over his flowered-print shirt and Bermuda shorts. "What's the big idea?"

"Sorry—I lost my doll." Kerry snapped out the quick apology and hurried back the way they'd come.

"You lost your *what?*" the stranger called after her, his eyes wide behind his thick glasses.

"Long story," Jake supplied, whipping a five-dollar bill out of his wallet and handing it to the man to cover his spilled drink. "She never got over her childhood."

Leaving the man and his wife standing and staring openmouthed, Jake dodged countless groups of thrill seekers and caught up to Kerry as she rummaged through the flowered bushes almost a hundred feet ahead.

"Uh, Kerry, I don't think you would have dropped it in there," he said, smiling nervously at a curious worker standing nearby. The teenaged boy swept a crumpled ice cream wrapper from the blacktop into his metal dustpan, his eyes on Kerry the whole time.

"She lost her doll," Jake explained with a shrug, as she continued to beat the bushes, then parted them and stuck her head and shoulders all the way in.

"Check lost and found," the teen answered, slowly backing away.

"Thanks, we'll do that." Once the boy was out of earshot, Jake grabbed Kerry's arm, pulling her from the greenery. "What in the world were you doing in there? I wouldn't be surprised if he calls security and they kick us out of the park."

"I spotted something white, but it was just a big rock." Disappointment clouded her eyes, and she pulled a leaf from her hair. "I thought the sack might have gotten kicked to the side, in the bushes. But maybe he's right and someone turned it in."

They located a map, and the lost and found, but came up empty. Nor had anyone spotted a white sack at any of the rides they'd previously ridden. They backtracked for an hour—but no doll.

"Don't worry about it," Jake said. "I'll buy you another."

"It was the last one on the shelf. I wanted Ashley to have it for her birthday."

"I'm sorry, Kerry. I don't know where else to look."

She threw him a sheepish glance. "It's not your fault, Jake. You're not the absentminded klutz; I am. In fact, you're a pretty special guy for gallivanting all over the place to help me search." They neared the entrance to the park. "I think I'm ready to call it a day now, though."

She did look tired, but Jake didn't want their time together to end yet. "Hungry? Before I take you home, I'll treat you to dinner."

Kerry made a face and put a hand to her stomach. "No, thanks. I've had way too many sweets and junk food. But hey, that reminds me. Dani wanted me to invite you to her apartment for dinner next Friday night. She wants to meet you."

Jake groaned, wishing he didn't have other plans. "I can't. I have to go to the zoo and help with a gorilla Friday. And I'm not sure when I'll be free."

Kerry stopped and stared at him as though he'd just

beamed down from another planet. "That's the *craziest* excuse I've ever heard. Gorilla-sitting at the zoo?"

He laughed. "I thought I told you. I'm a veterinarian, Kerry. I have a friend who works there, and he's asked for my help. He and three local vets, including me, are performing surgery on a gorilla. He's been having stomach problems."

Kerry shook her head. "A vet. . .wow, I would've never guessed, though I often wondered what you did for a living. You sure have easy working hours."

"I was on vacation when we met." He gently squeezed her hand as they left the park and waited for the tram to take them to Jake's car twelve rows away. "I can make it next Saturday, if that'll work okay for your sister."

"I'll make sure it does," she said, a huge smile lighting her face.

Jake's heart soared. He was glad he'd gotten in touch with Kerry again. He hadn't been able to forget her; she'd been on his mind constantly. Fact was, he'd never noticed how bland life was without her spicing things up. Even Pastor Mark had encouraged Jake to see her again, assuring him God hadn't intended for man to be alone. In the counseling sessions, he'd also told Jake that he needed to tell Kerry about Ruth as soon as possible.

And though he knew Pastor Mark was right, Jake hesitated. He didn't want to scare Kerry off when he'd so recently let go of the self-condemnation of wanting to see her again. This day had been terrific, despite the chase for the missing doll.

Tomorrow. He'd tell her about Ruth tomorrow.

Six

"I like him," Dani said as she stirred concentrate and water together in a glass pitcher. "And you two complement each other well. Both in looks and personalities."

A hot flush rose to Kerry's face, and she busied herself with retrieving three glasses from the overhead cupboard. "It does look promising. Dinner was great, by the way."

"So was your blueberry pie. Thanks for bringing it."

"Menade!" Ashley demanded from the nearby playpen. She clutched the padded green rail, lifting her small, bare foot to the white webbing, and tried to climb out.

"Whoa there, little one!" Kerry chuckled and poured a small amount of lemonade in the sipper cup, slapping on the plastic spout top. "You know, Dani, she'll soon find a way out of there. She's growing like a dandelion."

Dani turned, one eyebrow lifted. "A dandelion?"

"Sounds nicer than a weed," Kerry explained, offering the cherub her drink. Ashley took it in dimpled hands and raised it to her mouth with a big smile.

Dani laughed. "Here, oh silver-tongued one, take this

to your boyfriend." She handed a full glass to Kerry. "Hope he likes pink lemonade."

"Who wouldn't on a scorching day like this?" Kerry shot back to cover her embarrassment.

She took the iced drink to the den. Jake had moved from the sofa to the outside balcony, his back to her as he stood at the rail, talking on his cell phone. Kerry debated waiting, then decided she'd just hand him the glass and walk away. It really was hot out there, and she didn't see how he could stand it. She walked to the sliding door, which he'd left cracked open.

"I found us a place." His low words to the person on the other end of the phone drifted to Kerry, and her hand froze on the handle of the door. "It's perfect. Has a big backyard with lots of trees." He paused then chuckled. "No, but we can plant an apple tree there."

Dread hit Kerry. She felt it settle in her legs like wet cement. She couldn't budge them.

"I miss you too, Sweetheart, but I enjoyed the time we spent with one another last night," he murmured. "Soon we'll be together again. I promise. . . . Yeah, I love you, too. . . ."

Backing from the door, Kerry blinked away hot tears. She whirled around, sloshing lemonade over her hand, and plunked the glass on the coffee table. Grabbing her purse from the chair, she retraced her steps to the kitchen. "I've got to go. I'll talk to you later."

Dani swung around, the surprise on her face turning to concern. "What happened?"

Kerry shook her head. "I have to go."

"But what about Jake?"

Several derogatory comments came to mind, but she squelched them all. "Tell him something came up."

Without another word, Kerry turned and fled the apartment, running down the stone steps to the sidewalk. Jake called to her from the balcony, but she ignored him, walking fast and concentrating on getting to the safety of her car.

The drive to her apartment was muddled. Kerry drove purely by instinct, angrily swiping the tears away, thankful she didn't have a wreck. Only when she locked herself in her apartment did she break down and have a good cry.

She had suspected Sarah of being Jake's girlfriend—but had never thought to ask him if he had a different girl! The two-timing Casanova—pretending to be a Christian. . .kissing her when he had another woman hidden away somewhere. From his phone conversation, it sounded as if they were ready for the altar—unless he was married already! The low-life jerk. . .

Unwittingly, her mind went to two nights ago when Jake took her out to dinner. After he brought her home, he'd kissed her on her doorstep. A kiss completely different from the one at the amusement park. One that soon turned to passion and set Kerry on fire.

The phone rang, the message clicked on, and Jake's steady voice filled her apartment. "Kerry? Dani told me you were upset. I think I know why, and I'd like to explain. . ."

"Not in a million years," Kerry growled at the black

box, turning the volume down with a snap. "I despise you, Jake Hartwell." She brushed new moisture from her eyes. "And I hope your new place falls down around your ears!"

The phone rang again, but Kerry left the volume down so she couldn't hear the message. Woodenly she fixed herself a cup of cappuccino, sat at the table, and stared at the mug. A knock at her apartment door a short time later startled her. She padded across the carpet and glanced out the peephole.

Jake's tense face stared back.

Clenching her lips tight, Kerry spun away from the door and headed for her bedroom. She had no intention of hearing any of his lame excuses or feeble explanations.

Another sharp knock followed, then pounding.

Kerry turned on the shower, drowning out the noise from the front room. She stripped off her clothes and stepped inside the cubicle, allowing the hot water to ease her tight muscles. A good ten minutes later, when the water had gone cold, she turned off the tap and stepped out. After toweling off, she threw a short silk robe around her, belting it tight. Though she figured he would be gone, she tiptoed to the door and peeked through the peephole to make sure. The porch was empty.

The phone rang several more times that night before Kerry went to bed. In the morning, it was what woke her. Groggily, she plucked up the receiver.

"Kerry?" Dani's worry was evident. "Are you okay? I tried to call you last night."

Memory of Jake's treachery came to mind and Kerry grimaced. "I don't want to talk about it now. Another time maybe. I just woke up and need to get busy on that new line of cards." After assuring her sister she was all right, Kerry hung up the phone.

She scrounged up some toast and a good strong cup of regular coffee then sat at the table, noticing the untouched cappuccino from last night. Frowning, she poured it in the sink. The phone rang. Suddenly remembering Mike told her last week that he'd call her today, she turned up the volume on the answering machine.

"Kerry?" His voice came on the recorder, and she grabbed up the phone.

"Yeah, I'm here."

"Didn't you get my E-mails? I sent five of them. How are you coming along on the new line?" He rarely bothered with a greeting.

"I should have them finished by Friday. . ."

"Something wrong?"

Kerry blew out a breath. "Life."

"You sound as if you could use a break. I'm free tomorrow after six. How about dinner?"

Kerry hesitated. Usually she turned Mike's offers down, but her bruised emotions needed a boost, and she'd made it clear to him a long time ago that their relationship was on a friends-only basis. What harm could it do to go out with him this once?

"Okay. I'll be ready at seven."

Jake drove down the busy street, his mind again on Kerry. Obviously his explanation about Ruth over the phone hadn't made one bit of difference. He'd wanted to tell

Kerry the truth in person, but since she wouldn't let him in her apartment, he'd resorted to calling her later and explaining over the phone. Maybe it was better this way. No use going out with a woman who couldn't accept the fact that he had a young daughter.

Aggravated, he stopped at yet another red light, his fingers drumming the wheel. His gaze swept the area— the fast-food restaurant on the corner, its colorful sign featuring a full meal for under three bucks—before he casually glanced at the car in the lane next to him. His eyes widened.

Kerry sat on the passenger side of a slick, red sports car. A young man in a business suit, several gold rings flashing from his fingers, sat behind the wheel. Kerry's disinterested gaze traveled over a couple of pedestrians rushing across the street, then flicked Jake's way—meeting his solemn stare.

Her mouth dropped partway open, her brows rising in surprise, before she clamped her lips shut and lifted her chin, glaring back at him.

Jake's mouth tightened. What did she have to be mad about? He was the one who should be angry! Standing outside and pounding on her door like a lovesick fool, repeatedly calling her on the phone. And who was the stuffed shirt with her? A new boyfriend?

Jake watched the car turn left. A honk behind startled him back to reality and the fact the light had turned green. Compressing his lips, he put his foot on the gas and sped forward.

It was high time to forget Kerry Bradford. Trouble

was. . .that was easier said than done.

Drizzle fell from an October gray sky, dampening Kerry's mood. She clutched the large manila envelope to her chest, debating on what to do. She'd met her deadline weeks ago and wanted to get this proposal for a new line of cards sent off soon. At least it had stopped raining so heavily.

She grabbed her pink windbreaker, threw it over her head, and whisked out the door to her car. The streets were slick, and it probably wasn't the smartest idea to go now, but a virus had forced her to remain cooped up in her apartment all week, and she was close to going stir-crazy. Besides, the post office was only five minutes away, if all the lights stayed green.

Kerry opted for a shortcut and turned onto a little-used road with few houses scattered down the lane. She thought about her last conversation with Dani. Surprisingly her big sister had been annoyed, telling Kerry she hadn't been fair to Jake. Evidently Dani knew something Kerry didn't but wouldn't say what, explaining it was Jake's place to tell her. Kerry's expression softened.

After her initial heated reaction to Jake's duplicity, she'd mellowed over the weeks. She'd been surprised when a parcel service delivered a package to her door, containing the Indian doll she'd lost, with a note tucked inside the box.

I contacted lost and found. Apparently someone turned it in after we looked there.

Jake

Tears came to Kerry's eyes. It had been a sweet gesture on his part to locate the doll and send it to her. An act opposite from the picture of the fiend she'd conjured up in her mind.

Something dark lying to the side of the road caught her attention. She slowed down, realizing with horror that it was a medium-sized dog. A car must have hit it.

Kerry drove to the shoulder of the road, put her emergency brake on and shifted into park. Jumping out, she ignored the rain and hurried to the dog's side. Its matted fur was bloody. The hit must have been recent. "You poor thing," Kerry murmured, putting a hand to his head when she heard a whimper.

She looked around as though help might magically appear from beyond the rows of bare trees lining the single lane road, then hurried to her car and opened the passenger door. Returning to the dog, which looked little more than a puppy, Kerry gently scooped him from the ground and settled him onto her backseat. The mutt whimpered again, and she cringed.

She had to find a vet. Scouring her mind for memory of a local animal hospital she might have seen in the past, she slid behind the wheel and pulled out onto the road. At least there was no chance of her running into Jake, since his office was located on the other side of Dallas.

She came to the street with the post office. Hadn't she once seen a tall sign somewhere on this road with a smiling cartoon dog and cat cuddling up next to each other? Chances were good it was an animal hospital. Combing her mind, she turned left. It had been next to a large grocery store, in a shopping center. . .

There! Elated to spot the friendly sign, she pulled into a parking space in front of the clinic. Realizing she couldn't open the heavy glass door with the dog in her arms, she hurried inside.

A dark-headed woman behind the counter looked with surprise at Kerry's bloodstained windbreaker and T-shirt. "Can I help you?"

"I have an injured dog in my backseat. He was hit by a car, I think."

"I'll get a doctor." The woman headed for the hallway.

Biting her lower lip and furrowing her brow, Kerry crossed her arms against her chest, clutching her elbows. Swiveling, she stared out the huge front window at her car. She hoped the poor little fellow was going to be okay and that it wasn't too late. . .

Rapid footsteps on tile arrested her attention and she swung around. The woman emerged from the hallway, followed by a tall man wearing a white lab coat. Kerry felt her knees go weak.

Jake.

Seven

Kerry!" Jake's eyes widened in alarm. "I heard a dog was injured—but you have blood all over you! Are you okay? Did you get hurt, too?"

"I–I'm fine," Kerry managed. "The dog is in my car." On stiff legs, she led the way. The shock of seeing Jake made her movements jerky. She opened the passenger side for him, almost hitting him with the door in the process. He gently scooped up the mutt, and Kerry slammed her car door then opened the clinic door for him, escape on her mind.

Jake must have sensed her eagerness to leave, for his steady gaze trapped her fluttering one. "Stay," he demanded softly. "We need some information. And then I'd like to talk to you."

Kerry was about to refuse—she still had her errand at the post office after all—and she really didn't want to dredge up the past. But something in his serious eyes stilled her tongue and she nodded, following him inside.

She answered as many of the receptionist's questions concerning the incident as she could while Jake disappeared with the dog. Afterward the woman led Kerry down the hallway and to a door. "Dr. Hartwell asked that you wait for him in his office." Her dark eyes studied Kerry with curiosity, but thankfully she didn't say anything more.

Kerry took a seat on a vinyl chair facing the modern desk. On its surface a cardboard box stood open, and two more sat on the flat gray carpet. Books lay stacked in a pile to one side; half were on a shelf on the wall. She remembered Jake had mentioned months ago that he was planning to relocate to the area, but she hadn't realized he'd already moved. How ironic that she picked his place of business to bring the dog. Of course, with her track record of blunders, it really shouldn't come as a surprise.

Sighing, Kerry studied the crumpled packing paper. Her gaze wandered to the back of a picture frame. She knew she shouldn't look, but curiosity won. Grabbing the metal rim, she turned the frame. A young girl smiled at her from the professional portrait, freckled nose wrinkled, displaying all her teeth—the front two missing. Her dark hair hung in long ponytails over her red tank top. Big brown eyes sparkled with mischief and fun. . .

"That's Ruth," Jake's voice said quietly behind Kerry. "My daughter."

Kerry spun around, shock making her blue eyes go wide.

Jake moved into the room and closed the door behind him. "That picture was taken two years ago, before she decided to chop off her hair." He smiled, though it felt stiff. What was Kerry thinking? And why did she look at him like he was the villain in an old B movie?

"So." Her brows slanted downward. "You *are* married."

"No. My wife died over a year ago—like I told you on your answering machine that night you ran out on me. After you overheard my phone conversation with Ruth."

Kerry blinked slowly, anger fading from her features. She shook her head, as though she were trying to get a grip on reality. Sudden knowledge filled Jake.

"You never got the message, did you?"

"I erased the messages without listening to them," she admitted, lowering her gaze. "Oh, Jake. . .I'm so sorry. But why didn't you tell me you had a daughter?"

"I've asked myself that same question many times these past months." He walked away from her, thrusting his hands deep into his coat pockets. "I never intended to get serious about anybody again, not after Anna. We had some real problems before her accident. . . ." He stared at the painted wall. "I found Christ after we married, but Anna didn't want anything to do with the new me. It led to countless fights between us. After her death, I blamed myself and didn't think I deserved another chance at love.

"But I've been counseling with Pastor Mark and have learned to release the guilt and pain. I learned to forgive myself for all that happened in the past. And I'm ready to go on with the present. . . ." He turned to face her, his eyes intense. "Do you understand what I'm saying, Kerry?"

Confusion clouded her face, and she shook her head.

"I was afraid telling you about Ruth would scare you away. I didn't understand my feelings at the time. But now I do." He covered the distance between them and knelt in front of her, taking her cold hands in his. "At first I told myself I was only seeking your friendship, but that wasn't entirely true. These past months have been so empty without you. I love you, Kerry. And one day I hope. . ."

Alarm brought her eyes wide and she struggled to her feet, breaking his hold. "I have to go."

He knitted his brows. "Right now?"

"Yes, I—I'm sorry," she stammered and hurried to the door. She stopped and turned. "The dog. Is the dog all right?"

Jake nodded in hurt confusion. Here he was baring his heart, and she wanted to talk about the dog? "Dr. Clifford is taking care of him. The injury wasn't as serious as it looked, though he'll have to have his leg in a splint for a while. Kerry, about us—"

"I'm glad he's okay," she interrupted. "Well, I better go. Just send me the bill."

He stood. "Kerry. . .?"

"I. . .I'll call you sometime." She fled the room, as though hot coals burned under her feet.

"Kerry Bradford, you're a fool!"

Kerry berated herself for the umpteenth time since the day she'd escaped Jake's office. It had been bad enough to discover she'd jumped to conclusions yet again where Jake was concerned. Then she'd barely had time to recover from the shock of finding out he was a widower with a daughter before she heard him declaring his love.

Kerry groaned. Yes, she loved Jake. She had thought about him every day and dreamed about him at night. But he was right. The idea of taking on his daughter scared her silly; Ruth would probably hate her. Kerry could barely manage keeping herself out of trouble—much less a child! And from Jake's last words to Kerry, she'd been sure a marriage proposal wasn't far off.

She threw down her pencil and glared at the drawing of two teens on the curve of a high roller coaster, the whites of their eyes showing, their teeth bared in fright. On the front she'd written, "Do things feel like they're speeding out of control. . .?"

"Well, better bail out while there's time," Kerry muttered, finishing the sentiment, "because you'll probably get flattened like a pancake if you don't."

Frustrated, she crumpled the paper into a tight ball and pushed away from the table. She was in no frame of mind to compose verse today, and the drawing was less than adequate. She hadn't been able to do any good work this past week, since she'd run from Jake. Her gaze landed on her Bible; it had been some time since she'd read it.

Sheepishly, Kerry picked it up and went into the den to settle on her sofa, hoping time in God's Word would improve her day. Her eyes immediately lit on the red words of Luke 6:37 that she'd highlighted in pink. "Do not judge, and you will not be judged. Do not condemn, and you will not be condemned. Forgive, and you will be forgiven."

Kerry let out a groan and closed her eyes. "Okay, God, I get the point."

Do you?

Kerry thought a moment. She'd judged Ruth would dislike her before she'd met the girl; she'd condemned Jake many times—recently for withholding information about

Ruth. . . And she'd never forgiven her brother-in-law for what he'd done to Dani.

"But God, that's asking too much! Bruce is a creep!" And, she admitted, he was another reason she held back from seeing Jake. Things had gotten far too serious too fast between them. She didn't want to end up like Dani.

Unless you forgive Bruce, your Heavenly Father cannot forgive you.

Kerry flinched as the soft words trickled through her mind. Deep down she knew they were true, but. . . "You'll have to help me then, Lord. Because even though I know I should, it's hard. I love Dani so much and hate to see her hurt. So. . .I ask You to make me willing to forgive him. Help me do it, Lord."

Peace enveloped Kerry, washing through her like a warm balm. But the smile soon disappeared from her face. Now what should she do about Jake?

Kerry blew out a soft breath, her attention going back to her Bible. She'd pray about it and seek direction. Like she should have done from the start.

The shrill ring of the phone near her ear diverted Kerry a few weeks later. She picked up the receiver before the answering machine in the front room could click on. "Hello?" she said, distracted.

"Kerry, could you pick up the balloons?" Dani's words came out rushed. "I'm not going to be able to get off work as early as I thought. And Ashley's party is in a few hours."

"Sure. Not a problem."

Kerry muttered a quick good-bye then turned back to

her drawing. An hour and a half later she looked at her finished product—not as polished as her usual work—but it made its point. A yellow road sign bore the message: "I've always been told, 'Walk, don't run.'"

Then below: "I've jumped to conclusions. I've careened into trouble. And it's gotten me nowhere."

On the inside she'd written: "Now I'm ready to follow directions. Will you let my first step be the one back into your life. . .and into your arms again?"

Satisfied, she stuffed the card into an envelope and checked the clock. Good. She still had time to drop this off before she bought the balloons at the local gift shop where she'd been working since early November. She only hoped Jake's car would be at the apartment complex. Dani had told her he'd been visiting Sarah every weekend.

"I'm off, Puddles," she said to the mutt who'd taken up residence on her sofa. When she discovered the dog she'd rescued was a stray, Kerry had entertained no choice but to adopt him after he left the animal hospital. "Sorry I can't take you with me, but there wouldn't be room for you and the balloons. Wish me success."

Puddles lifted his head from his paws and wagged his tail, issuing a farewell bark.

Ten minutes later, Kerry pulled into the parking lot, thankful to see Jake's blue sports car parked near the office. She slipped from behind the wheel, hurried over to his windshield, and tucked the card underneath the wiper. Then with a quick look to the office to make sure she still went unobserved, she ran back to her car and drove away.

Muttering under her breath, Kerry drove down the lane to Dani's apartment. Dani had said fifteen helium balloons should be plenty. She wasn't kidding. It had been a test of Kerry's skill to drive with one hand and keep the balloons away from her. And the warm air blowing from the vent made them bounce around even more.

A large pink oval sneaked by and slipped in front of Kerry's face, blocking her vision.

"Aggghhh!" Kerry pushed the balloon away, her eyes widening in horror when she saw that she was on the wrong side of the road—and a blue car was coming straight for her.

With a squeal of tires, she jerked the wheel to the right, shot back across her lane and into the brown grass. The other car did the same.

Pulse-pounding seconds ticked by as her heart knocked painfully against her rib cage. She took a deep, steadying breath, dropping her forehead to the wheel. Her door was wrenched open.

"Kerry! Are you all right?"

"Jake! That was you?" At his familiar dear face, she shakily stepped out of the car—and into his arms. She laid her head on his shoulder. "I'm so sorry for almost running you over! I couldn't see, a—and then when I—I saw I was in the wrong lane—"

"Shh. It's okay. I just want to know one thing." He moved away a fraction and tipped her chin until she met his intent gaze. "Did you mean what you wrote in the card?"

She nodded. "But I need to take it slow."

His smile beamed wide. "As slow as you want it."

"And if Ruth doesn't like me—"

"She'll love you. Just like I do."

A strange shyness came over Kerry. "I love you, too—oh no!"

Memory of her errand came to mind and, eyes wide, she spun around to watch as the last latex balloon bobbed out of the open car door and sailed upward. Fourteen more pink and white ovals drifted higher in the powder blue sky. "Ashley's birthday balloons!" she moaned.

"Forget the balloons," Jake insisted softly, turning her to face him again. "I'll buy you several dozen—the whole store of them if you want. Did you just say what I think you said? That you love me?"

She nodded, and his hands went to either side of her face, his thumbs caressing her cheeks. "You've made me a very happy man today, Hannah Kerry Bradford," he breathed before his lips settled on hers in a toe-curling kiss.

Kerry wrapped her arms around his waist, the balloons forgotten.

🐾

"Is my veil straight? Do I look okay?" Kerry turned her back toward the full-length mirror, her anxious gaze traveling over every inch of the ivory lace gown.

"You look fine," Dani said as she closed the door behind her. "You make a lovely spring bride. But hey—you'll never guess who's out there, in the congregation."

"Who?"

"Aunt Harriet!"

Surprised, Kerry turned to her sister. "All the way

from California? Are you sure?"

"Well, I didn't get a good look. She's sitting in the middle, and I only got a glimpse of her when I checked on Ashley and Mom. But the woman is wearing a gigantic floppy straw hat with mounds of yellow and white daisies and a long dress with huge orange and yellow flowers."

Both girls smiled. "Aunt Harriet," they said in unison.

"I'm so glad she could come." Kerry was thrilled her great-aunt had flown in. It had been years since she'd seen her, ever since she'd given Kerry the dachshund figurine. But worry soon wrinkled her brow again, and she faced the mirror.

"What's the matter? Do you want me to go get Mom?"

"No, we already talked, and besides, she's busy with Ashley. It's just that. . .oh, Dani, I know something's going to go wrong! The rehearsal went too smoothly, and you know what they say. That it's the rehearsal that ends in a nightmare, but the actual ceremony goes without a hitch. Mine will probably turn out opposite. . . ."

Dani heaved an exasperated breath. "Do you love him?"

Kerry looked at her sister's reflection in the mirror. "Of course I love him. What kind of question is that?"

Dani grinned. "Well, then stop borrowing trouble, and just concentrate on Jake."

A loud knock shook the door. Dani moved to let their father in. "Ready, Sugar? It's time." His blue eyes twinkled at Kerry. "You make a fine bride!"

Dani grabbed her bouquet of cream roses and smoothed the skirt of the peach satin dress she wore as matron of honor. "I better get out there. Just remember,

Sis, take it one step at a time—and stop worrying!"

"Thanks, Dani." Kerry hugged her sister. Despite her fears, she was elated to have glimpsed Dani having what looked like a long, serious talk with Pastor Mark at the rehearsal dinner. Perhaps her sister's salvation was close at hand.

They took their place at the back of the church, hidden from view of curious guests. The smell of orange blossoms turned her queasy stomach and Kerry was suddenly sure she was going to be sick. Now, wouldn't *that* make a fine entrance?

At last, the moment of truth arrived. The organ pealed the announcement of the bride, and the music switched to Lohengrin's "Wedding March." Jake stood at the front next to his best man, his gaze glued to Kerry, and she inhaled sharply. Her fiancé was devastatingly handsome in his black tuxedo. She looked away and concentrated on her mission to reach his side without making a fool of herself. At least she had her father's arm to hold onto.

Throughout the endless trek, she put one foot slowly in front of the other, focusing on the large metal cross on the wall ahead, trying not to tremble so hard. "And one, two. And one, two," she recited under her breath, remembering to measure her footsteps. As she neared the front pew, Kerry's gaze lowered to her soon-to-be-daughter, Ruth, and she almost broke out laughing.

One jean leg had slipped from where the little flower girl had rolled it up under her dress to conceal it. Several inches of blue denim could be seen beneath the peach-colored lace hem. Obviously Jake had been too preoccupied to check into the tomboy's wardrobe this morning. Kerry's gaze swung his way.

His green eyes glowed with love and admiration, trapping her with their intensity. Heat blanketed her, and she struggled to take the next breath. Her father released her arm. Moving forward, she raised her foot to the carpeted step to join Jake and to her horror, misjudged the rise and tripped.

Before she could plummet to the floor in a mountainous froth of ivory lace, Jake grabbed her, catching her against him. His eyes twinkled as he met her embarrassed gaze.

"From this day forward," he murmured for her ears alone, "I promise to always be there, to catch you when you stumble."

Her lips slowly swept upward. "And I'll always be there for you, too, Jake. To encourage you when you're down."

They looked deeply into one another's eyes, until an amused clearing of the throat signaled near Jake's elbow.

Jake grinned. "Shall we take that first step together, Kerry?" He moved to offer her his arm.

"Together." She nodded. "I like the sound of that."

Linking her arm through his, Kerry stood tall and walked to the altar beside the man she loved, confident that she was going in the right direction. At last.

*I guide you in the way of wisdom and
lead you along straight paths.*
PROVERBS 4:11

PAMELA GRIFFIN

Pamela Griffin lives in Texas and divides her time between family, church activities, and writing. She has two novels with **Heartsong Presents,** as well as various novellas. Prolific in her work, she enjoys writing both historical and contemporary romances—and doesn't consider it work at all! A reformed prodigal, Pamela is grateful to the Lord for every good thing in her life, and gives Him full credit for where she is today. She welcomes you to visit her at her website: http://home.att.net/~words_of_honey/Pamela.htm

Dog Park

by Dina Leonhardt Koehly

Dedication

My heartfelt love and a lifetime of thanks to:
Mom, Dad, Craig, Nicole, Madelyn,
DW, LL, Blake, Tanner, Mom K, Dad K,
and Aunt Betty Carr

One

Lynne backed out of the driveway, then headed down the palm-lined street. Bamboo barked. The rust red and white Welsh corgi knew where they were headed. The dog park was to Bamboo what Disneyland was to a child.

After Lynne parked the car she checked the mirror. Her short blond hair was disheveled. With no hairbrush in sight, she reached for her baseball cap and sunglasses. What did it matter what she looked like? It was only the dog park. Clipping the leash on Bamboo's collar, Lynne headed for the gated entrance.

Lynne and Bamboo were familiar with most of the dogs. Bamboo knew them by scent; Lynne knew them by sight. Most of them were friendly; if they weren't, they had to leave the park. Those were the rules.

Stepping inside and closing the gate behind her, she unleashed Bamboo. The stocky little corgi darted away to freedom. Bamboo really got into the spirit of play with the other boisterous dogs and found delight in the chaos of barking and charging about. It was a terrific outlet for her boundless energy.

Lynne smiled as she headed for a park bench. Sitting down, she pulled out a novel and started to read. The dog park was not only a joy to Bamboo; it was to her as well.

Looking up, she checked on Bamboo's whereabouts. Lynne chuckled. Bamboo was chasing a fawn-colored pug dog. It was Phoebe; she was a regular at the park. Lynne watched as the pug turned abruptly and stopped, making Bamboo trip and roll. Phoebe took off again, enjoying the chase.

Lynne viewed her surroundings with appreciation. The scent of pine and eucalyptus filled the air, and the morning dew clung to the grass. It was another beautiful day in Southern California. She picked up her book again and continued to read.

"Excuse me," a deep-sounding voice said.

Lynne glanced up. A tall, attractive man with wavy, black hair stood before her. "Yes?"

"Is that your dog over there?" he asked, pointing to a small dog in the distance.

It was Bamboo. "Yes. Why do you want to know?"

He whistled. "Brutus, come." A large white and black Great Dane came limping over. "Look at what your dog did to Brutus." The man pointed to the right back leg. It had a gash and was bleeding.

Aghast, Lynne shook her head. She swallowed hard. After an interminable silence, she spoke. "No, Bamboo didn't do that. She wouldn't hurt a flea let alone a Great Dane," she responded like a woman protective of her pet. Lynne had raised Bamboo from a puppy, and had trained her to be a mannerly and loving dog.

"Ma'am, I beg to differ." His dark brown eyes bore into hers. "Your dog chased Brutus, then bit his leg. Isn't your dog a Welsh corgi?"

"Yes, so what of it?" she asked as she stood up. Lynne squelched back the words she *really* wanted to use. She felt like a midget standing next to him. He had to be well over six feet, easily dwarfing her five-foot-three-inch frame.

"My neighbor had one of those dogs and it was belligerently aggressive. That breed herds animals by nipping them in the heels," he informed her.

"Preposterous," she said as she looked at Bamboo, the picture of canine decorum.

"Vicious corgi," he mumbled as he snapped the Great Dane's leash back on.

"How dare you insinuate that my dog is vicious." Anger pulsated from the veins in her neck.

"I suggest that you pay the vet bill and we'll call a truce."

"Are you nuts?" she fumed. "Can I ask you something?"

"What?" He raised his eyebrows, giving her a penetrating look.

"Did you see my corgi bite your dog in the leg?"

"Well. . .uh. . .no, not exactly," he stumbled. "I heard Brutus yelp. I turned and saw your dog chasing him. I felt it safe to assume that the corgi was the guilty party."

"I don't know if it's safe to *assume* anything," she huffed. "It's either a yes or no. Did you see Bamboo bite Brutus?"

"No, but—"

"Aha, sorry," she interrupted, "but I'm not paying the vet bill." Lynne turned and stomped off. She was shaking inside as she called Bamboo to come. Bamboo met her at the gate. Lynne picked her up and hugged her tightly. "You're not vicious, Boo," she murmured into her ear. As she closed the gate, she glanced through the mesh fence. He was staring at her and he didn't look happy.

Pulling the key from her pocket, she unlocked the door with shaky hands. Lynne pulled out onto the highway. "So much for a peaceful day at the dog park," she grumbled.

She turned to see Bamboo hanging her head out the open window. Her tongue was flapping in the wind. "Bamboo, you didn't bite that big dog, huh."

Bamboo stuck her head in and looked at Lynne with her big, chocolate brown eyes.

"No, I know you wouldn't hurt anything," she said, convinced of her dog's innocence.

A huge rush of emotion seized her as she reached her home, the lovely townhouse she had inherited from her parents. Lynne wished that she could talk to her mom right now. She needed to hear her mother's calming voice.

Her parents had died in a plane crash when she was sixteen. She had no siblings. Feeling quite alone, she went to live with her aunt Andrea, uncle Chip, and cousin, Margo. They were her lifelines. They gave her hope that there could be life even with the loss of her parents. At two years her junior, Margo had become like a sister to her. Now a decade later, Margo and Lynne shared living space at the townhouse.

Once inside her home, Lynne unleashed Bamboo.

The little dog ran straight to Margo, who was sitting in the kitchen.

"Hi, Boo, how was your morning?" Margo asked. Her brown eyes sparkled as she stroked Bamboo on the head. "Did you cause any dog riots? Did those male dogs fall over their paws to get to you?"

"Oh, Margo, you won't believe what happened," Lynne groaned. She flopped down on a chair and grabbed a banana from the bowl.

"You don't look well," Margo commented as she lifted Bamboo up onto her lap.

"I feel dreadful," Lynne said, explaining what had taken place at the park.

"Have you ever seen him there before?" Margo asked.

"No, I haven't. Why?"

"Well, maybe he's got a scam going. This is Southern California where the cost of living is particularly high and people can use all kinds of methods and tricks to swindle money out of innocent people. For all you know that dog could have scraped himself in the dog park accidentally."

"Hmm, maybe you're right," Lynne said.

"Don't worry another minute over it. We both know that Bamboo is a sweet little girl," Margo said, scratching Bamboo under the chin.

"You're right; I'll put it out of my mind."

Margo poured herself a cup of coffee, then said, "Oh, by the way, Pastor Drew's wife called for you."

"Lana? Did she leave a message?" Lynne asked.

"Yes, she said that tomorrow morning's service had a change in the program. The choir was going to sing an extra song. She now wants you to do your solo next Sunday instead."

"That's fine with me," Lynne said. "Did she mention why they were changing it?"

Margo nodded. "The new youth pastor, Matt Hunter, has arrived. Pastor Drew will introduce him to the congregation, then the choir will do a special song to welcome him."

"I thought he was arriving next week," Lynne remarked. Being one of the church secretaries, she knew all the events planned at church, and this event wasn't slated on this week's schedule.

"Lana said that Pastor Hunter was anxious to meet everyone and get settled. He called Pastor Drew yesterday and said that he'd be in church tomorrow."

"Well, that at least explains why I didn't know," Lynne said. "I'm looking forward to meeting him."

"Robert is here," Margo called. "Why don't you carpool with us to church?"

Lynne raced down the stairs with Bible in hand. "Thanks, I will."

Robert was Margo's fiancé. Robert was a likeable man. Big and bearlike, he had the heart of a gentle lamb. He donated much of his time to helping the youth at church and that is how Margo had met him.

"Hey, Ladies, I met our new youth pastor yesterday," Robert exclaimed as Lynne and Margo piled into the car.

"What's he like?" Margo asked as she leaned over and kissed him on the cheek.

"Well, I'll say this, all of the single ladies at church will be fighting over him," Robert said, then chuckled. "All except you." He winked at Margo.

"And tell us why the ladies will be fighting over him?" Lynne asked.

"The guy is tall, good-looking, single, brilliant, and loaded."

"Loaded?" Margo repeated.

"He's so wealthy that he's not going to take a penny in salary from the church."

"Did he tell you that?" Lynne wondered how inside information always seemed to circulate so fast.

"No, I heard Pastor Drew mention it to an elder," Robert said.

"Well, he's just what West Coast Community Church needs," Margo said.

Once they arrived at church, they made their way into the sanctuary and took their seats. After the choir finished, Pastor Drew introduced the new youth pastor.

Lynne caught her breath and felt faint. There, on the stage, stood the man from the dog park. How could it be? *The rude dog owner is the new youth pastor.*

Her mind recalled what Robert had told them earlier. . . this man was wealthy. So why had he demanded money from her to pay the vet bill? It didn't make sense.

The rest of the service was a blur. Lynne barely heard a word of the sermon. Her eyes were transfixed on *that* man sitting behind the pastor. So this was Matt Hunter.

When the service was over, Lynne walked toward the

back. She froze. Matt Hunter was at the double doors shaking hands with the parishioners. Spinning around on her heels she quickly headed for the side door. Lynne had to escape. She wasn't willing to talk with *that* man again.

"Lynne, I'm so glad I caught you," Lana Martin, the pastor's wife said, tapping her on the shoulder. "I'd like you to meet Matt Hunter."

"Lana, I'm kind of in a hurry—"

"No, no. . .this will take just a minute," she insisted.

Lynne's heart pounded in her ears. Her feet felt like lead. What would she say to this man? *Lord, help me,* she pleaded. Maybe he wouldn't recognize her. After all, she had had her baseball cap and sunglasses on.

"Matt, I'd like you to meet one of our church's secretaries, who also happens to be one of our church soloists, Miss Lynne Wilson."

She gave a small shrug and forced herself to look up. "Hello." She could feel her skin starting to heat up and her head started to ache.

Matt stared at her then exclaimed, "You!"

"Do you know Lynne?" Lana questioned.

"Uh. . . ," he stumbled, "we met at the dog park the other day."

"Well then, I'll leave you two alone to talk," Lana said as she patted Lynne on the arm.

Lynne cringed. She wished that she could blink her eyes and disappear. "So, you're the new youth pastor?"

"And you're the church secretary and church soloist," he said as he raised a brow. "Wouldn't have guessed."

Her eyes narrowed as her face flushed with color.

"What's that supposed to mean?"

"How many hats do you wear in this church?" he questioned, not answering her.

"Just two; that's enough," she replied, feeling awkward.

"Lynne," Margo exclaimed, "you've met Pastor Hunter."

"Yes," she said. "My ride is here. I'd better go. Nice chatting with you," she said through gritted teeth. She turned, pulling Margo's arm.

"Why are you yanking me so hard?" Margo whispered.

"I need to get out of here fast," she said in a low voice as she pushed the doors open to the outside courtyard.

Margo stopped. "What's wrong with you?"

"That man was the bozo at the park," she stated in a low voice.

Margo grabbed Lynne's arm. "Pastor Hunter? This is too funny for words. Are you sure?"

Lynne stomped her foot. "Yes, I'm sure and it's not funny."

"Do you know that you just called our youth pastor a *bozo?*" Margo asked, repressing a grin. "Although I guess that isn't a bad word; after all, Bozo was a cute clown."

"He's no clown, he's rude. He called Bamboo 'vicious,' " Lynne reminded her.

Margo chuckled. "This is so funny."

"There's nothing more mean than laughing when your cousin is in emotional anguish," Lynne voiced.

"I'm sorry, Lynne. I guess he isn't a scam artist. By what Robert said, he certainly doesn't need your money," Margo conceded.

"Then why did he want me to pay the vet bill?" Lynne asked.

"Good question. Maybe you'll have to ask the man to find out," Margo suggested.

"No way," Lynne said. "I'm never talking to him again." She knew that was impossible. Being a worker in the church, they would inevitably bump into each other.

"Such a shame," Margo said.

"Why?" Lynne creased her eyebrows.

"He's so good-looking," Margo commented. "Did you see his gorgeous brown eyes?"

Lynne snorted. "I thought they were black."

Margo laughed, then nudged her. "You noticed, Cousin."

"I did not," Lynne said adamantly.

"Then why are your cheeks so red?" Margo asked.

"Anger," Lynne said. "Just whose side are you on?"

Margo smiled as she placed an arm around her cousin. "I'm on yours, of course."

"Hey, Ladies," Robert said. "Don't mean to interrupt, but Pastor Drew and his wife invited us to have lunch with them and Pastor Hunter."

"No thanks," Lynne said all too quickly. Her feet were itching to run. She needed to get out of there.

"Whoa, Lynne, you're not on another diet are you?" Robert asked.

"Uh-huh, I'm on a man diet, can't see another one today," she said huffily.

"Wow, what happened to you?" he questioned, noting her hostile tone.

"I'll explain later," Margo said.

"You two go on. I'll get a ride home with Cece," Lynne insisted. Cece was the church librarian and lived in the same neighborhood as Lynne.

"Are you sure?" Margo asked.

"Yes, go on and have fun," Lynne said, then added, "and see if you can find out if Pastor Hunter's dog survived his injury."

Margo smiled. "I'll report back to you later."

"Thanks, Cousin." Lynne smiled. "Now, if you'll excuse me, I'm going to go home and pray. I suddenly don't feel like much of a Christian."

Lynne resented harboring such angry feelings. Being a Christian was no easy task. Her mother and father had been such good examples to model one's life after. They had lived their faith in words and deeds. They were good-hearted, giving, and forgiving. Could Lynne forgive this man? After all, he had been so rude and being a pastor, one would expect him to be more courteous.

Lynne felt an urgency to pray. She knew the Lord would help her deal with this abominable man.

Two

Hearing the front door open, Lynne called from the bathroom, "How was your lunch?"

"Delicious," Margo said. "You should have been there."

Lynne walked out into the hallway. "Did you find out if his dog lived?"

"No, he's in bad shape. . .his leg got infected and they might have to amputate."

"Oh no, that's horrible," Lynne moaned. She stared at Margo, stunned by her words.

Margo laughed. "I was just teasing."

Lynne smacked her cousin on the shoulder. "You scared me, Margo. I feel weak all over."

"The dog is fine," she reassured her. "He said that Brutus's leg is better and they even dared to go to that dangerous dog park again."

"Did he mention anything about Bamboo?" she asked.

"Oh yes, he told Pastor Drew and Lana everything," Margo said.

"Oh great," Lynne fumed. "Now Pastor Drew and

Lana will think I have an aggressive attack dog."

"No, quite the opposite. Pastor Drew defended you and Bamboo. Then Lana suggested to Pastor Hunter that he put the incident behind him."

"Whew, I feel relieved," she said as she followed Margo into the living room.

"I should mention though that Pastor Hunter still seemed upset over the episode," Margo said, flopping down on the leather sofa.

"How could you tell?" Lynne sat down next to her.

"When Pastor Drew was talking about you, I saw Pastor Hunter squeezing his napkin into a tight little ball, then he unraveled it and squeezed it again."

"Maybe it's a nervous disorder," Lynne suggested as a giggle escaped.

Margo shook her head. "I doubt it. The only time he squeezed the napkin was when your name came up in the conversation."

"Oh, puh-leeze, I think the man has problems," Lynne said, shaking her head.

"I think the problem is you," Margo said, grinning.

"And what is that supposed to mean?"

"Where's Bamboo?"

"Don't change the subject," Lynne said. "Oh no, I left Bamboo in the bathtub!"

Lynne raced back to the bathroom and opened the door. Margo walked in behind her. "I can't believe it. Your dog is swimming in the bathtub."

Lynne laughed. Bamboo stopped. Placing her drenched paws on the side of the tub, she barked.

"I think you're clean now, Boo," Lynne said as she opened the stopper to let the water drain. She threw Margo a towel, then she grabbed one herself. "We better both work on drying this mutt, or we'll both end up getting wet."

"Good idea," Margo said as she lifted the drenched corgi out of the tub. "Say, are we scheduled to play at the Coffee Club tomorrow night?"

"Yes, I thought you already knew. The schedule is posted on the refrigerator."

"I know. I wanted to make sure. That new manager is always changing our work nights," she commented.

"We should rehearse that new song later tonight," Lynne suggested.

Lynne loved her part-time night job. She sang what was dubbed as "The Gospel Blues" at a popular restaurant and jazz club called the Coffee Club. Her cousin accompanied Lynne on the piano. Margo had played the piano since the age of six. Lynne had sung in the shower since she was a toddler. Everyone knew it was inevitable that the two of them would be in a musical group when they grew up. Although neither one of them desired to commit to a full week, they enjoyed playing and singing two or so nights a week.

Together Lynne and Margo made quite a team. They both knew their talent was a blessing from God. Their music always carried a message of hope and love.

Lynne felt the rush of adrenaline as Margo began to play the piano. Lynne's rich sultry voice sang out on cue. The words and haunting melody filled the dimly lit room.

Dressed in a long black gown with matching long satin gloves, her voice mesmerized the crowd.

Tonight the Coffee Club was filled to capacity. It was a popular place to chat, have coffee, and listen to the gospel blues. The owner, Bill Peters, told Lynne and Margo that ever since he had booked their show the Coffee Club was a sellout the nights they performed.

The Coffee Club was unpretentious. It was filled with gospel and jazz memorabilia and the walls were decorated with a collage of famous faces. The tables were close together, making it nearly impossible for the waiters to maneuver between them. Their menu was simple: sandwiches, non-alcoholic drinks, and dessert.

Taking a break after an hour of singing, Lynne reached for the tall glass of mineral water the waiter had brought her. She walked over to Margo and rested her arm on the piano.

"Let's start the second set with the new song 'Loving You, Lord,'" she suggested.

Margo nodded. "Sounds good."

"Is Robert coming tonight? I don't see him out there," Lynne commented.

"He's probably running late," she said as she took a sip of juice. "Robert was going to bring a friend along."

Lynne groaned. "I hope he's not going to try to fix me up with another of his friends."

"Oh no," Margo said as a smile appeared. "He knows you won't like this friend."

Lynne felt suddenly uneasy. "Who is it?"

Margo pointed to the clock. "Our break is over."

"Margo, who is it?" she repeated.

"I guess you'll find out soon enough." Margo smiled weakly. "Pastor Hunter."

Lynne felt ill. Her stomach lurched. Her throat tightened as she whispered, "I can't sing with that man in the audience."

"Lynne, you're going to be singing at church Sunday. He'll be there, too, and don't forget that you'll probably run into each other during the week while you're working at the church office," Margo reminded her.

She shook her head. "He's scheduled to go on the youth camp retreat this week, so I won't have to see him until Sunday."

"Okay, then you can do it. . .go grab that microphone," Margo urged.

"Margo, really, I can't do this—"

"Get ahold of yourself, Girl," Margo interrupted. "If you walk out now, there goes our job."

Lynne bit her lip. This was a nightmare. She didn't like this man and resented him being there.

"Lynne, are you okay?" Margo asked with concern.

"Yes, I'll be fine," Lynne said as she pulled the microphone off the stand. *Lord, help me get through this night*, she prayed.

Halfway through the first chorus, Lynne saw Robert and Pastor Hunter take a seat in the back. She could barely hear the piano, her heart was pounding so loudly in her ears. Lynne focused her attention on the crowd seated in front of her. Familiar faces smiled up at her, instantly calming her racing heart.

Lynne breathed a sigh of relief after she sang the last note. The audience gave her and Margo a deafening round of applause.

After their final song, Lynne bowed and waved to the crowd. "Thank you all for coming tonight." Bending down by the piano, she grabbed her belongings. She leaned over to Margo. "Is Robert going to give you a lift home, or are you coming with me?"

"I'll go with Robert if you'd like to make the great escape," Margo said with a smile.

"Thanks, I owe you," Lynne said. She quickly headed for the back door.

"Lynne, could I talk to you for a moment?"

Lynne turned to see Jackie, one of the waitresses who worked at the Coffee Club. "Sure."

"When you sang that new song, 'Loving You, Lord,' tears filled my eyes," Jackie confessed. "I'm not a Christian, but that song moved me and I don't understand it."

Lynne was not surprised. She too had felt that same way when she first heard the lyrics to the song. "I feel like crying when I sing that song," she admitted.

Jackie nodded. "My mom used to sing songs like that when I was little. Then my dad died when I was ten. My mom started drinking. She became an alcoholic. After that, we never went to church again."

"We have something in common," Lynne said as she touched Jackie's arm. "My mother and father died when I was young. My father was a pilot. My parents were flying to a convention when they had engine trouble. The plane crashed. That same day I had received my driver's license and felt on top of the world. Then I was informed that my parents had died. My whole world crashed down around me."

"Oh, Lynne, I'm so sorry," Jackie said. "Can I ask you something?" Lynne nodded. "Why aren't you angry with God?"

"I remember feeling angry after it had first happened, but later that anger dissolved and I felt a gratitude to the Lord because He never left me through that dark valley. I always felt Him so near. Also, Margo, Aunt Andrea, and Uncle Chip were a godsend. They helped me through that deep sorrow. They encouraged me to sing and that was healing in itself."

"Don't you miss your parents?" she asked, her voice choked up.

"Of course. I loved and adored my parents." Lynne's eyes welled up as she continued, "They were the source of my happiness, but because they instilled in me that there was everlasting life through God's gift, His Son, Jesus, I have the strength to go on even though they aren't here with me."

Jackie's eyes grew misty. "Lynne, I feel like the anger has disappeared. Do you think God can forgive me for being so hateful?"

"Of course He can, and will," Lynne said as she hugged her. "He's been waiting for you to have a change of heart. Perhaps the Lord used that song to bring you back to Him."

Jackie brushed a hand across her eyes. "I feel like a load has been lifted from my shoulders."

"Come to church with us on Sunday," Lynne encouraged. "Margo and I can pick you up on the way."

"Oh, you don't have to do that. I know where West Coast Community is," Jackie said, smiling. "I'd better be getting back to work. I'm on cleanup duty."

"See you on Sunday then," Lynne said. As she walked out the back door, the joy overwhelmed her. Maybe that song would bring a lost soul back home. She couldn't wait to share the good news with Margo.

"You shouldn't be walking alone in dark parking lots," a familiar voice warned.

Lynne jumped. "Do you make a practice of scaring women in parking lots, Pastor?"

Tension hung between them, and neither said anything for a moment. Suddenly, he chuckled. "You're like your dog. . .feisty."

"And you're like a pest. . .annoying," she threw back in quick rebuttal. Lynne turned abruptly and walked to her car. She couldn't believe what had just come out of her mouth. Instantly, she turned back around. "I apologize; I shouldn't have said that. I don't know what came over me."

Standing where she had left him, Pastor Hunter smiled. "I apologize too for what I said. I shouldn't have compared you to your dog."

Why didn't his apology sound like one? She grimaced as she said, "Well. . .uh, good night."

"You have a nice voice," he said.

Startled at his comment, she flushed. Fortunately, it was dark. "Thank you."

"So is this how the church gets new members?" he asked.

"What do you mean?"

"That young woman was touched by one of your songs," he commented. "I heard you invite her to church."

"Didn't your mama tell you it's rude to eavesdrop?" she asked.

"No," he said with a grin. "Lynne. . ." He paused a moment. "May I call you Lynne or do you prefer Miss Wilson?"

"Lynne," she said.

"Lynne," he repeated, "may I walk you to your car?"

"It's right here," she said, pointing to the car on her right. "But thank you for the offer."

"Well, good night, then," he said, sounding reluctant.

"Good night." Lynne unlocked her car door and jumped in. She thought about their conversation on the drive home. Matt had been nice to her. She didn't know what to make of it.

Walking into the townhouse, she heard Bamboo running to greet her. Lynne bent down and picked her up. She cradled her in her arms like a baby. "How's my little Boo-girl?" Bamboo licked her cheek.

"Where have you been?" Margo asked as she came into the hallway. "You had me worried."

"I was talking to Jackie, then Pastor Hunter stopped by to talk," she explained. Lynne set Bamboo back down. She quickly disappeared down the hall.

Margo smiled. "Hmm, sounds interesting."

"Don't even read into it," she warned. Lynne turned as she heard the clicking of toenails on the hardwood floor. Bamboo came back and sat down by her feet.

Lynne glanced down. "Why is Bamboo chewing on a toothbrush?"

"Uh, I was trying to brush her teeth, but she bit down on the brush and took off running. She hid the brush and I couldn't find it," Margo explained.

"Naughty girl," Lynne scolded. "Bamboo, give me the toothbrush."

Bamboo's ears flipped down as she dropped the toothbrush into her hand. Lynne pried her mouth open, then proceeded to brush Bamboo's teeth.

"Why does she sit still for you and not me?" Margo questioned.

"Because you're not firm enough," she explained. "You let her walk all over you, excuse the pun."

"I guess you're right," she admitted, then yawned. "Well, I'm off to bed. Oh, and by the way, Robert told me that Pastor Hunter said that we were talented."

"Hmm, he might be nice after all," Lynne said.

"Does that mean he's off your *bozo* list?" Margo asked, giggling.

"I don't know. I think he's still on probation." Lynne grinned. Time would tell.

Three

Butterflies danced in her stomach as she stepped onto the stage. Never before had Lynne been so nervous about singing in church. She knew the reason. Matt Hunter was causing her to feel all kinds of emotions lately. The most comfortable emotion she felt toward him was annoyance. But since their encounter in the Coffee Club's parking lot, her feelings had changed. She was starting to like him.

As Lynne took the microphone in her hand, she glanced down to the front row to where Matt was seated. His eyes met hers; she turned quickly as the intro began. Her mind went blank. She panicked as she searched the audience for her cousin. She spotted Margo. She was signing the words "Holy Spirit." Lynne smiled as relief flooded her. She remembered the words to the song instantly. What was happening to her? She never forgot the words to a song.

After the service had ended, Lynne found her cousin. "Thank you for saving my neck," she said, then asked, "but how did you know I had forgotten the words?"

"I don't know exactly. You looked strange, not your normal calm self," Margo said.

Lynne nodded. "Feeling barely able to breathe for a moment, I suddenly felt faced with myriad insecurities."

"Would it have something to do with our new youth pastor?" Margo asked.

Lynne shook her head, denying it all too quickly. "No, but now that you bring his name up, will you help me find him?"

"He's right around the corner," Margo said as she pulled Lynne through the church lobby. "Say, by the way, how come Jackie didn't come to church this morning? I thought you had invited her."

"I did," Lynne said glumly.

"We'll have to make sure she makes it next Sunday," Margo said.

The two women stopped a few feet behind Pastor Hunter. Not wanting to interrupt him as he talked with an elder of the church, they waited off to the side. Lynne's ears perked up when she heard her name mentioned.

"Yes, Miss Wilson seems nice, but it's her dog that I fear," Pastor Hunter said. He chuckled.

Lynne fumed. Margo grabbed her arm to pull her back, but Lynne twisted away, marching directly over to the pastor. "Excuse me, Pastor Hunter," she said.

Pastor Hunter turned. A distressed look suddenly appeared on his face. "Hello, Lynne," he said as the elder conveniently slipped out the side door.

"Here is the money I owe you," Lynne said as she slipped an envelope containing a one-hundred-dollar bill in his hand. She silently willed herself to let go of the envelope. It had been a hard decision to make, but Lynne knew she had to do it. "I hope this will be enough to cover the expenses for your dog's injury."

He shook his head. "No, no, I can't take this money," he said. "It's not necessary."

"Oh, but it is," she replied angrily. "Then maybe you'll stop talking about my dog."

He grimaced. He seemed quite uncomfortable. "Lynne, I'm sorry that you heard me say that—"

Not letting him finish, Lynne turned and walked out the door. One minute she liked him, the next she couldn't stand him.

"What happened?" Margo asked as she caught up to her.

"Margo, he makes me so upset. It's not right to feel this way, especially in church. I feel that my angry thoughts of him are justified, but then I feel guilty and think perhaps I'm being overly sensitive. He's like a thorn in my side. It seems like every time I have a conversation with him, I feel the need to go pray and repent for the ill thoughts I have of him."

Margo smiled. "Let it go. Plain and simple, men sometimes say the dumbest things. Believe me I know; Robert is always putting his foot in his mouth, but I love him just the same."

Lynne nodded. "You're right. I need to let this go."

Finished with her prayer of repentance, Lynne changed into a pair of shorts and a pink sleeveless shirt. She called out to Bamboo, "Let's go for a walk."

Bamboo charged into the room and sat down by her feet. Lynne clipped the leash on her collar, then headed out the door. She needed some fresh air to perk her up. As she neared the sidewalk, a van pulled up and parked at the curb. A man carrying a beautiful array of flowers walked up the sidewalk and stopped at her side. "I'm looking for Lynne Wilson," he said.

"I'm her."

"These are for you then," he said and smiled as he handed her a clipboard. "Please sign here."

She signed her name, then took the flowers. Lynne breathed in the fragrance of the bouquet. They were lovely. She walked back to the porch and set the flowers next to her as she sat down.

Bamboo sniffed at them as Lynne pulled the card from the florist pick. Opening the envelope, she pulled the card out. Her heart skipped a beat as a one-hundred-dollar bill fell out into her hand. Her eyes were drawn to the words on the card.

> *Lynne, please forgive me. It was wrong to talk badly about your dog. I am sorry.*
>
> *Matt*

She smiled as she bent down to pick up the vase. "No, no, Bamboo," she said, aghast at what she saw. A pink Gerber daisy dangled from Bamboo's mouth as she chewed on the stem.

Lynne ripped the daisy from Bamboo's mouth, then

wagged her finger at the corgi. "You're pathetic," she muttered.

She walked back into the house and placed the flowers in the center of the kitchen table. Gazing at the bouquet, she chuckled. Lynne was now glad that she had repented of her ill thoughts before she had received the flowers.

"Bamboo, I think we can return to the dog park," she said. With the mention of those words, Bamboo raced to the door. Lynne grabbed her keys. She hadn't gone back to the dog park since the incident.

On the drive to the park, Bamboo couldn't sit still. Once they arrived, she darted for the park's gate as Lynne opened it. Lynne smiled. Bamboo barked. They were happy.

Pulling the gate closed, Lynne released Bamboo. Phoebe, Bamboo's pug friend, came up for a friendly sniff. The two dogs turned in circles, then ran off.

Lynne sat down on the grass under the shade of an old pine tree. Closing her eyes, she rested her head against the trunk. Her mind rehearsed the songs for the next evening's performance at the Coffee Club. When she sang the words, she felt closer to God. To her, singing was an addiction, one that gave her peace and one that brought her into a deeper worship with the Lord.

"Sounds good," a familiar voice said.

Lynne's heart raced as she opened her eyes. Looking up, she met the youth pastor's gaze. Tall, dark, and good-looking, that was Matt Hunter. "Hello," she said as her heart raced.

"What were you singing?" he asked as he sat down next to her.

"I didn't realize that I was singing out loud," she commented; then her eyes searched for Bamboo. She suddenly felt uneasy. She had to keep an eye on the dogs. This time Bamboo wasn't going to be blamed for anything.

"Lynne, did you hear me?" he asked.

"No. What did you say?" she asked, still staring at Bamboo.

"Why do I get the feeling that you're not paying attention to me?" he asked.

"Maybe because I'm not. For your information I'm just keeping an eye on my dog," she replied.

"He won't bite Brutus again, will he?" Matt said and winked.

"Really!" She glared at him. "First of all, Bamboo is a she, not a he. Secondly, she didn't bite Brutus the first time." Why was it that every time she was around him, her thoughts became muddled? She couldn't think straight. He was simply driving her to distraction.

"Do you know that your eyes turn a lighter shade of ice blue when you're angry?" he asked as a grin appeared on his face.

He was the biggest thorn she had ever met. Why did she suddenly have the urge to bite him on the leg? Revenge for Bamboo. Her thoughts were so absurd. She prayed quickly, *Lord, please help me to be kind.*

Lynne clenched her teeth. "Thank you for the lovely flowers." She decided not to thank him for returning her money.

"Sounds like you really liked them," he replied as a chuckle escaped.

"Bamboo especially enjoyed the pink Gerber daisies," she said. With that comment, she knew she needed counseling but couldn't resist adding, "She also found that fake money very tasty."

Matt roared with laughter. "Lynne, you have a delightful sense of humor."

"Thanks, it helps me to get over the potholes in the road."

"Am I a pothole?" he asked as a lopsided grin appeared.

"More like a crater," she muttered.

Matt grinned. "I think I've met my match."

Lynne smiled, then said, "Better watch your dog. Looks like he's growling at a rottweiler."

Matt shook his head as he looked from her to his dog. "Brutus, come," he called. The Great Dane raced over. Sitting down by Matt, Brutus panted heavily.

Lynne reached out her hand slowly as Brutus leaned forward to sniff her. "Hi, Brutus. How's the leg?" His tongue slapped a wet one on her hand.

"His leg has healed fine," Matt answered. He stood up and dusted himself off. "Are you going to be at the church softball game on Saturday?"

"I have to be," she said.

"Why? Do you sing the anthem?"

"Oh, aren't you funny." She creased her brows. "No, I'm the pitcher for the Righteous. What team did Pastor Drew place you on?" The pastor loved softball, and insisted on having the two church teams play once a month during the softball season.

"He put me on the best team, the Chosen," he said.

"We'll see which team is best." Lynne smiled. This pastor needed to be humbled.

Matt returned her smile. "I'll be looking forward to it. I must be going; I have to go get ready for the evening service."

She stood up. "Have a nice day."

"I will now," he said, then winked.

Her eyes followed the pair as they left the park. Brutus was a handsome and well-mannered dog, despite the fact that his owner was not well trained.

She thought about Matt's comment regarding Bamboo. She bristled. How dare he insinuate that Bamboo would bite Brutus again. Lynne would go to her grave knowing that her little corgi never bit Brutus the first time.

"As if his big mutt couldn't defend himself," she said grumbling.

Lynne glanced over at the gate. Matt hadn't left. He was talking with the woman who owned Phoebe, the pug. Lynne wished that she could hear what they were talking about. Whatever it was, Matt didn't look happy.

Lynne waited until Matt and Brutus left, then she walked over to the woman. She introduced herself. "Hello, my name is Lynne."

"You're Bamboo's mom," the woman replied in a friendly manner. "My name is Sharon."

Lynne smiled. "Phoebe's mom, right?"

Sharon nodded. "Our dogs love playing with each other."

"Bamboo is definitely more playful and happy around dogs her own size than the bigger dogs, like that Great

Dane that just left," Lynne said.

"Oh, I agree; same with Phoebe," Sharon commented. "I was just talking with the owner of that Great Dane. I noticed that the dog's leg had healed nicely."

Lynne stared at her. "How did you know that his leg had been hurt?"

"I saw him stumble over a broken sprinkler head over there," Sharon explained. "The metal sprinkler head was stuck in the upright position. That's why he hit it. But the park crew fixed it so I wanted to let that gentleman know. He won't have to worry about his dog getting hurt again."

Lynne was giddy. "So you told him that you saw his Great Dane hit the sprinkler head?"

"Oh yes," she said. "But he didn't look too happy about it. He doesn't seem too friendly."

"I agree. Well, I'd better be going. It was nice meeting you," Lynne said.

"Nice to meet you too," Sharon said.

Lynne laughed as she jogged over to where Bamboo was playing. She was deliriously happy. Bamboo was proven innocent. "Boo, come here," she called.

Bamboo trotted over. Lynne picked her up and squeezed her tight. She couldn't contain her joy. "Boo-girl, you've been exonerated." Now Lynne wondered how long it would take Matt to share the news with her. Or maybe he wouldn't?

Arriving home, Lynne went directly to her room. She couldn't get Matt off of her mind. Her thoughts went to his laugh, then to his smile. How could he be charming and irritating at the same time? And why was she thinking about him all the time? Lynne picked up her weathered old Bible and flipped through the pages as she prayed. *I need help, Lord.*

Her eyes came to rest on the Scripture in the Book of Philippians. She smiled as she read the passage, "Let your gentleness be evident to all." *Okay, Lord, I know what You're saying. It's going to be hard to follow, but I'm going to try to be on my best behavior when I'm around him*, she promised silently.

She continued to read, "In everything, by prayer and petition, with thanksgiving, present your requests to God. And the peace of God, which transcends all understanding, will guard your hearts and your minds in Christ Jesus."

Lynne placed her Bible back on the nightstand. She felt better already.

Four

It had been a busy day at church. Lynne spent most of the day in her office filing. After taking a coffee break, she walked into the copy room. There stood Matt, casually dressed in jeans and a white shirt. His back was to her and she could hear him mumbling to himself. She moved back to the door, but not before Matt turned around.

"Caught you," he said, grinning. "You weren't trying to sneak out before I saw you?"

"Of course not," she said. "How are you adjusting to your new surroundings?"

"Good, except for the fact that I can't seem to operate this machine. I only need one copy," he explained.

"Matt, next time you need copies of something, drop it off on my desk and I'll run it for you. That's my job."

Matt smiled as he leaned back against the copy machine. "Do you do coffee runs also?"

Lynne smiled. "Only if you ask politely."

"I'm always polite." He winked.

Lynne snorted as she grabbed the sheet of paper out

of his hands. "This is how it works. Lift lid, place paper on the glass between the arrows, shut lid, press start and poof. . .here is your copy. Easy as one, two, three."

"Thanks," he said as he took the copy. "How about lunch?" He gazed down at her; his brown eyes sparkled as a lopsided grin appeared. "Please."

Why did he have to be so attractive? "I brought lunch, but thanks for the invite."

"Some other time perhaps?" he asked, not giving up.

Lynne found herself nodding. "Sure." She wondered when he was going to mention something about Brutus and the sprinkler episode. She decided not to say anything yet; she wanted him to tell her.

"How long have you been a secretary here at West Coast?" he asked, changing the subject.

"Four years and I've been a church soloist for six," she answered. "And how many years have you been in the ministry?"

"This is my third year as a youth pastor," he said.

"Really?" Lynne raised her eyebrows. "How did you choose this church to put in your application for youth pastor?"

"I didn't choose this church; God chose it," he said, smiling.

Intrigued, Lynne probed further. "Can you explain that in a little more detail?"

"Pastor Drew and Lana know my parents. When West Coast's youth pastor left here, Pastor Drew called me and asked me if I'd be interested in being the youth pastor here. I hesitated. West Coast Community was such a large church compared to the church that I had been the youth pastor at. I didn't think I could handle a youth group of that size," he admitted.

"What made you accept the offer?" Lynne asked.

Matt laughed. "Pastor Drew's persistence. He wouldn't leave me alone."

"Oh yes, he certainly can be that way, especially if God put it on his heart," Lynne shared.

"So, I prayed about it, and here I am," he said. Then with a smile he added, "Aren't you glad that I made that decision?"

"Oh, sure, I'm happy as a clam." She couldn't help but grin. When Matt chose to be, he was really a likeable man.

"That's what I was hoping you'd say." His eyes twinkled.

"So, tell me something else. . .I heard someone say that you're not taking a salary from the church."

"That's correct. I'd better get back to work now," he said abruptly.

Without another word, Matt left the room. "Was it something I said?" Lynne muttered. He was a hard man to figure out. Matt didn't even bring up the subject of Bamboo's innocence either. If she was smart, she would stay far away from that man.

"Jackie called in sick," Margo said after Lynne walked into the house. "This is the third day in a row. Maybe somebody should check in with her."

"I think I'll drop by her apartment before our gig at the Coffee Club," Lynne said as she closed the book she had been reading.

"You had better leave now or you won't have time," Margo suggested.

Lynne stood up. "You're right. I'll leave now."

Jackie's apartment was across town. She pulled up to the curb and parked. She walked down the tree-lined path to Jackie's apartment. When she knocked at the door, an older woman answered. "Can I help you?"

"Yes, is Jackie home? I'm Lynne Wilson. I work with Jackie," she explained.

The woman suddenly looked displeased. "She's sick."

"Maybe I should come back tomorrow," Lynne suggested.

"No, please don't," the woman said coldly.

Startled at her answer, Lynne replied, "Are you Jackie's mother?"

"Yes, and I don't appreciate you stuffing your religion down her throat," she said angrily.

Lynne swallowed hard and tried to remain calm. This was not going well. "I would never stuff Christianity down anyone's throat. Your daughter asked me about my faith and I simply invited her to church."

"*Simply* nothing, you've messed up her mind," Jackie's mother said. Without another word, she shut the door.

Lynne stood there motionless. She willed herself to move. What had she done? She had shared her faith with Jackie, nothing more nothing less. Lynne turned slowly and walked back down the pathway. She felt awful. How could she sing tonight? She needed prayer.

Lynne headed down the street to a gas station and parked. She walked over to the pay phone. Her fingers punched out the numbers to the church. Maybe Pastor Drew or Lana would still be there.

Finally on the seventh ring, someone answered, "Hello, West Coast Community. Can I help you?"

Lynne froze. She didn't want to talk to him.

"Hello," Matt repeated.

"Hello, is Pastor Drew in?" she asked.

"Lynne, is that you?"

"Yes, is Pastor Drew or Lana in?"

"No, but I am," he said.

She sighed. "Okay, well thanks. Bye."

"Wait, Lynne," he said. "You don't sound good. . .are you all right?"

She took a deep breath to steady her frayed nerves. "Yes. . .no. . .I mean, I'm okay," she mumbled.

"Did you have a tussle with your little doggie perhaps?" he asked with a chuckle.

"You're heartless. I'm sick of your jokes about my dog," Lynne said. Without warning she burst into tears. She felt miserable. She needed prayer and she wasn't getting it.

"Lynne, I'm sorry," he said. "I'm always saying stupid things when I'm around you. I was only trying to be humorous."

"Well, you're not," she said with a sniff.

"What's wrong, Lynne? Can I help you?"

"Since you're the only one I can get ahold of right now, I guess you'll have to do. I need prayer," she admitted reluctantly. "I feel like I can't sing. My confidence is shaken. I don't know what to do and honestly, I don't feel like talking to you about it."

"I deserved that," he admitted. "But listen, Lynne, I've been in some similar situations. Remember what I shared with you earlier about my reluctance to accept the position at West Coast? The Lord showed me that it was fear that was holding me back. There is a Scripture that helped me overcome the fear. It's 2 Timothy 1:7, and it says, 'For God did not give us a spirit of timidity, but a spirit of power, of love and of self-discipline.' Don't let your confidence be shaken. Don't let fear keep you down. You have a gifted voice; use it to glorify the Lord and don't worry about anything else."

"Thanks, I'll try to remember that. Good-bye, Matt," Lynne said.

She replaced the receiver and thought about the Scripture. She had felt fear. When Jackie's mom had berated her for sharing her faith with Jackie, Lynne felt terrified. She knew that fear could easily disable a person from doing the Lord's work. She was going to try to not let that happen, no matter how bad she felt.

As Lynne walked back to her car, she repeated the Scripture over and over. A calming peace fell over her. She slid into the driver's seat and headed for the Coffee Club. She remembered something that Pastor Drew had once told her: "Prayer was the tender nerve that moved the mighty hand of God." As she drove, even though she certainly didn't feel like it, she prayed for Jackie and her mother.

The next morning was uneventful. Pastor Drew and Matt

were in a meeting with the board members and all was quiet in the church office. Not even the phone had rung. Lynne stared at the computer screen as she thought of Matt. He was constantly on her mind. She thought of him way too much.

"Lynne?"

Lynne looked up. Jackie was standing in the doorway. "Hi, Jackie," she greeted. "Come in and sit down."

"Thanks," she said as she took a seat. "Am I interrupting your work?"

She shook her head. "I'm caught up with my work, so there's nothing to interrupt. Are you feeling better now?"

Jackie nodded. "I wanted to thank you for coming by yesterday."

Lynne raised her eyebrows. "Did your mom tell you that I came?"

"No, I heard Mom talking to you. I wanted to apologize for her rudeness," she explained.

"Oh, Jackie, that's all right," she said, fidgeting with her pen.

"No, it wasn't all right. Mom is angry because I want to go to church now. I asked her to come with me and she blew her top. Then I shared about that night and how your song touched my heart, and she grew more angry and told me to quit my job at the Coffee Club."

Now Lynne understood why Jackie's mom had been so upset. "Is that why you've been calling in sick?" she asked.

Jackie nodded. "Mom said that if I go back, I might as well find another place to live."

At twenty, Jackie probably didn't have enough money to move out. "Jackie, do you really want to go to church?"

"I do and I know the Lord wants me to," she admitted. "Don't get me wrong, I love my mom, but I know Mom doesn't want to go with me because of her drinking addiction. She used to call herself a Christian and she knows that what she's doing is wrong, and that is why she is so angry with me."

"You're probably right," Lynne said. "If you continued to work at the Coffee Club and went to church, do you think that your mom would really ask you to leave or is she just bluffing?"

"My mom may be an alcoholic, but she still loves me," Jackie said quietly. "No, I know she wouldn't make me leave."

"Then continue to work at the club and start going to church," Lynne said as she reached across the desk and squeezed Jackie's hand. "Trust in the Lord and He'll give you the strength to handle the situation with your mom."

Jackie stood up. "Thanks, Lynne, for talking with me. I feel better already."

Lynne followed Jackie to the door. "Remember the Lord is on your side," Lynne said as she hugged Jackie.

Five

Lynne was not happy; the Righteous were losing. They had scored one run and the other team had scored four. The Chosen were gloating and whooping it up. Normally this wouldn't have bothered her, but since Matt had hit a grand slam on her fast pitch, she was miserable. They had one hope left; Robert was up to bat.

"Come on, Honey, you can do it," Margo called out.

Robert smiled and puffed up his chest. Lynne held her breath as Pastor Drew threw the first pitch.

"Strike one," the umpire said.

"Robert, we're counting on you," Lynne called.

"Strike two," the umpire said.

Lynne groaned. Margo sighed. Then the sound of the ball cracking off the bat made the two women look up. Robert hit a high flyer. The ball sailed out of the park.

"Yippee!" Margo jumped up.

"Way to go, Robert," Lynne hollered. Three runs came in. The score was tied.

Margo was up to bat. Pastor Drew looked confident

as he threw three perfect pitches. Margo was out. The Chosen were up and it was the bottom of the last inning.

The afternoon sun was hot and the air was thick with humidity. Lynne took a gulp of water then took the mound. Her palms grew moist. Not a good sign. Wiping her hands on her pants, her eyes watched the batter step up to the plate. He was smiling. She needed to wipe that confident smile off Matt's face.

Lynne concentrated as the ball rolled off her fingers.

"Strike one," the umpire said.

"Yes," Lynne said under her breath as the people in the stands clapped.

"Strike two," the umpire called again.

"One more," Lynne uttered. As the ball left her fingers, she knew instantly that it wasn't a good pitch.

Thwack! As Lynne watched in horror, the pitch curved then collided with Matt's leg. Matt fell to the ground. Moaning, he held onto his knee.

Lynne rushed to his side as others gathered around. "I'm so sorry," she said to Matt.

"Where did the ball hit you, Matt?" Lana questioned.

"On the knee," he groaned.

"Matt, let's get you to the doctor," Pastor Drew said as he squeezed in front of Lynne.

"I don't think I can get up just yet," he said in a raspy voice.

"We'll help you to the car," Robert said as he moved to Matt's side.

Pastor Drew and Robert helped Matt up. As they assisted Matt to Pastor Drew's car, Lynne followed behind. Feeling quite miserable she looked down at her hands. How could she have thrown such a lousy pitch?

"Lynne, I've never seen you pitch that awful," Margo said from behind her. "What happened, Girl?"

Lynne turned. "My hands were moist from nerves. The ball slipped off my hand wrong."

"You can say that again!" Margo exclaimed.

"Alright," Lynne said. "I feel terrible and you're not helping matters."

"It doesn't look good for you, though."

Lynne glared at her cousin. "What do you mean by that?"

"Well, everyone knows that you and Matt don't get along—"

"Oh, so everyone thinks I hit him on purpose," she interrupted.

Margo shrugged. "But I know you didn't."

"Wow, thanks for the vote of confidence," Lynne grumbled as she opened the car door.

Margo and Lynne drove silently to the emergency center. The two women caught up with the men as they entered the hospital. Lynne felt racked with guilt as she looked at Matt. He glanced her way, but his face was expressionless.

Lynne wanted to say something, but before she could, the nurse ushered him through a door and he disappeared.

Pastor Drew walked over and sat down next to Lynne. "Don't feel bad, Lynne," he said, patting her gently on the shoulder. "Accidents happen."

"Do you think it was an accident?" she questioned

sullenly, then glanced at Margo. "I know others will think I did it on purpose."

"Lynne, don't worry about what others think. I know you didn't intentionally hit Matt." Pastor Drew stood up and began to pace the hallway.

"I'll never pitch again," she mumbled, putting her head in her hands.

"Lynne, don't talk that way," Margo said as she put her arm around her cousin.

"Matt will be fine. He's tough," Robert chimed in.

"You'll forget about this by tomorrow," Margo said.

"Easy for you to say," she whispered. "You won't have the whole church glaring at you. I hit our new youth pastor in the leg and they obviously know that the two of us haven't gotten along well."

At that moment, Matt emerged from the exam room. Leaning on one crutch, he appeared to still be in pain. The doctor talked to him a few minutes before Matt hobbled over to them. Lynne tried to swallow the large knot that had formed in her throat.

"What's the prognosis, Matt?" Pastor Drew asked.

"It could have been worse," Matt said. "They took X-rays and fortunately I only have a bruised kneecap. He gave me an ice pack and some pain pills."

Lynne breathed a sigh of relief. "Thank You, Lord."

Matt smiled at her. "That's exactly what I said."

Lynne was relieved to see him smile. "How long will it take to heal?"

"The doctor said I'd feel back to normal in a week's time," he explained. "You have one mean pitch, Lady."

"Now, now, she didn't do it on purpose," Pastor Drew responded quickly.

Matt laughed. "I can see that you're doing your job of protecting the church secretary."

"She's a fine woman and a good softball pitcher," Pastor Drew said, then turned to Lynne. "Why don't you take Matt home? I'll take Margo and Robert back to the field with me."

"That's a great idea." Matt grinned.

"See, everything worked out okay," Margo whispered.

"The day's not over," Lynne whispered back.

The car was silent as they drove to Matt's house. He was renting a small home close to the church. After she parked in the driveway, she walked around to Matt's side.

"Can I help you out?" she asked.

"No, I can manage," he said as he leaned on the crutch for support. "Really, it's not bad at all."

"I'm certainly glad to hear that," she said as relief flooded her.

"Can you come in for a moment?" He looked hopeful.

"Yes, sure," she said as she followed him in. She turned and closed the door for him.

"No, Brutus," Matt called out suddenly.

Thud! Instantly Lynne fell against the door. A huge weight pinned her alongside the door, sending her face crashing against the hardwood frame.

"Brutus, down," he commanded. "Lynne, are you okay?"

As Brutus backed away, she was able to move. "I think so." She reached for her nose. The pain was excruciating. As she pulled her hand away, blood ran down her chin. "Do you have a towel or something?" she asked, turning around to face Matt.

"Oh, Lynne, I'm sorry," he said, then turned to Brutus. "Bad boy. Go lie down, Brutus."

"Woof." A deep bark came from Brutus as he plunked down on the wood floor, putting his head down between his large paws.

"I'll be right back with a towel," he said.

Lynne stood by the door, not moving. Brutus kept his big brown eyes fixed on her. She tilted her head back, hoping that it would slow the bleeding. Matt came hobbling back into the entryway with a towel.

"Can I move, or will he attack me again?" Lynne asked as she took the towel.

"He didn't attack you; that was his way of greeting you," he explained. "Doesn't Bamboo jump up to greet you when you come home?"

"Yes, but she's only a foot high so when she jumps up, she can't knock me over and break my nose."

Matt laughed despite the situation. "Point taken. Come and sit down. Brutus won't hurt you again, I promise."

"Put your hand on the Bible and promise, then I might believe you," Lynne said as she followed him into the small living room.

"Lynne, why is it that whenever we are together, sparks fly?" Matt asked. He carefully edged himself down next to her on the couch as he placed the crutch off to the side.

"Perhaps it's the way our relationship started off," she suggested. "After all, you did say Bamboo was a vicious corgi while demanding that I pay the vet bill for your pooch here—the one, I might add, that almost broke my nose just now."

"And you paid me back by whacking me with your crazy pitch," he reminded her.

Lynne laughed. "No wonder the sparks fly. . .I think we have it out for each other."

Matt chuckled. "I think we'd better start over." He reached out his hand and grabbed hers. "Hello, my name is Matt. Nice to meet you."

"Hello, my name is Lynne. Nice to meet you," she said as she shook his hand. She liked the feel of his warm hand around hers. Maybe they could be friends after all.

"Okay, we're off to a good start," he said. "How's your nose?"

Lynne took the towel away. "It's stopped bleeding now."

"Good. Can you stay for dinner or do you have to work at the Coffee Club tonight?"

"No, I have the night off. I'd love to stay for dinner."

"Great. Can you help me make spaghetti? I don't know how long I'll be able to stand with this sore knee, so I might need you to make the sauce."

"Since spaghetti is a no-brainer, how about if you show me where everything is, then I can make it and you rest," she suggested.

"Okay, that's a deal," he said.

Lynne helped him up and handed him the crutch. "Can Brutus get up now? He looks sad."

"He always gives me that look when he's in trouble," Matt said. "Come here, Brutus." Brutus ambled over, his long tail swishing behind him. Stopping in front of Matt, he whimpered.

"It's okay, Brutus. Let's call it a truce," Lynne said as she stretched her hand out slowly. Brutus sniffed it, then licked it. He was a sweet dog, but didn't know his own strength.

As Lynne looked past Brutus, she saw a picture on the side table. It was of an older woman standing next to Brutus. Perched on her head was a tall pink hat with feathers. "Not to be nosey, but who's the hat lady?"

Matt reached down and picked up the frame. "This is Aunt Harriet. She collects hats like Imelda Marcos collects shoes. And the more flamboyant the hat the better."

"Sounds like an interesting lady."

"She is, and I love her dearly."

Lynne fixed dinner while Matt set the table. The dining room looked out onto a large patio filled with ferns, Japanese maple trees, and an array of colorful impatiens cascading from terra-cotta planters. Matt opened the French doors that led out to the patio, letting in a cool breeze.

Lynne piled the spaghetti onto the plates and poured the iced tea into the tumblers, then sat down. After Matt prayed for the food, Lynne said, "You have a lovely house here. Rentals are not usually this nice and well taken care of."

"Katie, the kindergarten teacher at church, is renting it to me," he explained. "It's close to church and it's just the right size for Brutus and me."

Lynne glanced over at Matt. It was time for true confessions and she wanted to hear his. "So, Pastor Hunter, when are you going to tell me about Brutus and the broken sprinkler head?" she asked boldly.

Matt choked on his spaghetti. Coughing and sputtering, he stared at her in disbelief. "How. . .? When. . .?" he asked. Raising his glass, he gulped down some tea.

She raised an eyebrow, enjoying his discomfort and said, "The same day that you found out."

"Oh, wow." He sighed and raked a hand through his black hair. "I'm in trouble."

"Uh-huh." Lynne smiled.

Matt threw her a puzzled look. "Why are you smiling at me? Aren't you mad?"

"No, I think I know why you didn't say anything," she said.

"Why?"

She took a long, slow sip of her drink, deliberately making him wait for her answer. "First, you thought I'd gloat, then, second, I'd lecture you on how terrible it is to make wrong assumptions, then—"

"Okay, okay," he said with a chuckle as he raised his hands in the air. "I can't bear any more of this. I'm sorry. I was wrong. I'm an overprotective pet owner and I need counseling."

"You're forgiven." Lynne rested back in her chair, feeling quite happy with herself that the matter had been resolved.

Matt's eyes grew large. "That's it? I'm forgiven? That's way too easy."

Lynne laughed, then changed the subject. "Tell me something, did you raise Brutus from a puppy?"

"No, I adopted him a few years ago from an SPCA shelter," he explained. "Brutus had been abused by his previous owner and I guess that is why I'm overprotective concerning him. When I thought Bamboo had bitten him that day at the park, I went on the offensive—"

"That's an understatement," interjected Lynne. "You went kind of berserk."

"Okay, I was an obnoxious dog owner. I confess," he said as he leaned back in his chair. "I feel better now that it's out in the open."

"Yes, confession is good for the soul, Pastor." Lynne grinned, then glanced over at Brutus who was lying on the hardwood floor. "He's a nice dog, but his size is so intimidating."

"He's a gentle giant, trust me," Matt replied.

"Tell that to my aching nose." Lynne giggled.

"Yes, jumping on guests is not good," Matt agreed. "But really, he is quite mannerly. I take him with me a couple times a month to visit the children in the pediatrics division of the local hospitals."

Lynne was shocked. "You're kidding me. The hospitals let a big dog like that visit sick children?"

"It's all set up by the SPCA. They have a program called the Animal-Assisted Therapy. I learned of it after I had adopted Brutus. Pet owners take their pets to hospitals, nursing homes, and other institutions and let the patients pet, hug, and talk with their new animal friend."

"What a wonderful idea," Lynne remarked. "How long have you and Brutus been in the program?"

"For about a year now. After I saw the joy on the

children's faces when they were able to spend some time with Brutus, I became hooked," he said. "I've gotten to know some of the children's parents and since they know I'm a youth pastor, I've been able to share my faith with them."

Lynne leaned forward and smiled. "Where can Bamboo and I sign up?"

Matt perked up. "You'd like to participate in the program?"

She nodded happily. "Bamboo is great with kids."

"Next month on the first Saturday I have an appointment at the Children's Hospital of Orange. Would you like to join Brutus and me?"

"Oh yes," she readily agreed.

"After church service tomorrow morning, my youth group is having a picnic at the park across the street from the church. Can you and Bamboo join us? I'll bring Brutus, then we can see how they get along before we take them to the hospital together."

"Sure, that's a good idea."

"Also, the program requires the pet that is participating in AAT to go through a behavior test. They have to be reassured that the animal will be of good temperament, up-to-date on their vaccinations, and, of course, well-groomed."

"How do I get Bamboo tested?" she asked as she began to clear the dishes from the table.

"I'll make an appointment for her at the SPCA center this week and then you can take Bamboo there."

"Sounds good," she said. "Speaking of Bamboo, I know

she must be starving, so I'd better head home now."

"Thanks for fixing dinner for me." He reached for the crutch, and stood up slowly.

"You're welcome," she said. "How's your knee?"

"It's aching, but I think a couple of aspirin could cure that." He opened the front door for her. "How's your nose?"

"It's sore." She laughed. "We're a couple of wrecks."

Matt chuckled as he followed her to her car. He leaned up against it. "It's a clear night; the stars are bright tonight."

Lynne glanced skyward. The stars sparkled and the moon shone brightly against the dark sky. She looked at him; their eyes met. Lynne's heart skipped a beat. She watched as Matt reached out and took her hands in his.

"Lynne, are you feeling what I'm feeling?" he asked in a husky voice.

She tried to steady her breathing as she looked up at him. "Yes," she whispered.

He pulled her gently to him. Lynne melted against him as he placed a gentle kiss on her lips. "You're so beautiful," he murmured. His kiss deepened and she returned it willingly. He pulled back, taking a deep breath. "Lynne, I've never met anyone like you. Your zest for living is contagious. When I first heard you sing, you took my breath away. Your love for the Lord is evident in everything you do and I feel like I'm being drawn in by it. In fact, I find myself always thinking of you," he admitted.

Lynne, astonished by his admission, blushed. "Matt, I think of you quite often too."

"What's our next step?" he asked, grinning winsomely.

"Let me think about it. This is all happening quite fast," she remarked softly.

He nodded. "Okay, I'll leave the next step up to you. . . now go home and feed Bamboo."

Lynne smiled. "Thanks for reminding me." Right now her mind wasn't on anything but Matt. She climbed into the driver's seat, then looked up at him. "I'll see you at church."

Matt bent down, then whispered, "I loved it."

She raised a brow. "Loved what?"

"Your kiss." He grinned mischievously.

"Oh. . .uh. . .yes. . .well," she stuttered, "yours was. . . uh. . .it was good too."

He smiled. "See you tomorrow, Miss Wilson."

"Yes, good night," she said dreamily.

On the ride home, Lynne couldn't believe how her thoughts had changed concerning Matt Hunter. Suddenly she was thinking of him in serious terms. The more she got to know him, the more she loved to be around him. She thought of marriage, family, dogs. . . Her heart raced.

Lynne shook her head. She was loco. One kiss and she was thinking matrimony? She barely knew the man. She needed to know more. Her thoughts went suddenly to what Robert had said about him: He didn't take a salary from the church because he was loaded. Where did his money come from?

That night, with Bamboo nestled at the foot of the bed, Lynne's mind would not be quiet. It rambled on about Matt, robbing her of sleep. She was excited, yet apprehensive about starting a relationship with Matt. She was the church secretary, he was the youth pastor; they shouldn't just jump in with both feet without testing the waters first. *Lord, guide my paths. Keep my eyes open and my ears hearing. Help me know Your will concerning Matt and me*, Lynne prayed. Sleep eventually came, but not before she had tossed and turned a few more times.

Lynne picked up Bamboo after church and drove to the park for the youth group picnic. She had felt disappointed at the morning service; Jackie hadn't shown up at church once again. Lynne was determined to pray for Jackie every day until she saw her walk through those church doors.

When Lynne saw the youth group, she pulled over and parked. Bamboo bounced out of the vehicle, pulling hard on the leash. Whenever she saw a group of kids, she wanted to be in the midst of them.

She spotted Matt and Brutus; they were surrounded by teenagers. Immediately Matt saw her and waved her over.

Lynne hoped that Brutus and Bamboo would get along well. She couldn't help but smile for it felt like a double date.

Matt pulled himself away from the kids and walked over to her. She noticed that he didn't have his crutch for support.

Matt reached out and hugged her. "Nice to see you, Miss Wilson."

Surprised by the display of affection, Lynne suddenly felt shy. "Hello, Matt."

"Hi, Lynne," he greeted warmly, then looking at Bamboo he bent down. "Hello, little lady." He stroked her back as she wiggled around excitedly. Bamboo moved in closer, enjoying the attention.

A deep "woof" came from Brutus. His huge jowls shook as he stood up and walked over to Bamboo.

Bamboo hit the grass. "What is she doing?" Matt asked.

"She always lies down when an unfamiliar big dog approaches," she informed him.

Brutus sniffed her, then poked her with his nose. Bamboo didn't move. The Great Dane moved around her, continuing to check her out.

Matt shook his head. "How I ever could have thought that she had bitten Brutus is beyond me."

"It's beyond me too," Lynne agreed. "Now you know why I defended her with determination."

"She looks like a little fox with those pointy ears and her reddish and white coat," he remarked. "But it seems like she's missing a tail."

Lynne smiled. "The breeders clip it off when they're pups."

Bamboo finally stood up, walking slowly around Brutus. She was so short in comparison that she walked right under him and he didn't even notice her there. Lynne tried hard to keep them from getting tangled up in their leashes as they kept moving around each other.

"I think they like each other," Matt said with relief. "Let's leave them here on the leashes—*away* from the food." He chuckled. "I'll tie the ends around the pole so they can't get loose."

"Is your knee better? I noticed that you don't have your crutch," she remarked.

"It's over there by the tables. My knee is healing faster than I expected."

"I'm happy to hear that," Lynne said as she glanced over at all the food on the tables. Her stomach growled. "I'm starved."

"Let's eat now while the kids are playing football," he suggested as they walked toward the tables. "Then we can eat in peace and talk without them hearing us."

"Sounds good." Lynne reached for a plate, then started dishing the food onto it. She sat down at a table that was still shaded from the afternoon sun.

Matt sat down next to her, prayed for their meal, then informed her, "I made an appointment for Bamboo to be tested at the SPCA center. It's tomorrow morning at nine o'clock. Can you make it?"

"Sure, that's fine."

"Lynne, did I move too fast last night? I don't want to do anything that would scare you off," he said.

She shook her head. "No, but I think we need to know more about each other before this goes any farther."

Matt grinned. "You go first then. Tell me your life story."

"I have no family except for my cousin, Margo, Aunt Andrea, and Uncle Chip. I lost my parents in an airplane accident when I was sixteen."

Matt placed his hand on hers and squeezed it. "I'm so sorry for your loss, Lynne."

She nodded, then continued, "Since I was little, I've

felt a desire to serve the Lord. I've always wanted to sing for Him and be involved in ministry. After my parents died, though, I didn't sing for a while, but eventually Aunt Andrea, Uncle Chip, and Margo encouraged me to sing and it was healing for me. Then Margo started accompanying me on the piano, and that's how we began to sing and play together."

"How about the men in your life?" he probed.

"Men. . .hmm. . .well, there haven't been a lot," she confessed with honesty. "I think my expectations are too high."

"Not a bad way to be," Matt said. "You'd only accept the best then."

Lynne nodded. "Now why don't you share a little about yourself, Pastor?"

Matt grinned handsomely. "Okay, time to expose my inner feelings, my dreams, my goals and ambitions, right?"

Lynne smiled. "I don't think you'll have time for all that; it looks like the picnic kids are getting hungry."

Matt glanced over at the group of teenagers. They weren't moving so fast now. "I'll make this fast then. I was a rebel growing up. I resisted going to church with my parents. I thought serving the Lord was boring and I didn't want any part of it. My grandfather was the pastor of our church, and even though my attitude was awful, he was always so good to me. I couldn't figure it out. He took me to baseball games, well-chosen movies, and fishing trips. We were buddies. Even though he was so busy with his church, he always found time for me.

"When I was about to graduate from high school I remember Gramps asking me what I was going to do with my life. I had received a scholarship in baseball, so of course my dream was to be a major league baseball player. I shared that dream with him. He then asked me if I ever felt led to go into the ministry like he had. I had laughed at the thought. That was the farthest thing from my mind.

"The day of my graduation, Gramps was diagnosed with cancer. It was terminal. I was devastated. From that day on, I spent every day with Gramps. I really loved him, Lynne. He was such a good man and was always giving of himself and kind toward others, even when they didn't share his beliefs."

Matt's eyes grew misty. "Every day I let Gramps read the Bible to me. I didn't even argue when he'd pull that weathered old book out from his nightstand. Little did I know that it was his perfect opportunity to plant the seed of faith in his wayward grandson.

"Before Gramps died I found myself promising him that I would go to Bible college, then on to theological seminary. The aspiration to play baseball wasn't there anymore. A new desire was placed in my heart, a desire to serve the Lord. A transformation had taken place in me and frankly, I was amazed.

"Right after I told Gramps that, he raised his Bible and placed it against his heart. I'll never forget that moment in time. It was the first time I'd ever seen my grandfather cry. I wept. It had changed my life and I thank God to this day for that special time with Gramps."

A tear rolled down Lynne's cheek. "He was some grandfather, wasn't he?"

Matt nodded. "God allowed something wonderful to

happen during those last months of Gramps' life. God gave me a second chance to serve Him. I took it greedily."

"Oh, Matt, that is such an inspiring story," Lynne said as she wiped the tear from her cheek.

"Hey, Pastor Hunter, can we eat?" a teenager hollered as others walked over to Matt.

"Yeah, we're starving," another one said.

"Sure, let's say the blessing first," Matt said. After the prayer, the kids all ran over and grabbed plates.

"While they're eating, can we stretch our legs and walk the dogs?" Lynne asked.

"Good idea, but let's stay in this area so we can keep a close eye on the kids."

"Look, Matt." Lynne pointed to where the dogs were resting. Bamboo and Brutus were lying side by side. "I think that they like each other."

"What a relief," Matt remarked. He walked over and untied their leashes from the pole. Bamboo shot forward and Brutus followed with a gallop. "She's got quite a wiggle. All you see is this fluffy bottom with no tail."

Lynne laughed as Bamboo pulled her forward. "Cute, isn't she?"

He nodded. "And she's full of energy; I wonder if Brutus can keep up."

Lynne watched as the Great Dane lumbered alongside Bamboo. "I don't think he'll let her out of his sight."

"It's already evident that she has him wrapped around her furry little paws." Matt chuckled.

"What can I say?" Lynne shrugged. "She has a certain female charm that draws those big dogs to her."

"Just like her mom." Matt grinned.

"Does that mean you're a big dog?" Lynne said as a giggle escaped.

"A big dopey dog that's head over paws for you," he confessed.

Lynne pulled Bamboo to a halt. She stared at him. "Matt, we haven't even dated yet."

Matt stopped. Brutus came to sit by him. "I can easily remedy that. Miss Wilson, will you go out on a date with me tomorrow night?"

She frowned. "I have to work at the club."

"Can I meet you at the Coffee Club before you have to sing, then we could have dinner together?"

"It's a date, Pastor Hunter." Lynne smiled. She wanted to get to know Matt even more.

Six

Lynne took great pride in wearing little makeup. Her high cheekbones had a healthy pink glow and her blues eyes sparkled with anticipation of her date with Matt. She had anchored two jeweled hairpins in her hair, sprayed some perfume on, and was ready for the evening.

Lynne sat down at a table next to Margo in the back of the Coffee Club. The two women had decided to arrive a little early. They had practiced their music and still had time to spare before Matt arrived.

"It seems like you and Matt are becoming an item," Margo commented, then winked at her cousin. "You hit him in the knee and *boom,* he falls for you."

Lynne rolled her eyes and laughed. "You're so goofy."

"Seriously though, how are you two getting along?"

"Great, except that one thing is bugging me. I've yet to learn how he can work for the church without taking a salary," Lynne said.

"He's wealthy. Robert told us, remember?"

"But where did he get his money?" Lynne questioned.

"And why is he living in a rental home the size of a cottage if he has so much money?"

Margo raised her eyebrows. "Good question, but knowing you, you'll find out real soon."

"Hmm. . .I hope so."

"Well, I'm going to go tickle the ivories while you have dinner with Matt," Margo said.

Lynne smiled. "Are you providing us mood music?"

"You bet I am." Margo grinned.

"Thanks, Cuz." Lynne stood up and headed for the kitchen. The chef had prepared dinner for her and Matt. The plates of food were waiting under the heat lamps.

As she carried the turkey melt sandwiches back to the table, Matt walked into the club. He looked handsome dressed in dark pants, a crisp white shirt, and maroon-colored tie. She waved him over to the table.

"Perfect timing; dinner is served," she said cheerfully.

"Hello, Miss Wilson," he said, then took her hand and brought it to his lips. His kiss sent her heart aflutter. She saw Margo watching from behind the piano. Her eyes were as big as saucers. Margo gave her the thumbs-up signal. Lynne squelched back a giggle.

Matt pulled her chair out and she sat down. "Thank you, Pastor."

He grimaced. "Somehow when you call me Pastor, it takes the romance out of the evening."

Lynne smiled. "Okay, Matt, I won't do that. Why don't you pray for us?" Matt took her hand again and bowed his head. Lynne felt herself blushing. After his "amen," she withdrew her hand and poured some ice water from the carafe into their glasses. "I hope you like turkey melt sandwiches."

He grinned, then nodded. "I like when a woman orders for me."

"I did it to save time." Lynne smiled. "I have to be onstage for the dinner show in a half hour."

"Oh, does that mean that we have to eat and talk fast?" he questioned, reaching for part of his sandwich.

Lynne shook her head. "Take your time; you can sit here all night."

"How did the testing go at the SPCA center?"

"Bamboo passed, of course." She beamed. "I filled out some paperwork and gave them Bamboo's vaccination record. Before I left, they gave me the approval to go with you and Brutus to the hospital next month."

"That's great. You'll really enjoy the experience."

"I'm looking forward to it," she commented. After a moment she asked, "How was your day at church?"

"Busy. The youth group and I had a car wash today. We're trying to earn money to buy a new van for the field trips and youth events."

"Why can't you donate one?" Lynne blurted out, instantly regretting it. "I'm sorry, I shouldn't have said that. It's just that Robert said that you're wealthy. Oops," Lynne said as she felt her face turn a shade of crimson. "I'm sorry. I can't believe I said that."

"No, that's all right, Lynne," he said. "That's a good idea. I don't know why I didn't think of it."

Startled, Lynne asked, "You really could donate a van?"

"Yes, and thanks for the wonderful idea." He smiled

and squeezed her hand.

"Matt, how old are you?" she asked, changing the subject. She felt she had the right to know. After all, they were getting to know each other.

"I'm thirty-two years old. Am I too old for you?"

"Of course not," she said. "So why at such a young age do you have so much money?"

"It's not something I enjoy talking about," he admitted. "I don't feel comfortable about it and maybe never will."

That sounded ominous. She noticed that Matt was crinkling his napkin into a tight little ball. Obviously, she wasn't making him feel too comfortable. What was the big deal? Why couldn't he tell her?

"What do you mean?" she prodded.

"Hi," Robert said, interrupting them. "Mind if I join you?"

"No," Matt said all too quickly. He pulled out a chair. "Have a seat, my friend."

Lynne glared at Matt. It was their dinner date and she wasn't done with her questioning yet. Matt avoided eye contact with her.

"Robert, don't you want to talk with Margo before she goes onstage?" Lynne hoped Robert would get the hint to leave.

"I've already talked with my honey." He grinned, then started talking with Matt.

Lynne groaned inwardly. Men were sure dense sometimes. She glanced around the club and noticed that it was beginning to fill up with people. Her time was running out. She frowned as she glimpsed at her watch.

"Well, I have to go round up my cousin," she said as she stood up and straightened her teal-colored evening dress. "Enjoy yourselves."

Matt stood up. "Thanks for having dinner with me." He leaned over, placing a kiss on her cheek.

Lynne smiled, despite the fact that she was slightly annoyed with him. "You're welcome." Then over her shoulder she called, "Let's do it again sometime."

"Yes, let's," he agreed readily.

The month had flown by. Lynne had seen Matt regularly at church and when he dropped by the Coffee Club to visit with her. She had enjoyed getting to know him and felt herself wanting to be around him more and more.

Lynne glanced at the clock. It was almost time for her and Bamboo to leave for their appointment at the hospital. It had been a busy morning preparing Bamboo for her visit with the children. Lynne had given her a bath, sprayed her with doggie perfume, then added the finishing touch—a pink satin bow tied to her collar.

"Boo-girl, you are one gorgeous dog," Lynne said in admiration.

Bamboo's ears shot up when she saw Lynne pull out the leash. She raced to the door and sat waiting for Lynne. Grabbing the keys and directions to the hospital, Lynne walked over to Bamboo. She clipped the leash on and headed out the door.

Once at the hospital, Lynne and Bamboo walked in through the back door of the pediatric wing. Stepping inside, she felt butterflies begin to dance in her stomach.

She hoped it would go smoothly.

Gazing down at Bamboo she said, "Now you mind your manners and be extra loving to the children."

"Oh, she will," a familiar voice said from behind her. "You're right on time, Sweetheart."

The endearment made her blush. Matt smiled handsomely at her. "Glad you didn't chicken out on me."

"I do confess I am a little nervous."

"Did you do as I suggested?" he asked.

"Oh, yes, I did my homework. I know everything there is to know about a Pembroke Welsh corgi."

"You'd be amazed at all the interesting questions that the children ask about the dogs. The first time I went with Brutus, I found myself saying, "I don't know, but that's a good question.""

"I'm well prepared then." Lynne grinned.

"Follow me," Matt said as he gave Brutus's leash a tug.

Bamboo followed right behind Brutus. Matt led them into a dayroom filled with half a dozen children. The kids squealed in delight as the dogs walked into the room. A couple of the children in wheelchairs were hooked up to IV bags. Lynne's heart lightened as she saw the joy on their faces when they saw the dogs.

"Hello Pastor Hunter and Miss Wilson," greeted a blond nurse. "The children have their name tags on and are ready for you."

"Thank you, Heidi," Matt said. He turned to Lynne. "We'll sit down over there."

Matt and Lynne took their seats in front of the children. Brutus and Bamboo laid down in front of them.

Matt introduced the SPCA team, then talked for a few minutes about Brutus and Bamboo. "Okay, now it's time to pet your friends here and ask any question that you might have," Matt said.

Lynne followed Matt from child to child letting the children pet and talk to Bamboo. Her heart was warmed at seeing the delight on their faces when they were able to touch the dogs.

"Has Brutus ever bitten you?" asked a young boy named Kevin.

"No, but he drools on me all the time and that's worse," Matt said making a face. The kids laughed.

"Bamboo smells so pretty," a little girl named Amy exclaimed as she pet the corgi.

"Bamboo loves to take a bath because then she gets to swim in the bathtub," Lynne said.

"I wish I could swim with her," said Amy.

"You'd come out looking quite hairy. She sheds like crazy," Lynne explained. Amy giggled.

Lynne brought Bamboo over to a little boy named Sean. He hadn't said anything the whole time and his face was devoid of expression. Bamboo, without warning, jumped up and placed her paws on the side of Sean's wheelchair. The boy looked startled.

"She won't hurt you," Lynne explained gently. "Would you like to pet her?"

Sean nodded. He reached out timidly and touched Bamboo on the head. Bamboo moved her head and licked Sean's hand. He pulled his hand back.

"She likes you, Sean," Lynne said. "Would you like

to pet her again?"

He reached out and scratched her head. "Hi, Bamboo." He smiled. "You're a nice doggie."

Lynne's eyes grew misty. She was pleased that Bamboo had taken a liking to Sean. "I think you've made a new friend." She winked at Sean.

"Will Bamboo come and visit again?" he asked.

"Yes, I'll bring her back to visit you and the other children real soon."

When the session came to an end the children gave the dogs a hug before they left. Lynne felt wonderful. It had been an enchanting experience.

"Miss Wilson, will you be bringing Bamboo back?" the nurse asked.

"Yes, I hope to."

"Please do; it will make the children so happy, especially Sean," she said.

After they were outside the hospital, Matt turned to her and exclaimed, "A miracle occurred in there, Lynne."

"What do you mean?"

"Sean hasn't talked since he's been in the hospital," he remarked. "He was in a car accident and lost his mother."

"Oh, how tragic," she voiced.

"Bamboo brought him out of his shell," Matt said in awe. "That's why Heidi asked you if you were going bring Bamboo back."

"Oh, I certainly will," Lynne said, smiling. "Well, Matt, thanks for inviting us girls here today. It's been wonderful."

"Our day isn't over," Matt announced. "I have a spontaneous picnic planned for us and the kids at the park."

"The kids?" she repeated.

"Bamboo and Brutus," he said. "I already checked your schedule with Margo. You have no work tonight."

Lynne raised a brow. "You could have asked me."

He shook his head. "I wanted to surprise you."

"I'm surprised." She smiled.

"I'll drive." Matt took her by the arm and led her and Bamboo to his large black utility vehicle. He opened the side doors for the dogs. Lynne slid into the passenger seat. "Nice vehicle. I think it's bigger than your rental cottage," she teased.

"This is the one thing I've splurged on," he admitted.

The park was a few miles away from the hospital. It was heavily wooded, filled with trails, and had a large pond and nearby picnic area. They walked with the dogs to a shaded spot under a large peppertree.

Matt laid out the large plaid blanket he had carried and set down the picnic basket. Bamboo instantly stepped onto the blanket and started moving it around with her paws, making a cozy little nest for herself.

"Excuse me, Missy, but that's our picnic blanket," Matt chuckled as he scooted Bamboo onto the grass beside Brutus.

Lynne eyed the big wooden basket. "We're going to have a real problem here when you open that picnic basket full of food," she warned. "Bamboo has absolutely no manners when it comes to food."

"Got that covered." Matt grinned as he pulled out two meaty bones from the basket.

Lynne chuckled. Brutus and Bamboo moved over to

Matt quickly. The dogs took their bones and sat down in the grass.

Matt passed out the plates and soda, then opened the containers of food. "Hope you like chicken and potato salad."

"I eat anything," she said and helped herself to a piece of barbecue chicken.

Matt settled down across from Lynne on the blanket. He looked at her for a moment.

Lynne felt his stare and looked at him. "What?"

"Lynne, you amaze me," he said with appreciation. "You were so good with the children in the pediatric unit."

Lynne shrugged. "How could you not reach out to those sweet children?"

"It's not only today. Everything you do, you do with your heart. You are so loving and caring."

Lynne's eyes widened. "Wow, what did I do to deserve this?"

"Shh," he said, placing a finger to her lips. "There's more."

"I've never felt this deeply about a woman before and I have a confession to make." He paused, then said, "I had seen you twice at the dog park before the day we met under those unpleasant circumstances."

"Really?"

"The first time I saw you with that wild corgi, I was intrigued."

"Wild corgi?" She gave him a disapproving stare.

"Okay, is frisky a better word?"

Lynne nodded. She glanced over at Bamboo. Nothing

else mattered to the corgi at that moment except that bone. Brutus had finished chewing on his; now his head covered it, protecting his treasure from outside predators, namely Bamboo.

"So, you and Brutus were spying on us girls?"

Matt nodded. "I was about to get up the nerve to come over and talk with you when Brutus got hurt."

"By the sprinkler head," she amended.

"Yes, but I had thought Bamboo had done it. Being the overprotective pet owner that I am, it really upset me and it ruined our first meeting."

"You can say that again," Lynne said. "I'm glad we met, no matter the circumstances." She started filling the basket with the leftovers.

As Matt threw away the paper plates and empty soda cans, his pager beeped. He glanced down at the number on the pager's screen. It was the church's number. He glanced at Lynne. "Someone from the church office called. My cell phone is in the car. I'll be just a minute."

"Take your time. I'll wait here with the dogs."

"Thanks, I'll be right back."

Lynne watched Matt walk to the parking lot. She found herself wishing that their day together wouldn't end. She felt so comfortable and happy when she was around him. She wasn't particularly surprised at her feelings either, since he was always on her mind lately.

Ever since losing her parents in the airplane accident, Lynne had felt herself longing to belong to a family. Margo, Aunt Andrea, and Uncle Chip had been wonderful to her, but she still felt the need to have more. . .a family of her own. Was Matt that family? Was he marriage material? *Lord, let me know if he's the one,* she prayed.

Matt was frowning as he walked over to her. His tanned skin seemed suddenly pale. "What's wrong?" Lynne asked with concern.

"That was Lana. She said that Pastor Drew has a flu bug. He asked if I would lead the service tomorrow and preach the morning and evening services."

"Why don't you look more happy about that prospect?" she asked, noting the stressed look on his face.

"I can minister to the kids easily, but ministering to the adults of the congregation is a whole different matter. I don't think I can do this." He looked at her and brushed a hand through his hair in frustration. "The church service is tomorrow and I don't have a sermon planned."

"I'm sure Pastor Drew had a sermon ready; can't you borrow his?" Lynne asked.

"I already asked," he muttered. "Lana told me not to worry. The Lord would give me the perfect sermon."

Lynne chuckled. "Hmm. . .sounds like you just have to trust the Lord, Pastor."

He glared at her. "You're making fun of me."

"No, I'm not. Remember that day I called the church office in a panic and thought that I couldn't sing because I felt downtrodden as a result of Jackie's mom's anger? What did you tell me to do?"

Matt grimaced. "I told you not to fear and to use your gift for the Lord's glory."

Lynne smiled. "Uh-huh. Case closed."

"Okay, okay, I'll do it," he said. "Just remember me tonight in your prayers as I agonize over this sermon."

"Agonize?" she questioned.

"As I prepare for this sermon," he corrected himself.

"I'll be praying, Matt," she said as she reached out and gave him a hug.

"Thanks, I needed that." He grinned.

Lynne smiled. "Let's go. . .you've got work to do."

Seven

The shrill ring of the phone jarred Lynne out of a deep sleep. She fumbled for the phone. "Hello."

"Lynne, I'm sorry to bother you," Matt's voice came across the line.

"What time is it?" she asked, rubbing her eyes.

"One o'clock in the morning," he said. "Did I wake you up?"

"No, Bamboo and I were watching a movie and eating popcorn," she grumbled.

"I should have checked the time before I dialed your number. I'm not thinking straight," he admitted.

"What's up?" She could sense the tension in his voice.

"I need your help. The sermon isn't happening. I've sat at my desk for hours and nothing has come. I don't know what to do. I can't go to sleep until I have something."

"And I have a feeling I won't get any sleep until you have something," Lynne said teasingly.

"I probably seem like a failure to you," he said quietly.

"Matt, I can't believe you said that. I think no such thing," Lynne said. "Believe in the gift God has given you. You can do it."

"Why do I keep feeling that I can't?" he groaned.

"Because you don't want to do this. You are fighting against it," she informed him. "You're not a failure Matt Hunter, but you're a baby."

"Wow, thanks for the kind words," he said in a dismal tone.

"I'll say whatever it takes to snap you out of this pity party. Do the job you're called to do. I've never shared this with anyone, but occasionally I have stage fright. I have to pray myself onto that stage and trust God that He'll calm down my racing heart so I can sing the song that He's given me."

"Oh, Lynne, you're right. I am fighting against it. I give up." He sighed. "I'll let go and let God take over."

"That's a good boy," Lynne said. "Now as for topics for a sermon, use the best one of all."

"What's that?" Matt perked up.

"Human life experience," she informed him. "Share about your grandfather and how his death played a huge role in your commitment to the Lord's work."

"You are the woman," Matt exclaimed. "That's it. That's perfect. Lynne, if you were here I'd give you a huge kiss."

"I'll take a rain check." Lynne laughed.

Matt chuckled with gusto. "Okay, I'd better start writing this incredible sermon. Thank you with all my heart."

"You're welcome, Matt. Good night."

"Good night, Honey."

Lynne replaced the receiver on the phone, then laid back down. A warm fuzzy feeling washed over her. Was that cozy feeling called love? If so, it felt incredibly good.

Lynne laughed. She felt giddy. Was she in love with the youth pastor? Now she was the one who wouldn't get any sleep.

"This is exciting being able to hear Matt give the sermon this morning," Margo whispered.

Lynne sat down next to Margo and Robert in the church pew. "I have a feeling that it will be a very inspiring service."

"I saw him a few minutes ago and he looked tired," Robert mentioned.

Lynne smiled inwardly. She knew Matt probably had gotten very little sleep. Lynne glanced toward the front as Matt entered from the side with the choir director. She said a quick prayer for Matt.

After the choir sang a few songs, Matt was introduced to the congregation. Lynne's eyes were glued to Matt as he stood up and started toward the podium. Lynne's heart skipped a beat as she watched Matt trip over a step. The congregation was silent as they watched him drop his Bible and papers.

Matt appeared calm as he bent and picked up his belongings. His face was red as he came to stand behind the podium. "Hello, I'm Matt Hunter, your bumbling youth pastor."

The laughter in the church filled the sanctuary. Lynne was relieved that Matt seemed all right. Matt caught her eye and smiled.

"I'm going to be honest with you," he began. "I didn't

particularly want to preach a sermon in front of the whole church. I'm better with kids, and that is why I'm the youth pastor." He grinned. "But a dear friend of mine gave me a lecture and set me straight. I knew then that God wanted me to give this sermon, so I stopped fighting."

Matt opened his Bible and straightened out his papers. "My message is appropriately entitled, 'Let Go and Let God.' "

As Matt continued with the sermon, Lynne felt someone slide into the pew next to her. She turned and was greeted with Jackie's smiling face.

"So glad that you're here," she whispered as she squeezed Jackie's hand.

"Me too," Jackie whispered.

Lynne glanced around the sanctuary as Matt spoke about his grandfather and how his life changed as a result of his loving outreach. Everyone was listening intently to the sermon, even Jackie.

At the end of the service, Matt gave an altar call. Lynne's eyes grew misty when Jackie left the pew and moved down to the front. She had a feeling that the sermon that Matt preached was exactly what Jackie needed to hear.

"That was a marvelous story about Matt's grandfather and him," Margo said as they walked out into the lobby.

Lynne nodded. "Say, I was going to ask Matt to lunch. Would you and Robert like to come?"

"No, but thanks anyway for asking. Robert is coming over to change the oil in my car today," Margo explained. "While he's doing that I'll take Bamboo for a walk."

"Oh, Bamboo will love that," Lynne said. "I'll see you later today then."

Lynne walked back into the sanctuary. She was hoping to catch Matt before he left. She noticed Jackie sitting alone in the back of the church.

"Jackie, are you all right?" she asked as she sat down next to her.

Jackie smiled. "It's so strange."

"What's strange?"

"I should be feeling awful right now but I don't. My mom is angry that I'm here, but after that sermon I don't feel anxiety about it," she explained. "I know my mom may never change, but I can change my heart and attitude and hopefully in the end she'll come around. If not, I will still come to church."

Lynne put her arm around Jackie and gave her a hug. "When Mom and Dad died, I knew that God was not going to bring them back no matter how hard I cried and pleaded. I knew eventually that I had to accept that and get on with my life. No matter what happens around us, we are responsible for ourselves and how we live our lives. Life is a gift from God and how we live our lives is our gift to Him."

"Well, from this day forward, I'm going to let God take control of my life. Like Pastor Hunter said, I have to let go and let God."

"Amen, Sister," Matt said as he walked up behind them. "How would you two ladies like to join an old bachelor for lunch?"

Jackie stood up. "I ate before church, but thank you."

She turned to Lynne. "I'll see you this week at work and I'll see you, Pastor, next Sunday."

After they said their good-byes, Lynne said to Matt, "You can't ask me out to lunch because I was going to ask you out."

Matt grinned. "I accept."

"Let's go to the café up the street. Then we can walk there," she suggested, glad that she wore flat shoes.

He took her hand in his. "Let's go, little lady."

Lynne flushed as she felt that warm and fuzzy feeling again as he held her hand tight. She felt like teenager—a teenager in love. A giggle escaped from her lips.

"Care to share what's so funny?" he asked, looking down at her.

"When the time is right." She grinned. "Let's hurry, I'm hungry."

When they arrived at the café, they were seated outside under a large umbrella.

"Matt, tell me more about your grandfather," she said after they had ordered. "At what age did he start to pastor in church?"

"Not until he was in his late forties," he explained. "Gramps grew up working in and tending to his parents' citrus groves. His family owned hundreds of acres of land and only half of it had orchards on it. Eventually the land became very valuable."

"Was the property located here in California?" Lynne asked with interest.

"Yes, right here in Orange County." Matt paused as the waiter set their food down on the table, then continued,

"Over the years as Gramps' parents learned of his desire to go into the ministry, they sold off a small parcel of land that didn't have citrus on it. With that money, they provided a way for Gramps to go to a Bible college and seminary. During that time he had married my grandmother and they had one son, my father."

"Does your family still have the citrus groves?"

"No, Gramps parents sold all the land to a large home developer. When they passed away, Gramps was the sole heir. He became wealthy overnight."

"How did that affect his ministry?" Lynne asked.

"He'd been a pastor for a few years. When he received the inheritance he stopped taking a salary from the church. He and Grandmother then set up a shelter for abused women and their children and had people from the church run it. Years later when Grandmother passed away, Gramps opened up another shelter in honor of Grandmother and called it Gracie's Shelter."

"And now you are following in Gramps' footsteps. You're a pastor and you're not taking a dime from the ministry," she mentioned in reflection.

"When Gramps passed away, he left me money to be able to go to Bible college and seminary. I didn't have to worry about working. Two years ago, at thirty, I was able to receive the rest of the inheritance. That's the way Gramps had set up the distribution of the funds."

Lynne breathed a sigh of relief. "So that's why you don't take a salary either. I must admit that you made me suspicious because you never wanted to talk about it."

"I didn't want to talk about it because I'm uncomfortable with it," he explained.

"Uncomfortable?" she repeated. "Why?"

"Because I didn't earn it," Matt stated. His deep brown eyes held a sad glint.

Lynne stared at him. He was peculiar. Most men wouldn't care that they didn't earn it, they'd simply enjoy it. Matt was certainly different from any other man she had met before.

"Matt, we didn't earn salvation either. Does that mean we shouldn't accept it graciously?"

Matt shook his head and said, "Wow, Woman, you always put me in my place with lightning speed."

"Somebody's got to straighten you out," she said. "Look at all the good that can be done with money if it lands in the right hands. Like the fact that you can donate a van to the youth group for their field trips and a million other good things. The possibilities are endless." She gestured dramatically with her hands. "Matt, why do you rent such a small house if you have the wherewithal to buy a home?"

"I'm a bachelor, Lynne. I don't need a big house to be all alone in."

Lynne nodded. "I understand."

"Not to change the subject, but I need to ask you something personal," he said.

"Go ahead, Matt," she said as her heart skipped a beat.

"Lynne, I'm finding that the more time I spend with you, the more I want to be with you. When I'm not with you, I miss your smile, your laughter, your beautiful face. . . I get plain grumpy when I don't see you enough;

ask Brutus. . .he can testify to that."

Lynne smiled. She felt overwhelmed. He cared about her. But did he feel as deeply for her as she felt for him? "So what are you trying to say?"

"Lynne, I want to—" Matt stopped as the ringing of his cell phone interrupted him. He looked apologetically at her. "I'm sorry, this will be just a minute."

"Hello," he answered.

"Yes, that's okay, Margo," he said.

"No, when did it happen?"

Lynne didn't like the expression of worry that appeared on Matt's face. And why was Margo calling him?

"We'll be right over," Matt said, then put his phone on the table.

"What's wrong with Margo?" Lynne asked.

"It's not Margo. It's Bamboo. She ran off," he explained.

Lynne panicked. "What do you mean *ran off?*"

"Margo said that she took Bamboo for a walk and Bamboo's collar broke. She tried to catch her, but Bamboo kept running."

Lynne moaned. "She hasn't done that since she was a puppy. I don't understand why she would just run off now."

"Let's go," Matt said as he put some cash on the table. "We'll find her, don't worry." He took hold of her hand and they walked back to their cars in the church parking lot. "I'll follow you."

Lynne was a nervous wreck on the drive home. She drove slowly hoping that she would see Bamboo on the way. When she pulled into the driveway, Margo and

Robert were standing on the grass.

"I'm so sorry, Lynne," Margo said, running up to her.

"It's not your fault," Lynne replied as she got out of the car. Matt pulled up behind her and parked.

"We've combed every street in the neighborhood, but we haven't seen her," Robert said.

Lynne's eyes welled up with tears. "She's so careless; she never watches for traffic. I hope a car doesn't hit her. Oh, why did she have to run off?" she rambled on.

Matt came over and put his arm around Lynne to comfort her, then asked Margo, "How long has she been gone?"

"About a half hour."

"Okay, let's keep looking," Matt said.

"Let's go," Margo said to Robert.

The two couples drove off in different directions. Lynne was silent as they searched down each street. *Please Lord, let me find Bamboo*, she prayed over and over.

Lynne rolled down the window and began calling out Bamboo's name. Wiping a tear away from her cheek, she felt Matt's warm hand cover hers. He gently squeezed it. "We'll find her, Sweetheart."

Lynne nodded as a large knot formed in her throat. Bamboo was her baby; she couldn't bear to lose her. Street after street they drove up and down, but no little corgi. They drove around for a couple of hours, then headed back to the townhouse.

"I made some posters up with a description of Bamboo," Margo said as they walked over to her. "Robert and I are going back out to hang these up and then we'll look some more."

"Can I go with you?" Lynne asked. "Matt should be getting back to church."

"No, I have some time left before evening service," he argued. "Let me go with you again."

Lynne shook her head. "I'll call you if we find her."

Matt took hold of her arms. "Not *if*, but *when* you find her." He bent down, placing a tender kiss on her lips, then hugged her tightly. "I'll check in after the service is over," he whispered.

She watched Matt walk away as she slid into Robert's car. He was so caring and gentle. *Lord, thank You for Matt,* she prayed as the car backed out of the driveway.

Margo and Lynne tacked up all the posters, then continued to drive around. An hour later, Lynne walked into the townhouse. Robert and Margo went back out to look for Bamboo.

Lynne felt sick. Bamboo was gone. She noticed the message light on the answering machine was blinking. She pushed the button. It was Matt. "Lynne, I need you here at church. Come as fast as you can."

She noted the urgency in his voice. What was wrong now? Not wasting any time, she drove quickly to the church. Lynne hoped that she'd catch Matt before the service began.

When she arrived, she saw Matt standing by the doors of the sanctuary. He was smiling.

"Come with me," he said, taking her hand in his.

They walked over to the building where the children's Bible study was being held. Lynne heard laughter and giggles coming from the room. "Woof, woof."

She turned to Matt when she heard that familiar sound. "Matt, is it. . .?"

Matt nodded as he opened the door to the room.

"Bamboo!" Lynne cried out. There in the midst of the children was the frisky, red-haired corgi. Bamboo's ears perked up as she recognized the beloved voice, then bounded for the door.

Bending down, Lynne picked her up. Squeezing her tight, she turned to Matt and asked, "Where did you find her?"

"The dog park." He smiled. "I was on my way to church, then suddenly felt led to take a detour to the dog park. She was sitting by the outside gate."

Lynne set Bamboo down, then jumped up, throwing her arms around Matt. "Thank you for finding my Boo-girl."

The kids hooted and hollered as she gave Matt a kiss. She then picked Bamboo up and thanked the kids for baby-sitting.

Outside the door, the hallway was empty. Matt pulled her and Bamboo to him. "I have something I had wanted to ask you earlier. It can't wait any longer because I see that you girls need two boys to take care of you. Lynne Wilson, I'm madly in love with you and I want to spend the rest of my life with you. Please tell me that you feel the same way."

"I feel warm and fuzzy." Lynne started laughing joyously.

Matt looked down at her, puzzled. "Does that mean you love me?"

"Woof, woof." Bamboo barked.

Matt chuckled. "I know *you* love me, Bamboo."

"And I love you too, Matt Hunter," Lynne whispered.

Matt sighed. "That's music to my ears, Sweetheart."

"Will you marry me?" Lynne asked boldly.

Matt laughed. "I think that you stole my line. . .but yes, I'll marry you."

"Woof, woof." Bamboo licked Matt's face.

"That means she's included. It's a package deal." Lynne smiled up at him, then added, "You'd better get going, Pastor; service has started."

"Will you girls wait for me?" he asked, grinning.

"We'll wait forever."

Matt blew her a kiss as he dashed toward the sanctuary. Lynne could only imagine what an inspiring sermon he would have tonight.

DINA LEONHARDT KOEHLY

Dina and her husband Craig have two daughters. She is a California native and lives minutes from Disneyland, Knotts Berry Farm, the beach, and the mountains. She thinks it's an ideal spot for fiction writers.

Dina was blessed to be raised in a family that had two sets of grandparents who were strong Christians and were both married for over fifty years. Her parents and brother and his family are also Christians. Her passion for writing love stories stems from the fact that she has had the privilege of seeing so many wonderful marriages in her family succeed because the foundations were built on the Rock, Jesus Christ.

The Neighbor's Fence

by Gail Sattler

One

C an you please do something about that cat of yours?"

Heather Worchenski lowered the phone and reached to slip her fingers through the slats of the blinds but stopped before she touched them. She didn't have to see it to know what was happening. Not only could she hear what was going on, she expected so could the entire population of the townhouse complex.

She returned the phone to her ear. "It seems to me it's not my cat that's the problem, it's that barking dog of yours. I suggest you solve the problem by taking him inside. Good-bye, Bill."

Heather sighed as she picked up her red pen to continue marking the stack of test papers.

The students' answers were more disjointed than usual, an indication that the end of the school year was not far away. This year, Heather also found herself getting distracted from her agenda. For the first time in many years Heather had already planned her summer vacation, and she could hardly wait.

She laid the pen on the table and gazed at the picture on the fridge of her eccentric great-aunt Harriet, smiling from beneath her latest flamboyant hat sporting a bright red rim and matching feather. Instead of sending cards or gifts for her seventieth birthday, her favorite aunt requested that all her nieces and nephews visit her in California, and Heather was going.

Not only would she have fun with unpredictable Aunt Harriet, but for three weeks, she wouldn't have to put up with her neighbor Bill Wilson and his noisy dog.

Unfortunately, having the entire summer off meant that except for the three weeks she was gone, she wouldn't be able to get away from him. Living in a townhouse complex taught her the hard way what it was like to live close to one's neighbors.

Again, Heather tried to ignore the never-ending barking and mark the test papers, but this time the doorbell rang. She looked through the peephole before opening the door, and instead of seeing a whole person, a familiar hazel eye stared back at her.

Heather stepped back, dragged one palm down her face, and opened the door.

"Good afternoon, Bill. What would you like? As if I didn't know."

"I know we've been through this before, and I know your cat has just as much right to be in your backyard as my dog has to be in my backyard, but the neighbors are starting to complain."

"I've heard no complaints."

"That's because my dog makes more noise than your

cat. But they also see your cat walking back and forth along the back fence, deliberately teasing him. And they're getting tired of it."

Heather buried her face in her hands. They'd been through this same conversation more times in the last month since Bill moved in than she could count. Short of keeping Fluffy inside, she didn't know what to do. Fluffy didn't ever leave the yard, therefore she didn't ruin the neighbors' flower beds or otherwise cause trouble. Heather had done the responsible thing and had Fluffy spayed, as well as tattooed for identification. Most of the neighbors liked her cat.

"I really don't know what to do. I shouldn't be obligated to keep my cat inside because your dog barks at her."

Instead of replying, he glanced over his shoulder. A few of the other tenants were watching them through the blinds, and one elderly couple was actually standing outside, watching.

"May I come in? I'm judged enough on my dog without this."

Heather allowed him inside, but only to keep away from prying eyes.

Bill rammed his hands into his pockets. "I don't know what to do, either. All I know is that I don't want to be the main topic of conversation at the next tenants association meeting again."

She couldn't help but smile. She'd been to a few of those meetings. "I know. Me neither."

"The committee says we've got to do something."

Heather lost her smile, crossed her arms, and narrowed

her eyes. She didn't want the committee to talk about her as a "we" with Bill. All they'd ever done was argue through the fence about their pets.

She tapped her foot. "What do you have in mind?"

"I really have no idea. Your cat constantly taunts poor Fido from atop the fence, and naturally he barks at her. Do you think if we put them face-to-face for a while they might stop?"

Heather blinked and stared at him. "Are you crazy? They'd kill each other!"

"I know people who have a cat and a dog in the same house. They don't fight. Sometimes they play together."

"That only happens when one of them is a baby and it's the only way they've known. Cats and dogs are made to hate each other."

He shrugged his shoulders. "Got any better ideas?"

She opened her mouth to protest, but snapped it shut. She really didn't have any better ideas. She didn't have any ideas at all. However, she didn't want Bill to get an eviction notice on account of his barking dog. Even though it hurt to admit it, he was right. Despite the fact that it was his dog making all the noise and disturbing the neighborhood, it was because Fluffy walked back and forth on the fence between their two properties, making her equally responsible for all the noise.

"No, I don't."

"The best solution would be if you could get your cat to stop walking on the fence."

"I'm not going to keep my cat indoors all the time. Nor would I ask you to tie up your dog."

She stood and stared at him while he stared back.

The silence hung in the air until a low rumble echoed from Bill's stomach.

His ears turning red, he withdrew one hand from his pocket and rested it on his stomach. "Sorry. I skipped lunch."

Heather checked her wristwatch. She didn't know where the day had gone, either. Not only was it past lunchtime, it was halfway to suppertime. Knowing so reminded her that she had also skipped lunch, but at least her stomach wasn't making noises.

Bill checked his wristwatch. "How would you like to talk about our mutual problem over dinner?"

While she did want to find a simple solution, she didn't want to go out to talk about it. "I don't think that's a good idea."

"Come on. We can prove to the neighbors that we can get along, even if our pets can't."

Heather turned and swung one hand in the air, encompassing the papers and books spread on the kitchen table. "But I have test papers to mark. I have to finish them all today because I'm busy tomorrow."

"It's going to get worse if we don't do something right away. At least now my neighbors are still talking to me."

Heather looked up at Bill. Until now, she hadn't realized he was so tall because this was the first time she'd been so close to him. They'd spoken often, but it was always through the knotholes in the wooden fence between their yards so the only thing in particular she'd noticed about him was the unique color of his eyes.

She had seen him often from a distance when she looked out the back window into his yard, but now that she stood face-to-face with him, she could see that he was younger than she thought he was, closer to her own age of twenty-four. His dark brown hair was cut shorter on the sides than on top, and he wore it in the same gelled-up style as most of the men their age at her church. He wasn't bad-looking, despite his big nose, not that his looks mattered. After what happened with Jeff, Bill's good looks were a mark against him, in addition to his poor taste in animals.

She said nothing.

He jerked his thumb over his shoulder, in the direction of the main street. "We can go to the local hamburger joint, if you're in a hurry. It's still kind of early for supper, so we'd probably get a nice, private table."

Heather narrowed her eyes to think. She didn't want to go out anywhere with him, including a fast-food restaurant.

"It really isn't a good idea."

"I think it's a perfect idea. Summer is coming and both of them will be outside more often, and that will mean more noise. We should think of something now, before it gets any worse."

He was right, but she wasn't ready to go out with a man for any reason. She was still licking her wounds after the latest fiasco with Brenda.

Bill cleared his throat. "Maybe instead of going out, the best place to talk is right here. I was going to throw a couple of burgers on the barbecue for supper. I can always put on one more for you. That way we'll be able to better analyze the problem as we're discussing it. You've never seen what your cat does from the perspective of my side of the fence. I think it will be a real eye-opener for you."

"I guess so. Is there anything I can bring? I don't want to put you out on short notice."

"It's no problem."

Heather decided that as long as she wasn't gone too long, she would still have time to mark the papers today. "Okay. I'll leave Fluffy in the backyard so I can see what she does. I just have to lock up and we can go."

Two

Bill stood outside while he waited for his neighbor to lock her front door.

She was shorter up close than she seemed from a distance, but she was just as feisty. She wasn't exactly pretty, but she wasn't ugly, either. Her hair was such a light brown it was nearly blond, but not quite. Behind her dark, wire-framed glasses, she had pretty, blue eyes, which were her best feature. Overall, Heather was kind of cute, if he could ignore the way she constantly scrunched her eyebrows at him.

As soon as they arrived at his townhouse, Fido bounced up to greet him. He let the dog lick his cheek, patted him, and when the usual greeting ritual was complete, Fido ran back to the yard. Bill could tell the exact second Fido reached the back fence, because the barking resumed.

"Why did he jump up like that?"

Bill smiled. "He always greets me when I've been gone."

"You were only gone for five minutes."

"I know. Isn't he a great dog?"

When she didn't reply, Bill escorted Heather into the kitchen. "Can I get you something to drink? Coffee? A soft drink?"

"Coffee would be great. Thank you."

Bill washed his hands with a squirt of dish soap, then pulled a few hamburger patties and buns out of the freezer. He threw the meat into the microwave to defrost while he started making a pot of coffee. "Would you like to go into the backyard until it's ready?"

"Sure. I want to watch what happens before you start barbecuing, because Fido will stop watching Fluffy and start watching the food."

"How did you know that?"

"He's a dog."

Bill wasn't sure he wanted to ask any more about her observation or reasoning behind it, so he simply escorted her into the backyard. He pulled out another lawn chair and opened it beside the one he'd been sitting in earlier.

True to the routine, the cat walked back and forth along the fence a few times and when Fido gave up barking and sat down, the cat walked directly to where Fido was sitting, sat atop the fence, lifted one foot, and started licking her paw.

"See? Your cat is deliberately teasing him. Notice how she sat down exactly above him. Now watch the tail."

Within a few minutes, seeing that paw-licking wasn't getting a response, the cat started swishing her tail back and forth, flicking the end of it directly above the dog's nose just to drive him nuts. When Fido couldn't stand it anymore, he jumped, but at the exact second he did, the cat stood and raised her tail, swishing it in the air above him.

Continuing the routine, the cat resumed her performance, parading back and forth on the fence, waving her tail in the air in a proud flourish with every step, while Fido barked and jumped from beneath in frustration.

Heather raised both hands to her cheeks. "My goodness! Is that what happens every day?"

Bill leaned back in the lawn chair, crossed his arms over his chest, and nodded. "Yup. Every day."

"I don't know what to say!"

"You can start by saying that you're going to stop your cat from walking back and forth along the fence."

"I have no idea how I can stop her. Fluffy jumps up there with no effort at all. We can't make the fence taller. There are rules about uniformity and not altering anything on the grounds, and I would think that especially applies to the fences, as that's the most visible thing between the yards."

He recalled seeing barbed wire hoops strung along fences around prisons which he thought would certainly deter the cat, but he didn't think she would take well to that suggestion. He tried to think of a way to rig up a scaled-down version, but couldn't think of anything, so he kept his idea to himself. "There's got to be something we can do. Especially now that you've seen what I'm up against on this side."

"I don't know why your dog keeps jumping and barking. Surely he should be able to tell that he's never going to reach Fluffy."

"It's a dog thing. I don't know why your cat keeps

walking along the fence. Surely she must get bored, walking back and forth along that fence, day after day, when nothing ever changes."

"It's a cat thing."

Rather than lose his temper, Bill rose and strode into the house to get the coffee and the lighter for the barbecue. As far as he could see, the only way they would solve the problem was to do something about the fence.

He nearly dropped the mugs when he heard Heather's voice behind him. "The only way we're going to stop this is to do something about the fence."

Bill turned to face her as he spoke, but with her standing and facing him with her arms crossed over her chest, his anger faded. She was as caught up in the situation as he was. The only way to solve the problem was to work together, which she was finally willing to do. "Then we're going to have to do something discreet. It can't look ugly."

"Do you have, like, tools or something in your shed?"

His stomach grumbled again, but this time he didn't think she heard. "I have tools, but nothing to use for building. The lumber store closes at nine on Saturday, so we have plenty of time to eat. First, though, we have to talk about what we can do before we go shopping."

He thought her face paled slightly, but then she stiffened and crossed her arms. "I have no idea what we can do until I see what we have available to work with, which means going shopping first."

He wanted to drag his hand over his face, but instead he harnessed his frustration and began removing the ketchup, mustard, and relish containers from the fridge.

"Can I do something to help?"

He wanted to say that she could start cooperating now that they finally agreed on a course of action, but smiled politely instead as he picked up the lighter and reached for the microwave. "How about if you carry the coffee mugs outside, and I'll get the hamburgers on a plate and light the barbecue."

"Doesn't it have a starter button? Mine does."

"The starter button doesn't work so I have to use a lighter."

"That seems so inconvenient. Are you sure there isn't a way to fix it?"

"It was easier to buy a lighter than to fix it, and the lighter cost less than a new barbecue when this one works just fine. Do you have any more questions?"

"I'm sorry I asked."

Bill squeezed his eyes shut, then smiled without commenting further. The tone of her voice had told him that she wasn't sorry at all. He wondered if they could agree on anything, then praised God that at least they agreed on the most important thing, which was to do something about the fence. Once they rigged up something, then the only time they would need to see each other would be waving from the safe distance of their own yards, in peace and quiet.

As expected, as soon as he set the plate of burgers on the patio table and lit the barbecue, Fido quit barking and sat faithfully beside him, hoping for something to hit the ground. Bill couldn't remember ever dropping food when he was barbecuing, but he always considered a dog's most endearing quality to be its unending optimism. He also noticed that as soon as the dog gave up and left the fence, the cat went inside, too.

All was quiet while he cooked, allowing them to discuss a few possibilities for the fence. They came up with a couple of suggestions that sounded workable, and now that he had an idea of what they were going to do, he could go to the lumber store to buy what they needed.

When they had their full plates in their laps and were ready to start eating, Bill hesitated. He always paused for a moment to give thanks to God before he ate, which was fine when he was alone or with his friends. But in the company of a stranger or casual acquaintance he often felt awkward. He certainly didn't want to make Heather ill at ease. At work, where he was the only Christian, he always prayed over his lunch, but there everyone knew him and politely gave him the few seconds he needed even though no one prayed with him.

He tried to think of what to do and gave up. He was about to close his eyes for a brief second when he noticed that Heather was taking an inordinate amount of time shuffling her burger around on her plate instead of eating it. He was about to ask if there was something wrong when she stilled, bowed her head slightly, and closed her eyes.

The realization of what she was doing nearly made him drop his own plate on the ground, except that he was very aware of Fido beside him, waiting for exactly that to happen.

"Heather? Would you mind if I said grace before we ate?"

She flinched, then smiled timidly. His heart began to pound in his chest, and he couldn't figure out why.

"Yes, I'd like that very much."

Bill cleared his throat, bowed his head, and closed his eyes. "Thank You, Heavenly Father, for this food before us, and we pray Your blessing upon it. We also pray that we can find an agreeable solution to the problem before us. Amen."

"Amen."

As he looked up, she bit enthusiastically into the burger.

"This is good. Thank you for inviting me."

Bill bit into his burger and chewed slowly as he considered what he had just learned. Just because his neighbor was a Christian didn't change anything. He knew she was single and she had a cat, but he still found her to be too disagreeable, too hyper, and too opinionated to do anything with—except fix the fence. He wasn't sure they could do that either without wanting to strangle each other, which was probably a sin.

The best way to avoid temptation to sin was to stay away from it, so when they had the fence all fixed up, except for occasionally waving at her from his yard, he planned to stay far away from Heather Worchenski.

He swallowed and reached for his coffee mug. At his movement Fido shifted and moved closer.

When he looked up, Heather was staring at Fido very critically. He waited for her to say something, but after a few minutes of silence and giving his poor dog dirty looks, he couldn't stand it anymore.

"Why are you looking at him like that? He's done nothing."

"He's begging for food."

"He's not begging. He's just hoping for something to hit the ground."

"Does food usually hit the ground?"

"No. But sometimes I'll toss something into his bowl. I don't feed him from the table."

"But that *is* feeding him from the table."

"It certainly isn't. He's just hanging around, hoping for a crumb. Doesn't your cat hang around when you're eating?"

"Certainly not. She gets her dinner before I eat, and then she goes into her basket to sleep."

He couldn't imagine opening a can of smelly cat food and having the scent of the foul stuff lingering while he ate his own dinner. "Whatever," he mumbled, then took another bite of his burger before he said something he knew he'd regret.

He remained silent while she studied her wristwatch.

Bill could take a hint. He quickly finished the second burger except for the last bite, which he tossed at Fido, who caught it without letting a crumb hit the ground. They were in the backyard, so it wasn't feeding him from the table. "Let's go. I think I have an idea of what we can get."

"If we really have to go to the lumber store, first I have to go home to get my purse. I want to pay for my half, and all I've got on me are my keys. Besides, if you're going to leave Fido in the yard while we're gone, I have to lock Fluffy's pet door or the neighbors will be treated to constant barking the whole time we're gone. Also, I can't remember if I locked the back patio door. It doesn't matter if it's locked now, because I'm sitting here looking right at it."

Bill sighed, wondering why he hadn't noticed before that she was so chatty. He didn't need to hear her life history. He only wanted to go. "Not a problem," he said as he stood.

He left the plates in the sink and walked back to her townhouse with her. When she opened the door, all was quiet.

"Where's Fluffy?"

"She's probably in her basket, sleeping."

"Isn't she going to greet you at the door? Or at least check out who is walking in?"

"Why should she? She knows it's me. Who else would it be?"

For a brief second, Bill didn't want to consider who else might be walking into Heather's home, then wondered why he cared. "Your cat doesn't know me. She should at least be checking me out as a stranger."

Heather made a strange snorting sound, which Bill thought quite unfeminine. "I'll be right back."

She walked side by side with him in silence as they returned to his place to take his car, thankfully without having to discuss it first.

As he waited for a couple of cars to pass before they could exit the complex, instead of making conversation she kept glancing from left to right out the windows so many times that he was getting annoyed.

Bill should have enjoyed the silence, but he didn't. He sighed when once more she glanced back and forth at the passing cars. "I promise I'm a safe driver. I'm not going to hit anyone."

She turned to him and gave him a very shaky smile. "I know. I'm just looking for someone. You're single, right?"

His reply caught in his throat, but when she looked at him with her big, wide eyes, he had to answer. "Yes, I'm single. Why?"

She wouldn't look at him. "I was just thinking. . .in case we ran into someone I know."

He gritted his teeth. "Am I setting myself up to get punched out by a jealous ex-boyfriend?"

Her face turned a ghastly shade of white. "No, it's nothing like that. I'm sorry for asking."

When he turned onto the street and merged into traffic she sank back into the center of the seat and faced straight forward, sitting stiff as a board. During the entire trip, she didn't say a word; all she did was watch traffic, which was fine with Bill, although it did make the short trip seem longer than usual.

As he waited for a traffic light, her uncharacteristically quiet voice startled him. "I guess we can't do this another day, can we?"

The only reason he was doing this at all was so that he wouldn't get evicted. Rather than doing it another day, he would rather not have been going at all, but they didn't have a choice. "We're almost there," he muttered.

"Sorry," she mumbled, then stared out the side window, paying no attention whatsoever to him. Instead, she carefully checked out every other car on the road. When a little red pickup truck passed them, he heard her sharp intake of breath, but when she made eye contact with the driver, a gray-haired, elderly man, she sighed out loud.

To his relief, they finally pulled into the parking lot. "Here we are," he snapped.

He was about to ask her to get out first so he could flick the switch for the electronic door locks, but instead of moving to open the door, she turned to him. "I'd appreciate it if we could make this little excursion as quick as possible."

He couldn't stand it anymore. "Is it me, or do you have an aversion to hardware?"

"It's not you, but it's something I'd rather not discuss. Can we please get it over with?"

Bill gritted his teeth even tighter. She couldn't have made it clearer that she didn't want to be seen with him, and the knowledge grated on his nerves. He had always considered himself a nice guy, and so did a number of the single women from his church, even if he wasn't interested in a relationship. For someone who had recently asked him if he was single, she was behaving like she was ashamed to be seen with him, and the thought stung.

"Fine," he grumbled, then forced himself to smile. "After you."

Three

Heather swallowed hard and walked into the lumber store. She tried to convince herself that she was overreacting, but she couldn't help herself. She told herself she was behaving like an idiot, that there was no chance she would see Brenda, but when the pickup exactly like Brenda's passed them, she'd nearly fainted. Fortunately, it wasn't Brenda on her way to work, it was someone else.

She'd tried to tell herself that the chances of Brenda actually working today were minimal. Brenda worked a Monday to Friday shift, leaving the part-timers to work weekends.

She turned around, hoping that Bill would lead so she could hide behind him, since he was nearly a foot taller than she was. "I really have to get home quickly, so let's just get exactly what we have to, and leave."

"This isn't exactly a pleasure trip for me either," he mumbled, then turned down the first aisle they needed.

She selected a spool of wire and a few packages of springs while Bill scooped some nails out of a bin and dumped them into a plastic bag, along with a pile of brackets. They walked side by side in silence to the outdoors section to select a piece of clear fiberglass roofing, and then they made their way back inside and to the checkout.

Relief poured over Heather. They were on their way out, and they had not run into Brenda.

Since it was suppertime there were no long checkout lines. While Bill piled everything onto the counter, Heather stood to the side to check out a display of hanging plant baskets. She ran her hands over the colorful blossoms, then lifted a small arrangement, trying to think if would be light enough to hang from one of the brackets they were about to purchase.

"Heather? Over here! In checkout six!" a female voice chirped.

Heather's heart nearly stopped beating. "Brenda. . . ," she muttered, her voice trailing off. "What are you doing here on your day off?"

Quickly she glanced over at Bill, who had turned to see who she was talking to. She could tell the exact moment Bill saw her sister. His eyes opened wide, and he was staring.

Her sister was everything she wasn't. Tall. Beautiful. Poised. Confident. Perfectly groomed. Twenty-twenty vision. Even the blue and yellow staff smock couldn't hide Brenda's hourglass figure. Brenda's musical voice turned heads, especially men's. When she really went into action, Brenda could stop a crowd.

Heather shuffled away, hoping Bill would simply pay for everything and wait for her at the car while she tried to make a dignified escape. Before they attracted too much attention, Heather gathered her nerve and approached her sister.

Brenda's gorgeous smile made a few of the men standing nearby smile back, even though she wasn't smiling directly at them. Before Brenda actually spoke, she swiped one manicured hand under her full mane of blond curls and flicked it back. In doing so, she made brief eye contact with one of the men in line who was smiling at her. Noticing that she was acknowledging him, the man sucked in his stomach, and his smile widened.

Heather wanted to scream.

Brenda turned to Heather once she finished flaunting herself. "I got called in to work an extra shift today because someone called in sick. I must say it's a surprise to see you here."

"I was just on my way out. I'll probably catch you at Mom's sometime." Despite her current state of mind in relation to her sister, good manners demanded she not walk off in a huff.

She was about to say good-bye when Brenda smiled and winked at the man whose purchases she was supposed to be ringing through. "I'll be right back, do you mind?" Once the man muttered his consent, Brenda turned back to Heather. "You're not still mad at me over that little thing with Jeff, are you?"

Heather wasn't mad. She was crushed. Devastated. Heartbroken. Betrayed. She forced herself to smile. "I'll get over it. As usual."

Brenda giggled, obviously not getting the hint.

Heather didn't want to have this kind of discussion in public, especially since she was near tears with Brenda bringing her recent failure to the attention of anyone in the vicinity. She had loved Jeff. She'd even thought they might be married someday—until Brenda came along and poured her charms and feminine wiles on him. Like every other man Brenda had led away from her, Jeff had also strayed. But this time, it hurt worse than ever.

Heather cleared her throat. "I shouldn't disturb you while you're working. Maybe I'll—"

"Heather?" Bill's voice drifted from behind her. She turned to see him holding up the plant she had been inspecting when Brenda called to her. "If you like this plant, let me buy it for you as a peace offering."

For the first time in many years, Brenda's face went blank. Quickly she composed herself and fluttered her long, thick eyelashes at Bill. "Oh! You're with someone! He's kinda cute, too. And what's this about a peace offering? Did you and your new sweetie have a little squabble and he's trying to make up?"

Heather backed up a step. "It's nothing like that. I have to go."

She wanted to run outside, but didn't want to leave Bill on his own now that Brenda knew they were together. She was now responsible for what happened, and the thought made her feel ill.

The plant sat on the counter beside the bag while Bill stuffed his change into his wallet, indicating he really had bought it for her.

On top of the worry that Brenda associated them as

being together, now she added a measure of guilt for the plant. Calling it a "peace offering" could only mean that she had been as curt with him as she thought she'd been, and that wasn't right, either.

She picked up the plant and scurried out ahead of Bill.

"Buh-bye Heather!" Brenda's voice singsonged behind her.

The sliding door swooshed closed behind them, creating a safe barrier.

"Well, wasn't that a pleasant surprise to see someone you know."

"That's my sister. I didn't know she was going to be here today." If she'd known, she would have traveled across town to the higher-priced competition.

She shuffled her feet and stared at the ground while Bill unlocked the car, the whole time dreading that he would ask questions about her sister.

Heather started talking the second the car started moving. "I think we've got the perfect stuff. I don't know much about building, but I really think this is going to work. And thank you for the plant. That was so nice of you. I didn't mean to be so cranky to you. I just had something else on my mind."

"That's okay. Maybe it will distract Fluffy from—"

"That plant is so pretty. Have you seen Mrs. Vanderhoff's yard, at the end of our section? She's got plants hanging from some kind of contraption all along her fence, and it looks quite nice. I think she might have some of this same variety, only in a different color."

"I guess. I don't really look much at—"

"And I insist on paying for my half of all that stuff, after all, we agreed. I know you said you wanted to buy the plant for me, but I don't mind paying for half of that, too, if it makes it easier. I might just buy a small plant for each bracket we use, that way it might decorate the yard and make it look like it was done on purpose. Also the hanging plants might help deter Fluffy from jumping up there. I think it's going to look really nice. I might go back to the store and get a few more plants, but you don't have to come with me, after all it will be for my side of the fence. But I really like that one."

"It's okay, Heather. Settle down. It's just a plant. It's not a big deal."

Heather squeezed her lips shut and stared out the window as they made their way home. She tended to talk too much when she was nervous, something that had been pointed out to her many times over the years, and she'd done it again. "Sorry," she mumbled, and remained silent for the rest of their journey home.

Bill pulled up in front of her townhouse, and they carried everything to her cement patio.

"Are we going to do this today or tomorrow?"

"I know you said you wanted to mark your papers, but I'd really like to do this today, since I'm busy tomorrow all day at church."

"Yes, I am, too."

He got back into his car and rolled the window down. "I'll be right back with my tools."

Heather scurried inside to put on a pot of coffee while she tried to picture the structure they were going to add onto the fence. They were going to cut sections of the clear plastic into long strips and fasten them to the fence at a 45-degree angle to prevent the cat from being able to reach the top of the fence.

Bill returned wearing a tool belt and carrying a couple of hand tools. "Ready?"

She was more than ready. As much as she hated to admit it, after having run into Brenda, she needed a distraction to sort herself out before she could concentrate on anything that required thinking. They would have to quit building at sunset, which would give her plenty of time to do the papers before bed. Then, with the papers out of the way, her mind would be uncluttered for the worship service on Sunday.

All their conversation revolved around measuring and cutting the fiberglass pieces into narrow lengths, which was fine with Heather.

When they had the first section hanging on the fence, Bill unplugged the circular saw and picked up the hammer. "Now here comes the hard part. We have to take a guess at how many springs to use per section so it will only support the weight of the plastic, but tip with the weight of the cat."

"How will we know?"

He shrugged his shoulders. "Trial and error. Where's Fluffy?"

Heather crossed her arms at the realization of what he meant. "You mean you expect me to put the cat on it and see if it collapses beneath her weight?"

He turned to sort out the hardware he needed for the

first section. "Something like that."

She waved her hands in the air as she spoke. "But I can't just put her on it and see if she falls down!"

Bill didn't look at her as he spoke. He simply continued to pick out the right number of springs, brackets, and nails as he spoke, which infuriated her even more. "Then how are we going to tell if the section will collapse beneath Fluffy when she jumps? We have to do this right."

"I'll use something that weighs the same, but I am *not* subjecting my cat to that!"

Heather stomped off to weigh Fluffy, then to find a comparable-weighted object. There was no "we" about this project. This supposed cat barrier was his conception, not hers.

"Wait! Don't go now! I need you to hold the tape measure."

She stomped back and held the tape measure in silence, allowing him to make his marks where he would fasten in the brackets, and then stomped inside to weigh Fluffy.

Four

Bill shook his head as Heather disappeared, then he started to hang the brackets.

Doing anything with Heather was a lesson in frustration. He didn't particularly like cats, but he would never be mean to one. He was only teasing when he suggested she use her cat to test the weight capacity once they had the first piece of the barrier in place, but she acted like she thought he meant it.

Either the woman had no sense of humor, or whatever made her go into hyper-drive at the lumber store threw her so badly she couldn't tell he was joking. And if that were the case, he would have to do something about it. The reason he'd bought her the plant was to try to make up for whatever it was he might have done, but now he was beginning to think that maybe it wasn't him at all.

Not that he'd looked at Heather's sister for very long, but in the one minute he had, the woman had winked and flirted with three different customers, including him. Except for the family resemblance in their chins they didn't look at all alike. Aside from her natural beauty, Bill found Heather's sister's perfect hair and flawless makeup out of place for someone working at the lumber store.

Even though she was much prettier than Heather, Heather was real, even though she was crabby.

He had attached all the brackets in place when Heather reappeared with a small frozen turkey.

"What are you doing with that?"

"This was the closest I could come to the weight of Fluffy."

He almost made a joke connecting the turkey with cats but clamped his mouth shut at the last minute. She didn't think his last joke was very funny, so he decided not to push his luck.

Together they raised the fiberglass section to the right angle and wired up the springs to hold it steady. Heather gently placed the turkey on it, and sure enough, it collapsed, dumping the turkey on the ground, then sprang back into place when the weight was gone.

"Wow!" he exclaimed as he ran his fingers through his hair. "I didn't really expect it to work the first time. Since we don't have to play with any adjustments or go buy different springs, we'll probably get the whole thing finished today."

"That's great. Just let me put the turkey back in the freezer, and we can get right to it."

She came back in considerably less time than it took to get the turkey in the first place, and things went well with the rest of the construction, which was probably because she wasn't talking a mile a minute. He'd actually found what little conversation they had pleasant.

When all was complete, they both stood back to admire their work.

"Not bad, even if I do say so myself."

Heather nodded. "That was a good idea to use the clear stuff. You can barely see it. . .it's perfect. Fluffy will only have to try it a few times and she'll give up. And that was a good idea to use those extra pieces to block her from using the side fence to get to the back."

"Whatever does the job." The faint ring of the doorbell sounded from inside Heather's home. "I think you've got company."

"I don't know who it is. I'm not expecting anyone. Please excuse me."

Bill scooped up his tools and hurried after her so he could leave when she opened the door for her guest.

"Brenda! What are you doing here?"

Now Bill knew it wasn't his imagination that whatever was wrong had something to do with Heather's sister. He was no expert on women, but even he couldn't miss the chill in Heather's voice when greeting her sister.

Brenda ignored the cold welcome. "I just thought I'd stop in to say hello, and. . ." She covered her lips with one hand as she turned to face him. "Oh! You have company!" The hand fell, and a smile that would have done any Hollywood actress proud came across her face, making her more beautiful than any woman he'd met in his life. She extended one hand. "My name is Brenda. I'm Heather's sister. And you are. . .?"

If he hadn't already seen her in action at the store, Bill might have been taken in by the sudden coy act. Besides, one Worchenski sister was enough. "Leaving. Good day, ladies."

Without shaking her hand, mentally giving himself the excuse that his hands were full, he nodded and walked out.

Of course Fido was at the door waiting to greet him. He bent on one knee and laid the circular saw on the ground to give Fido a good welcome. "I did it, Fido, old boy. That rotten cat won't be bothering you anymore. And that means I won't have to see Heather again, either."

His smile dropped as he started to gather up his tools to put them away. In the rush, he'd forgotten his drill at Heather's.

He made Fido's dinner, then stood at the back patio door looking out into the backyard while Fido ate. From his side, all that was visible was what he'd done to block the cat from walking up the side fence to the back, and that was only because he knew it was there and knew what to look for. They had done a good job at making a nearly invisible cat-proof barrier.

He was about to turn away when he saw Heather's curtain move. She stood at the patio door without going outside, also looking at the back fence. Since she was now alone, it was the perfect time to go get his drill.

Just as he always did, he rang the doorbell and peeked back through the hole, waiting for the movement to indicate she had seen him, but there was none.

Bill stood straight and ran his fingers through his hair. Her car was parked in her carport, and it couldn't have taken him more than a minute to jog up from his place. He knew she was home, and that she wasn't already in bed.

He banged on the door. "Heather! It's me, Bill! I forgot my drill!" he called through the closed door.

Bill stepped back. His stomach churned, knowing that accidents in the home happened all the time. He checked his watch. If she didn't answer the door in thirty seconds, he was going to break it down and call an ambulance.

At twenty-nine seconds, he raised his fist to bang on the door one more time, but the door opened before he made contact.

He stood, frozen, his fist still clenched in the air. She stood in the doorway holding his drill, but she wouldn't look at him. She kept her face downward, but it didn't prevent him from seeing her red nose and bloodshot, puffy eyes.

She thrust the drill into his hands as she spoke. "Here's your drill. Thanks again for your help."

"Heather? Is something wrong?"

"No, nothing's wrong. Good-bye, Bill."

And the door closed in his face.

Bill sat at the kitchen table, his face buried in his hands. The barking was driving him nuts. He didn't want to think of what the neighbors were thinking. He especially didn't want to think of the next tenants association meeting.

He didn't have to look up the number. He had it memorized.

"Hi, Heather. I guess you know why I'm calling."

"Hello, Bill. I guess you know what I'm going to say."

"It's not my fault that they found another way to annoy each other. The fence barrier worked just fine."

Her ragged sigh coming through the phone directly in his ear felt much more personal than he was sure it was meant. "I know. I would never have thought they would poke at each other through the knotholes. I don't suppose we can plug them?"

He stared out into the backyard where Fido currently had quieted momentarily because he had his nose poked through the largest knothole. The dog backed up, then started barking again when the cat's paw appeared through the same knothole.

Bill sighed back. "I guess we can try some wood putty, although I doubt it will work in the larger holes."

"We won't know until we try. When do you want to start?"

He checked his watch. He didn't have any wood putty in his tool shed, so that meant he had to go to the lumber store before it closed. Only this time, he was going to be smart and go alone. "I'll meet you at the back fence in half an hour."

Fortunately, the traffic lights were in his favor, and most fortunately, he didn't see Heather's sister at the store. He made it to the fence in exactly half an hour, where Heather was waiting for him.

All he could see of her was her eyes and the top half of her nose, and he knew she was standing on her tiptoes to get that high. He also knew better than to tease her about it.

Fido sat at the foot of the fence beneath her, barking his head off. Every once in a while, a cat paw came shooting through a knothole, made a quick swipe in the air, and retracted, which made Fido quit barking at Heather and plunge for the knothole, never quite catching his quarry.

Bill opened the container and handed a trowel over the fence. "Let's start with the smaller ones until we get the hang of this." He poked his finger through a nearby hole. "See my finger? Let's do this one first."

When she pressed the trowel against her side of the hole, he pressed enough wood putty in to fill it. "Next one!" he called.

He could tell the exact second she moved because the putty disappeared out of the knothole.

Bill struggled to tamp his irritation. "You took the putty with you."

"I guess this isn't going to work then. It's stuck to the thingy you gave me."

"It stuck to the *trowel* because you just pulled it back. You're supposed to slide it down the fence, not pull it away."

"Oh. Like icing a cake."

He'd never iced a cake in his life, but if that's how she could relate to troweling, then whatever worked. "I guess."

"Here's your stuff back. Let's try again."

The putty came back at him through the same knothole, wadded up into a ball. She pressed the trowel against the hole again. "Ready."

This time, she swiped the trowel properly and the knothole stayed full.

"Great. I think this is going to work." He poked his finger through each knothole as they worked their way across the fence while Fido and Fluffy continued to go at each other through the larger knotholes at the far end of the fence.

During the lulls in barking they made pleasant small talk, although Bill felt as though he was talking to the fence instead of a person. Since she was too short to talk over the top of the fence they also communicated through the knotholes while they worked. He felt a strange relief that they were only plugging the lower holes, leaving the top ones still open so he would still be able to see Heather through them, although he didn't know why he cared. Soon, they would have no reason to talk so it wouldn't matter if the upper knotholes were filled or not.

After being bent over for a while Bill paused to stretch, which allowed him to look down over the fence and through the clear plastic roofing panel at Heather. Instead of being hunched over, as he was, she knelt in the grass while staring intently at the fence. When she noticed his shadow above her she flinched, nearly dropping the trowel.

He grinned down at her. "Sorry, I didn't mean to scare you. I had to stretch my back."

She smiled back. "I was waiting for your finger. I was beginning to wonder what was taking so long. If you're getting a little stiff, would you like to take a break? I think I have some iced tea in the fridge."

Bill opened his mouth, but no words came out. Earlier in the week, he had thought Heather quite plain, especially next to her sister. Now he could see that he was wrong. In the short month since they had shared the back fence the only thing special he'd noticed about her was her nice eyes. Today was different. Pretty flowers surrounded her where she sat, and the natural sunlight made her complexion glow. For the first time since they'd met she wasn't wearing her glasses, and she was genuinely smiling. She wore no makeup, but she didn't need to. Her eyes were stunning. He liked the unusual blue gray color, especially outside. Usually he thought blue eyes to be cold, but when Heather smiled, it made him feel all warm inside.

"You're not wearing your glasses."

She shrugged her shoulders, but otherwise didn't move. "I don't wear them all the time. I just need them for reading or driving or when I'm concentrating on something. I don't think that includes pressing this thing up against the fence and waiting for you to tell me it's okay to move."

Her reminder of what they were supposed to be doing should have made him get back to it, but he didn't want to move. "So how have you been the past few days? Is everything okay?"

Her pretty smile dropped as one corner of her mouth tipped down and she scrunched her eyebrows while she was thinking. Today it didn't annoy him. Today he thought it was kind of cute. "Of course everything is okay. Why wouldn't it be?"

"You looked upset on Saturday after your sister left."

Suddenly, she lowered her head so he could no longer see her face, focusing all her attention on the trowel in her hands. "Oh. That was nothing. I'm okay now," she mumbled.

He didn't think it was nothing, but didn't want to contradict her. Instead, he felt bad for bringing it up. "Let's get back to work. We can probably finish this today."

As soon as he moved, Fido ran to the knothole in front of him and started barking. The cat's paw came shooting through, but instead of retracting quickly, the cat swiped in the air a few times before the paw disappeared.

"Rotten cat. . . ," he muttered under his breath, still staring at the hole. He could see the cat was getting over-confident in its quest to bat Fido's vulnerable nose.

The light behind the hole went dark again. Fido lunged at the fence, smacking his front paws against it while he barked in fury. Bill dropped to his knees and grabbed him by the collar, dragging him away. At the same time, he saw the light shift again behind the hole. Something started to come through. "I'll show that cat," he grumbled, half to Fido, half to himself. With the speed of light he grabbed. . .a finger.

He heard Heather gasp. Bill froze, not letting go.

Heather's voice squeaked from the other side of the fence. "Can we fill this one next?"

He was touching her. Her finger was. . .soft. It was tiny. And delicate. Just like the rest of her. He could still see her in his mind's eye, sitting on the ground amongst the flowers. Today she had smiled at him, but a few days ago he had seen tears in her eyes. Even though it was his dog making all the noise, she readily accepted half the responsibility without argument. Nor did she hesitate when it came time to get dirty doing the work to rectify it.

Last week she had paused to give thanks to God for her meal in front of him when he was still a stranger. In a strange way, it impressed him that she didn't pretend to always be happy and cheerful. She was properly polite, but yet forthright enough not to hide that she was in a crabby mood.

On Sunday morning he'd seen her leaving the complex, walking. She was all dressed up and had stopped to chat to a number of the elderly ladies on her way to the big church across the street.

He wondered what she was like to her students, and what grade she taught. And he wondered if she was as single as he thought she was.

"Bill?"

"Oops. Sorry." He allowed her to pull her finger out of his hand and back through the hole. "Yes, we'll do this one next," he muttered as he scooped a large amount of putty out of the pail, and they continued filling the rest of the holes.

The sun set just as they finished the last knothole.

Heather reached over the cat barrier to return the trowel, then stood well back from the fence so she didn't have to duck beneath it. Bill wished it wasn't so dark so he could see her better.

She wiped her hands on her pants. "That's it then, we did it. Hopefully this will be the end of the squabbling between them. Good night, Bill. And let me know how much that stuff cost, so I can pay for my half."

Instead of turning, he watched until she was inside her home.

He wished he had an excuse to keep talking, but he didn't.

Five

Heather stopped walking and scanned the church parking lot. Someone had called her name, but she couldn't tell where the voice had come from.

"Heather! Wait up!"

She spun to face the street. After a car drove by, Bill ran toward her from across the street.

Her stomach knotted. She didn't want to know what Fluffy and Fido were doing now. Against her better judgment, she had left the cat free rein to go outside while she was away at church. She'd only left two minutes ago, and already there were problems.

"Hi. Thanks for waiting." He inhaled deeply a few times to catch his breath after the short jog. "I was shopping for a church in the neighborhood and I thought I'd try this one. Usually I prefer a small congregation, but when the church is right across the street from home, it's pretty hard to resist. Been coming here long?"

He started walking toward the building, giving her no choice but to follow. "About two years. It may be a large congregation, but there are plenty of smaller home groups to plug into. I really like it here. I think you'll find that everyone is really friendly, and the pastor is a very gifted speaker."

Heather listened politely while he told her a little about the small church from his old neighborhood. The whole time he talked she expected to hear about the latest cat and dog fight, but nothing was said.

She introduced him to a number of people once they were inside, but instead of finding a seat for himself when the service was about to begin, he sat beside her.

"Thanks for inviting me," he said as the lights started to dim.

She didn't recall inviting him, so she chose not to comment.

He knew all the songs but one, and she noticed that he had no difficulty finding the Bible verses during the sermon. When the congregation stood for the closing hymn, he sang in harmony, not missing too many of the notes, which Heather thought better than she could do.

"How would you like to take a short walk and join me for lunch? I see there's a little café on the corner. Is it any good?"

"Yes, it is good. They have different lunch specials, and a lot of the church crowd goes there."

As soon as the words came out of her mouth, she realized that by not immediately declining, she had accepted his lunch invitation.

She didn't know exactly what he wanted to talk about, but one thing she did know, it would be about

Fluffy, and she wouldn't like it.

Heather peeked through the kitchen blinds and stared outside—past Fluffy, who was sitting in the middle of the yard, and past the back fence—to Bill's patio door.

All she could do was stare at his closed curtains and wonder what he was doing and what he was thinking.

During lunch on Sunday he hadn't said a word about Fluffy or Fido, or the back fence, or complained about anything. He talked about his favorite television programs, his family, the last book he'd read, the weather—all normal stuff. And she couldn't figure it out. He'd gone into detail about his job as a computer technician and proudly told her that he got everything he needed for his many projects at wholesale prices. Before she knew it, not only was she getting her computer upgraded, she somehow had invited him for supper on Friday instead of paying for the parts.

Tomorrow was Friday.

Heather stepped away from the blinds and buried her face in her hands.

She didn't know when it happened or why, but something had changed. Bill was her grumpy neighbor. He had a dumb, annoying dog. Up until the last couple of weeks, every time she talked to him all they did was argue.

But now, he was being. . .nice. She didn't want to like him. She didn't want to have anything in common with him. She wanted the old Bill back. The old Bill was safe.

Heather opened the patio door and stuck her head out into the cool evening air. She had to run to the grocery store, and this time she wouldn't leave the cat outside while she was gone. "Fluffy, come on, Girl, come inside."

The cat remained sitting in the middle of the yard, staring at the back fence. Today Heather didn't have time to convince Fluffy to come nicely, so she walked outside to pick Fluffy up.

To her surprise, Fluffy jumped out of her arms and ran to the back of the yard, sitting a few feet from the fence.

Heather stomped through the yard to pick her up again, but a strange sound distracted her. Cautiously, she approached the fence, trying to identify the noise when suddenly Bill's dog popped out from beneath the fence like a gopher out of a hole.

Fluffy yowled.

Fido barked.

Heather screamed.

Fido made a beeline for Fluffy, who sprinted into the house with the dog behind her at full speed, nipping at her tail with every step.

Heather gave chase to the both of them, screaming and running at top speed behind them.

Something upstairs echoed with a resounding crash.

Bill muttered under his breath at the sudden burst of noise the animals made outside, but when he heard a scream, he thunked his coffee mug to the table and ran to the door. He pushed the curtain aside just in time to see Heather running into her house. He flung the patio door open to hear a loud crash from inside her townhouse.

His stomach tightened into a painful knot when he

saw that Fido was not in the yard and there was a huge pile of dirt next to a big hole under the fence.

Running as fast as he could, he sprinted to the back and prayed the fence would hold his weight. Taking advantage of the momentum, he jumped into the air with his last step, rested his hands on the top board of the fence, and scrambled unceremoniously over the top. He landed on the cat barrier with a *bang*. It collapsed beneath him, scratching his back as he slid down and landed on the ground. Clambering to his feet, he ran into Heather's townhouse.

He didn't miss a step as he followed the din up the stairs and into a bedroom.

His feet skidded to a halt. A floor lamp was lying on its side with broken glass strewn around it. All he could see of Heather was her jean-clad bottom in the air as she held up the ruffle of the bedspread with one hand. Her head and other arm were under the bed as she begged Fluffy to come out. Fido had his head under the foot of the bed with his rear end in the air in exactly the same position as Heather, barking like mad, his tail wagging a mile a minute. From beneath the bed came the most horrible squall he'd heard in his life.

Quickly, he crunched through the broken glass and scooped up Fido, holding him tightly to quell the frantic struggling.

"Heather! Are you okay?"

Even over all the noise, he heard a *clunk* as she hit her head on the bottom of the bed frame.

She skidded backward and stood, pressing one palm to

the back of her head. Her other arm waved in the air to encompass the commotion and damage. "Look at what your dog has done!" she screamed over the cat's wailing. "Just take him and get out!"

He opened his mouth to apologize, but the fire in her eyes stopped him. "I'm going. . . ," he muttered as he backed out of the room. He hurried down the stairs without putting Fido down and let himself out the front door. He almost called out for her to lock it after him but decided not to push his luck.

Despite Fido's size, he barely felt the forty pounds of panting dog in his arms as he carried his wayward pet home. His heart pounded, but not from the short run. This time, he really was in deep trouble.

Without a doubt, he would replace the broken lamp—provided it wasn't an irreplaceable family heirloom. He didn't want to think of what would happen if it was. However, the first priority would be to prevent Fido from ever digging under the fence again. And that meant another trip to the lumber store.

The entire drive he tried to figure if there was an easier way, but knew he was only trying to fool himself. The only solution was to dig under the fence and bury a length of wire mesh from one end to the other.

He didn't want to think of what his back would feel like after all that digging. He wasn't in bad shape considering he sat behind a desk most of the day, but he wasn't used to heavy physical labor. Especially when he had to do it all in one day.

Since his employer owed him some time, Bill figured

he'd take tomorrow off and get it over with. If Heather took mercy on him after seeing what he'd done, maybe the invitation he'd barely managed to squeeze out of her for dinner tomorrow would still be on.

Once inside the lumber store, which was becoming much too familiar lately, he headed straight for the customer service department to ask the clerk to cut a length of mesh.

His heart nearly stopped when the blond woman behind the counter turned to help him.

"I know you! You're Bill, right?"

Brenda, Heather's sister, was the last person on earth he wanted to see right now. "Uh, yes. Could you please cut a piece of that wire mesh for me?"

She plunked her elbows on the counter, leaned toward him, and cupped her chin in her palms. Bill backed up a step to put some distance between them.

Her voice dropped to a conspiratorial whisper. "So how are things between you and Sis?"

For the moment they weren't that great, but he wasn't going to talk about it to Heather's sister in the middle of the lumber store. "The mesh I need is the one-inch. Over there." He pointed, but she continued stare at him, directly into his eyes. He couldn't look away. He'd never seen a more beautiful woman in his life, especially up close.

She fluttered her eyelashes and gazed at him with the most perfect blue eyes he'd ever seen. "The store closes in ten minutes. You could take me out for coffee, and I could tell you all about Heather."

Bill swallowed hard. He didn't want to be rude, but he

didn't want to go out with Heather's sister, for any reason. In his mind's eye, he pictured Heather with tears in her eyes after her sister had left, and then the way Brenda had shamelessly flirted with every man in the store the first time he'd seen her. Instinctively, he didn't trust Brenda.

"I'm really in a hurry," he said, being very obvious about checking his watch.

Brenda shuffled closer. "Or if you and Heather are past news, we can still go out and. . .you know. . .talk. My lips are sealed." To emphasize the point, she positioned her lips in a kissable pout that would have sent most men reeling.

Bill narrowed his eyes. Two could play at this game.

He stepped forward to the counter to rest one elbow on it, leaned his hip against the counter, rested all his weight on one foot, casually crossed his other foot over his ankle, then leaned toward her and dropped his voice to a low, husky whisper. "We're far from old news, if you catch my drift," he said as he smirked boldly. They weren't exactly present news either, but he wasn't going to tell her that. "So why don't you be a sweetie and get me that mesh? Or should I call for someone else?"

Her eyes widened, she backed up, and gave a slight gasp. "Certainly! Sorry! How much do you need?"

"Thirty-five feet."

Brenda scurried off with the wire cutters and efficiently measured and cut the wire, and soon Bill was on his way home.

Even if it meant a week of physical therapy, at the crack of dawn, he knew what he'd be doing.

Six

For the first time since she'd moved into the townhouse complex, Heather didn't open the pet door
to give Fluffy free access to go outside during the
daytime while she was gone at work. It wasn't that she
didn't trust Fluffy, but if Bill gave his aggravating dog
free rein of the yard there would be no one home when
disaster struck. And she knew it would. She'd seen Bill
filling up the hole last night, but all the dog had to do was
pick another spot and they would have the same problem
all over again.

Knowing that Bill would already have gone to work,
Heather walked into the yard to inspect her side of the
hole.

"Good morning!"

Heather fumbled her coffee mug, nearly dropping it.
"Bill! What are you doing out here?"

He walked to the fence and leaned one elbow on the
top of it. "I'm preventing Fido from digging another
hole. Wanna see?"

She pressed down the spring-loaded cat barrier and

stood on her tiptoes to see into his yard. He had started digging a trench along the bottom of the back fence. A roll of wire mesh lay nearby.

"If he ever digs again, he'll hit the wire and he won't be able to get any further. Great idea, huh?"

"Uh. . .yes. . . ," she drawled. "Isn't that a lot of work?"

He swiped his forearm across his forehead. "I guess. But it's the only thing I can think of to prevent him from getting under the fence again."

She wondered if it would have been simpler to move, but kept the idea to herself. "I suppose." Heather cleared her throat. "I was curious about the hole and just thought I'd have a quick peek before work. And speaking of work, shouldn't you be gone by now?"

"Usually, yes, but I took the day off to do this."

Her stomach churned. So far, they'd worked together to keep the animals separate, and this time, he hadn't asked her to help. A wave of guilt washed through her at the way she'd screamed at him last night. Yes, it was his dog, but it wasn't his fault the dog had dug under the fence and done what dogs naturally do, which is chase cats.

It served her right. What little good relationship they'd worked to build was now destroyed, and it was her own fault for losing her temper.

She opened her mouth to speak, but Bill beat her to it.

"I'm really sorry about what happened last night. I want to replace that lamp Fido knocked over."

She cleared her throat. "Don't worry about it. It's not a big deal, just something I thought was the right color and picked up at a garage sale."

His face brightened. "Do you like garage sales? Every once in a while I go cruising the garage sales during the summertime. I want to buy you the right color lamp at the store, but maybe one day we can do garage sales together."

"But. . .I. . ."

"Great! The weather is supposed to hold out all weekend. Why don't we do it tomorrow?"

"Tomorrow?"

"You don't have other plans, do you?"

"Well, no. . ."

"Great. We can discuss it tonight during supper. Is five o'clock okay? And weren't you on your way to work?"

Heather gasped as she checked her watch. "Oh no! I'm going to be late! Bye!" Heather waved over her shoulder and ran to her car, wondering what she'd just committed herself to. In addition to spending all day Saturday with him, it seemed they were still on for supper tonight.

The timer for the lasagna went off at 5:00, exactly the same time as the doorbell rang.

This time she didn't look through the peephole. She knew who it was.

The last time he came in, he wore a tool belt and carried a drill and his circular saw. Today, he carried a briefcase in his hand and a duffel bag over his shoulder.

He smiled, causing Heather to reassess her previous opinion of him. Instead of taking away from his appeal, his rather large nose made him look distinguished.

"Hi, Bill. Do you think we'll have any surprises tonight?"

He deposited everything beside the door. "I hope not. Quite frankly I don't think there's anything more they could do. I'm sure we've covered it all."

"I have to take supper out of the oven. Please excuse me."

Instead of making himself comfortable in the living room, he followed her into the kitchen. "Anything I can do to help?"

"No, not really. The table is all set. I just have to heat up the garlic bread, and we can eat. How are you feeling after all your hard work today?"

He pressed his fists into the small of his back, twisting and stretching at the same time. "Stiff, but not bad. The walk tomorrow will do me good."

So much for her excuse to cancel their garage sale excursion.

He dropped himself onto one of the kitchen chairs, stretched his long legs out in front of him, leaned back, and clasped his fingers behind his head.

"I like what you did to your kitchen. This is really comfy."

"Thank you." Feeling ill at ease at having her decorating analyzed, Heather opened the fridge and removed the salad she'd prepared in advance, then poured two glasses of milk.

"Who's that lady in the picture you've got on the fridge?"

Heather smiled. "That's my aunt Harriet. She's rather eccentric."

"No kidding? The loud hat with the red feather might give it away."

Heather laughed. "She's really a lot of fun. I'm going to visit her this summer for her birthday."

Bill smiled back, and something inside her stomach fluttered. "It must be nice to be close to your family. And speaking of family, I saw your sister at the lumber store yesterday. She recognized me."

Heather nearly dropped the milk jug. She didn't want to talk about Brenda, especially now. The wounds were still too fresh. "That's nice," she mumbled.

"She asked about you."

"I'll bet she did." She knew what Brenda would have asked, too. Her sister would only have mentioned Heather in passing. Bill would have been the focus of Brenda's interest.

It had started this way with Jeff, too.

Every time Heather began dating someone, Brenda moved in, and every time she had lost another man to Brenda's allure and charm. Even when Brenda showed no interest, men still abandoned Heather for Brenda in the faint hope of sparking Brenda's fancy.

Her biggest mistake had been thinking Jeff would be different, but it hadn't taken long for Brenda to have Jeff in the palm of her hand, too. When that happened, her interest waned and Jeff became history, for both of them.

Knowing that the same was going to happen with Bill shouldn't have mattered; after all, there was nothing between them except the start of a good neighbor friendship. No matter what Bill was like, after the last time with Jeff, Heather refused to set herself up for another heartbreak in the shadow of her sister. She'd rather be single all her life than go through that again.

Still, she didn't want to see Bill used as a pawn. She didn't want to see anyone set himself up for a broken heart because she knew firsthand what it felt like. Once Brenda had a man's devotion, she quickly grew bored of her conquest. And as always, the conquests Brenda tired of fastest were Heather's losses.

"Yes. She asked if I wanted to join her for coffee after work."

She nearly felt sick, thinking of Bill and Brenda together. He didn't deserve what Brenda would do to him. Bill was a nice man. He even treated his dog nicely, even when the dog's behavior was despicable.

Heather didn't really want to know the answer, but she had to ask. "Did you go?"

"Nope."

She waited, hoping he would expound on his decision, but he didn't. Part of her wanted to warn him what he was in for, since it was obvious to her that Brenda had made an erroneous connection between herself and Bill and was starting to play her usual games. Heather didn't want to insult his intelligence or his pride by disclosing that once marked by Brenda, she would get him, no matter how he felt now. But she'd never seen a man who didn't fall for Brenda, once Brenda set her mind to it.

She busied herself with slicing the lasagna and setting the pan on the table. "Here we are, supper's ready. Would you like to pray before we eat?"

Heather folded her hands in front of her on the small table and bowed her head, waiting for him to speak, but instead of hearing his voice, she heard the gentle scrape of the lasagna tray being pushed on the table. Her heart nearly stopped when his warm hands covered hers.

His prayer was short, but very sincere, and her poor heart pounded all the way through it. At his closing "amen," she yanked her hands out of his and fumbled with her cutlery.

Just like the last time they ate together, he made no mention of Fluffy or Fido. Before long, he had her laughing at his amusing stories, and she thoroughly enjoyed herself.

He continued to tell jokes while they tidied the kitchen. When it came time to do the dishes he made a few macho-male jokes, which was especially amusing because he had his arms immersed in sudsy water up to his elbows at the time.

While he washed up the last few things, Heather stood on her tiptoes and stretched to put her good salad bowl back on the top shelf where it would stay until the next time she had company for dinner.

"What are you doing? Here, let me do that for you."

She started to tell him that she could do it just fine by herself, but when she turned, instead of finding him at the kitchen sink she bumped him in the stomach with the bowl.

"Let me take that."

Heather raised her head and looked up at him. She was barely aware of the bowl being taken out of her hands, but when it was, Bill stepped closer and she couldn't break eye contact. He held the bowl with one hand, and with his free hand he slowly and gently ran his fingers through her hair.

"You're short," he said, his voice strangely lower in pitch than usual.

She wanted to tell him he was tall, but the words wouldn't come out of her clogged throat.

Something was very wrong. She couldn't breathe properly, her heart was pounding again, and her feet wouldn't obey her brain, which was trying to tell her to move away because it looked like Bill, her neighbor with the screwy dog, was going to kiss her.

Bill's eyes closed as he lowered his head. Heather couldn't help herself, but her eyes drifted shut, too.

She could feel the heat of his breath on her cheek, and knew his lips were about to touch hers, and she wasn't going to stop him.

Fluffy let out a horrible wail from the backyard.

Fido started howling at the top of his lungs.

Heather's eyes shot open, and on a delayed reaction, she shuffled backward until the small of her back pressed into the edge of the counter. Bill's hand dropped from her hair and he stood straight, but he otherwise didn't move.

The squall in the backyard increased in volume. They stood, staring at each other until one of the neighbors yelled out a string of expletives.

Heather and Bill ran into the yard at top speed.

She never thought she would be grateful for another cat and dog squabble.

Seven

At precisely 9:00 A.M. Bill knocked on Heather's door and waited.

Bill squeezed his eyes shut for a split second, then stiffened, trying to appear normal and carefree by not fidgeting with the bag in his hand.

He would have kissed Heather last night if it hadn't been for Fluffy and Fido going at it again.

The trouble was, it hadn't been entirely spontaneous—he'd been thinking about it for days and he still wanted to kiss her now. Despite her bothersome cat, as time went on he needed to be with her more and more. He'd never believed in love at first sight but since they'd started spending time together, whatever relationship they had was changing, and it was changing fast. He wondered if this was what it was like to be falling in love, because he'd never been in love before.

Heather answered the door wearing very crinkled clothes and no glasses. Her uncombed hair stuck out at all angles, and she looked adorable.

"I'm sorry, I slept in. I guess this means we're really

going to hunt for garage sales today."

He held the bag in the air and waved it back and forth. "Yup. And even better, I have a surprise for you."

She squinted to read the logo as he continued to wave the bag. Since he didn't know exactly how clearly she could see without her glasses on, he whipped the bag behind his back. "No cheating. I'll just sit on the couch and wait. Take your time, but remember, the best bargains are early. The early bird gets the worm."

She walked away mumbling something about birds and buckshot and squashed worms after the rain, but he chose not to pay attention. The second she disappeared from sight, he sauntered over to Fluffy's bed in the corner of the living room, where Fluffy was still curled up in a ball sleeping. He couldn't imagine having an animal that didn't sleep faithfully in his bed, and failing that, at least greet him in the morning.

He peeked in the bag, smiled, and returned to the couch to wait.

Heather returned in fresh jeans and a comfortably worn T-shirt, her face scrubbed and free of makeup, and her hair combed neatly, but not curled. This time she was wearing her glasses. "Do I have time to make a quick piece of toast, or will all the bargains be gone by then?"

Bill laughed. He couldn't care less about the stuff for sale. He wanted to walk around with Heather all day, along with his little surprise. She may have just dragged herself out of bed, but he'd been up since seven. "Take all the time you want, but remember, if you take too long, you'll have to feed me lunch."

Her face paled. She checked her wristwatch and scurried into the kitchen. Soon the aroma of toast drifted toward him, followed by the scraping of the knife. He could have clocked her with a stopwatch, because she appeared in the doorway in record time.

"I just have to brush my teeth," she mumbled around her last mouthful, then swallowed. "I'll only be a minute."

It was less than a minute, and she had returned. "So what's in the bag?"

He reached inside it but didn't withdraw the contents. "The discount pet mart opens at eight on Saturday."

She craned her neck, so he held the bag away. "Are you going to show me or not?"

"It's not for you. It's for Fluffy."

"Fluffy? But. . ." Her voice trailed off when he pulled out the brand-new cat harness and leash. "You've got to be kidding." She crossed her arms over her chest and tapped her foot.

He shrugged his shoulders. "I don't know what else to do. We've done everything possible to keep them separated, and now that they can't get at each other they sit and howl at each other. We can't have that, so let's get them together in a tightly controlled setting so they can get used to each other. They both need to be out of their own territory, you know, someplace where neither one is confident of their surroundings. Once we have that accomplished, they both need a certain degree of restraint. I figure that getting them both out on a leash is the solution."

She blinked a few times. "You're telling me that you think we can just put them on leashes and walk down the street? A cat and a dog?"

"That's what I'm saying."

"Does insanity run in your family?"

"I told you before that I know people who have a cat and a dog, and they get along just fine."

"And I told you before that only happens when one of them was young when they first were put together."

They both stood in silence. He turned toward Fluffy, who still hadn't moved out of her bed, although Bill was almost positive the cat was now awake. "I suppose you have a better idea?"

"No, I don't. But you can't take a cat and a dog out together. It's not natural."

"It's not natural for animals to live in captivity, either, but the human race has pets all over the planet. I don't consider that a valid argument."

She stomped over to Fluffy and picked her up. The cat cuddled in and started purring when Heather stroked her fur. "Fluffy doesn't go for walks."

"I know she doesn't. That's why she's so fat."

"*Fat!*"

He ran one palm down his face. "Heather, I know not a lot of people take their cats for walks, but the fact is that I bought a cat leash and cat harness from the store, which proves that enough people actually do it for them to manufacture such things."

She sighed loudly, which he didn't think was quite as endearing as he had in the past. "Do you really think this is going to work?"

"I have no idea, but it's the last thing I can think of."

His heart went into overdrive as she thought about it. It was true that he didn't want to get kicked out because his dog made too much noise, and now that Heather's cat had joined in the chorus he didn't think she would want to get kicked out, either.

In addition to getting the animals used to each other, he simply looked forward to going out with Heather often, because when they walked through the neighborhood with the animals, it was neutral ground for them, too.

"She's not going to like this thing strapped to her, you know."

"The lady at the store said she might not like it the first couple of times, but she'll get used to it. She also said to use a harness because a cat can slip out of a collar if you have to pull hard on it in case of an emergency."

"Do I want to ask what kind of emergency we might face?"

"I don't think that takes a lot of imagination."

She sighed again. "No, I don't suppose it does. Well, I might as well try it; we've got nothing to lose. By the way, if we're going to walk both of them together, where's Fido?"

He jerked his thumb over his shoulder. "He's outside tied to the tree, waiting."

"Waiting? You left your dog out there all this time?"

Bill shrugged his shoulders. "Waiting is what dogs do best."

He struggled not to comment as Heather slowly and tenderly put the harness on the cat, talking gently to her and stroking her fur the whole time. The cat had stopped purring, which made him wonder if the cat knew they were up to something she wouldn't like.

"When I bring out the leash at home, Fido jumps up and down and gets all excited. I wonder if cats do that."

"I guess there's only one way to find out." Bill left first to untie Fido before Heather came out with Fluffy. He positioned the leash firmly in his hand, then wrapped it around his wrist twice for good measure.

Heather's door opened and she came out, dragging a very uncooperative cat behind her. Bill stiffened and braced himself, ready for Fido's reaction when he saw Fluffy.

This was it, the moment of truth.

Heather slid into the bench at church to wait for the service to begin, and Bill slid in beside her.

Today it seemed natural to be in church with Bill, because all they could do now about their problem was to pray.

Yesterday had not gone well. She didn't have a lot of hope for any change, despite Bill's assurances to the contrary.

She'd never been so embarrassed, and she'd never had a more stressful day, including when she'd been in charge of the cafeteria at the high school the day the students had a food fight.

Exactly what she'd expected had happened, only worse. Fido had charged at Fluffy the moment he saw her. Bill had been ready, but Heather was positive that the sudden jolt had wrenched his already sore back. And just like she'd expected, Fluffy tried to run away when she saw Fido, and then had gone ballistic at being restrained. She'd had Fluffy since kittenhood, but Heather didn't dare to try to pick Fluffy up in fear of being mauled. She felt so helpless as the cat desperately tried to escape, and all she could do was stand there and hold the leash, fighting and pulling against the strain of the frantic cat.

After awhile, probably because of exhaustion, they'd both settled down and Heather and Bill had begun their planned walk.

On opposite sides of the street.

Every once in awhile Fido would lunge, even with the distance of the street between them. Patiently and countless times, Bill pulled Fido back until once again the dog heeled at Bill's side.

Fluffy hadn't been quite so easy to make walk nicely. The cat alternated between bucking and pulling on the leash, to curling around Heather's legs to be picked up, to simply falling onto her side and going stiff, making Heather literally drag Fluffy like she was dead.

Since they couldn't go to a restaurant for lunch, in desperation they'd gone to the concession at the park. Bill had tried to tie Fido to a tree and join Heather and Fluffy, but Fido barked more frantically than ever when he saw Bill go near the cat while he was unable to be near his master.

If that wasn't bad enough, all day people had pointed at the strange woman with her uncooperative cat on a leash.

And they hadn't gone to a single garage sale.

The lights dimmed. Heather needed this time of prayer and worship to her Lord God. She didn't know what to do about Fluffy and Fido or about Bill, so she prayed for God's will to be done.

The same as the week before, they walked to the café on the corner for lunch after church. Again, Bill entertained her with cheerful conversation, but this time he was different in ways that were almost subtle, but not quite. He held onto her hands while they prayed, but after her "amen" he didn't let go. To her surprise, he gave her hands a gentle squeeze, then ran his thumb up and down her wrist a few times, smiling at her in a way she couldn't figure out.

Also, this time his conversation wasn't so light and teasing. They talked in a very different way, about things that helped them to know each other in a more personal way. She nearly choked on her sandwich when he hinted about taking her out for dinner to a place Heather had always associated with a romantic date. If she didn't know any better, she might have thought he was flirting, but of course he wasn't. This was Bill, her neighbor.

She almost considered calling his bluff. The trouble was, something told her that he really would have taken her out. With Brenda in the wings, she didn't dare. This time, the joke would be on Brenda because this time, Bill and Heather had no relationship to split up. But more and more, she didn't want to see Bill hurt when Brenda tired of him.

Bill annoyed her by paying for the whole lunch, even though Heather argued with him that they agreed to split all costs to do with their pets down the middle. She considered this lunch a consultation, except as they were walking home it occurred to her that neither the cat nor the dog had entered the conversation even once.

As they turned the corner into their townhouse complex, a familiar little red pickup sat in a visitor parking space. Despite the warmth of the spring day, a chill ran through Heather from head to toe when she saw a movement in front of her townhouse door.

"Yoo-hoo! Heather! Bill! I've been waiting for you!"

"Brenda," she choked out. "What are you doing here?"

Eight

Bill could tell the exact moment Heather saw her sister. Her face paled, and her step faltered almost indiscernibly.

"I was just in the neighborhood, and thought I'd stop in."

"Oh, really?" Heather said as she checked her watch. "If you're on your way to work, then you should have started half an hour ago."

Brenda gave an airy laugh and waved her hand in the air once. "I'm not working today. I'm free all afternoon and I thought I'd come and visit you." The whole time she was talking to Heather, Brenda kept glancing at Bill until she turned completely to him, ignoring Heather. "Do you think we can convince Heather to make us a nice pot of that delicious coffee she's so good at?"

He couldn't believe the gall of Brenda to word her question to subtly pair them together and insinuate that Heather was on the outside, looking in. Heather also caught the sly shift, because he heard a small, in-haled gasp.

He knew Heather would never make an issue of it. As far as she was concerned, they weren't officially together, although the last time he'd seen Brenda he had tried to leave the impression that he and Heather already had established a relationship. He'd meant to discourage her and he wondered how she couldn't have understood his hint.

Bill stepped next to Heather and slid his arm around her waist. She stiffened slightly and turned sideways to look up into his face. Bill smiled and gazed into her eyes. "I guess we can make a pot of coffee for your sister while she's here, can't we, Honey?"

If she hadn't gone stiff enough before, she went absolutely rigid with his endearment. "I. . .I guess so."

He hoped that Brenda couldn't see Heather's hands shaking as much as he did as she unlocked her front door.

Since his townhouse was an exact mirror image of hers, he was able to head confidently to the kitchen and find the supplies without much effort, hoping he was giving Brenda the impression that he belonged there, and that he'd done this before. To complete the picture, he picked up Heather's hand when they were done and gave it a gentle squeeze to let her know he wasn't letting go, and led her into the living room while Brenda followed.

Knowing Heather wouldn't make a scene in front of her sister, he sat in the corner of the couch, tugging Heather's hand so she had no alternative but to sit right up close beside him. To emphasize the point that they were holding hands, Bill covered their joined hands with his other one for just a second, smiled at her, then leaned back continuing to hold hands, like it was commonplace.

"So, Brenda, how long have you been working at the lumber store?"

He could see the exact moment Brenda recovered from watching his little display. "About three years. I was wondering why I hadn't seen you before, but Heather told me you only recently moved into the neighborhood."

"That's right. Buying this townhouse is one of the best things I've ever done, in more ways than one, right Honey?" He raised Heather's hand and patted it again.

Heather jumped to her feet, her movement so unexpected that her hand slipped out of his. "I think the coffee is ready."

He rose and smiled at Brenda. "Excuse us then."

Brenda smiled back, but hers wasn't the same polite, friendly smile he'd given her. Brenda narrowed her eyes and gave him the most sultry smile he'd seen from a real person. "Certainly," she said in a honeyed whisper.

Heather had left the room without him, so he hurried into the kitchen where he found her lining up three cups getting ready to do the pouring.

He picked up the coffee pot. "How about if I pour and you get the cream and sugar out."

She slapped her palms to the countertop. "What are you doing?"

"I'm helping pour the coffee for company."

"Don't be obtuse, Bill. You know what I mean. Why are you doing this?"

His obvious excuse was to put on a show in front of Brenda, but if he was going to be totally honest, it wasn't just to give the impression that they were seriously involved; he wanted that involvement to be real, on both sides.

He tried to dream up a convoluted answer to distract her from her question, but at the same time he opened his mouth to speak, out of the corner of his eye he saw Brenda approaching from down the hall on her way to the kitchen.

In two steps he was directly in front of Heather, blocking her view of the doorway. "Just because," he mumbled as he slipped two fingers under her chin, tipped it up, and kissed her.

Kissing Heather was everything he hoped it could be, and more. Because he knew that kissing her would have been the last thing she would expect he was careful not to be forceful. As much as he wanted to, he didn't slip his hands around her back to hold her tight. He kissed her softly and gently, allowing her to back away if she wanted to. At first he felt her flinch at his initial contact, but it only lasted for a second, and she softened and leaned against him to return his kiss.

Fireworks went off in his head. When she slipped her arms around his back he thought he might have died and gone to heaven. Instead of the quick kiss he'd meant, he wrapped his arms around her and poured all the love in his heart into kissing Heather.

Somewhere on the outer edges of his consciousness, he heard the tap of heels on the linoleum floor, then a scrape when Brenda skidded to a halt. "Oh!" she gasped.

Heather wrenched away from him, her face turned a

ghastly white, then flushed deep pink. She wouldn't look at him.

Bill tried to get his brain to function as he slowly turned around. He'd known Brenda was coming, but the touch of Heather's soft lips and the press of her tiny hands into his back made all else flee his mind.

Brenda's blue eyes opened as wide as saucers and her pouty mouth hung open. She abruptly backed up a step. "I was just coming in to see if I could help. I guess not. I think I'll go wait in the living room." Without another word, she turned and hurried out.

Silence hung in the air for almost thirty seconds.

"She saw us!" Heather ground out in a stage whisper.

He looked at Heather, focusing on her mouth—the mouth he'd just kissed—and grinned. He hoped his smile didn't look as goofy as it felt. "Yeah. . ." He let his voice trail off.

"You don't know what you're in for!" she exclaimed in a forced whisper.

Heather had kissed him back, and as far as he was concerned, he knew exactly what he was in for, which was the start of a beautiful relationship. He let his thoughts drift to how much he'd enjoyed kissing her and wondered when he could do it again.

"Bill! What's wrong with you? You don't know what you've just done!"

He reached forward to touch her hands. "I think I do know."

She yanked her hands out from his. "No, you don't. She wants you."

"But I'm not interested in Brenda. I'm interested in you. She couldn't possibly think otherwise after what she just saw."

Heather shook her head, then buried her face in her hands, which Bill didn't think was a good sign. "You don't understand my sister. This is what she always does. I don't know what it is with her, but whenever I start something with a man, she moves in and before I know it, he's lost interest in me and has fallen for her."

"Then all those other guys were idiots, and their loss is my gain."

She shook her head so fast her glasses slipped down her nose. She didn't bother to push them back up. "You don't know what it's like to have Brenda pour all her charm on you. Jeff said the same thing, but in the end, he lost interest in me the same as everyone else."

Bill's gut clenched. If she was singling out one man, that meant he had special significance. "Jeff? What's so special about Jeff?"

She stared at him, her eyes glassing over and welling up with tears. She tried to blink them back but couldn't. She lifted her glasses and swiped the moisture away with the back of her hand, then repositioned her glasses. "Nothing is special about Jeff anymore. But at the time, I thought we were going to get engaged. Even as serious as I thought we were, he still strayed into Brenda's open arms."

Bill reached toward her in an attempt to pull her in for a hug, which he thought she needed, but she avoided his touch. "That's not going to happen. I promise you."

"You can't promise what you don't know. Jeff knew

what she was like, but his last words to me were that this time Brenda had changed. . .she really loved him, and it wasn't a game anymore. Maybe it wasn't, I don't know. But a week later, Jeff and Brenda had split up. I don't understand my sister, but one thing I do know is that I'm not going to lay my heart open and bare only to get it stomped into the ground again."

He cringed at her bald-faced description. There was no doubt that Heather had been hurt deeply, and he wished there was some way to convince her that he wouldn't be sidetracked by Brenda's practiced charms. "What can I do to make you trust me?"

"I'm sorry, there's nothing you can do."

Bill didn't believe that for a minute, but he couldn't argue with her. As soon as he was alone he knew what he would be praying for, which was for God to give him the strength to be tested by fire. He would prove to Heather that he would not be led astray by that which moth and rust would destroy. The treasure he sought was not what showed, but what lay deep within.

"Okay, let's give your sister the coffee. And as soon as she leaves, we should try again taking the animals for a walk. We're going to have to take them out every day to make this work."

He gritted his teeth at her answering groan. He hadn't meant to, but he'd just given her something else to worry about.

Nine

If she hadn't experienced it herself, Heather wouldn't have believed it had really happened. It had been a gradual process, but over the course of many weeks they had met their goal. First, they managed to walk on opposite sides of the street without Fido and Fluffy pulling and straining at the leashes to either get at each other or to flee. The next week they could walk on opposite sides of the street without Fido barking or Fluffy meowing back. Following that, they walked down deserted residential streets from Monday to Friday, and on the weekends in the deserted parking lots at the industrial complex. There they had enough room to walk close to each other, but still far enough away so that if both animals pulled on their leashes to get at each other, they would not be able to touch.

The next step was to allow them to touch noses while at the far reaches of the leashes. To Heather's complete and utter disbelief, they didn't fight. At first they were both so stiff she thought if she blew on them they would topple, but eventually the animals relaxed. They could touch each other without fighting, and they were even comfortable with each other.

Today, Heather and Bill were walking side by side with their pets on leashes, holding a normal, totally relaxed conversation.

Miracles really did happen.

Every day, Heather had been praying for this moment even though she really didn't believe it would come to pass, yet here they were.

She listened to Bill's suggestion that they open a section of the back fence with a flap door so the dog and cat could have access to each other's yards, allowing them to play together. They shared a good laugh, recounting in detail their trouble and expense to keep the animals separated.

Besides the cat and dog walking side by side without a care, something else had happened she thought would never come to pass.

Brenda had not been able to earn Bill's attention. Like most men, Bill appreciated her beauty and charm, but unlike most, he wasn't affected. That being the case, Brenda had tried something different.

Last week, Brenda had come to church for the first time in years. Their family had attended church together all her life, but Brenda had pushed God aside when she graduated from high school, much to their parents' regret. Brenda knew the routine well enough to fit back in like she'd never left. Bill seemed genuinely happy to see her there but expressed nothing beyond a kindred friendship for a Christian sister.

Heather was having difficulty trying to sort it all out.

On one hand, she was ecstatic to see her sister back in church, but she was understandably cautious as to Brenda's reason. Had Brenda really felt the touch of God in her life, or was she there only to impress Bill? During the service, Bill hadn't let go of Heather's hand. Had he done it because he was sending signals to Brenda not to bother him, or was he showing Heather in front of the competition, that his heart really was with her?

Holding his hand during church reminded her of the other time he'd held her hand, which was the first time Brenda had dropped in unexpectedly. That was the day Bill had kissed her so beautifully she nearly melted into a little puddle on the floor.

The sun had nearly set by the time they entered the front gate of the townhouse complex. The brilliant pink and purple hues of the clouds and sky created an ambiance of awe, along with the suggestion of romance.

For the last week, she had the impression that Bill wanted to kiss her good night, but he never did.

On the way to her townhouse, she saw a familiar red pickup truck in a visitor parking space.

Heather's heart sank. Brenda was waiting beside her front door.

"There you two are! Look what I've got!" She held out a small plaque. "I got the Employee of the Year award!"

Heather dug in her pocket for her keys while Bill examined the award.

"And look what else they gave me!" She held out half of the photographs to Heather, making her abandon her search for the keys, and gave the other half to Bill.

"Isn't this the company president?"

"Yes! They took a picture of him giving me the award and a few others from the banquet, but I have to give them back. Here, I'll take Fido so you can look at them without bending them."

Heather continued to search for her keys while Bill looked at the pictures. "Maybe we should go inside where I can turn on the light."

"Oh, give me Fluffy's leash so you can find your keys then. You know you look ridiculous walking a cat, Sis."

Heather grinned as she handed over the leash, leaving Brenda to hold both animals. She knew how stupid she looked walking Fluffy, but it was worth it. Through all the time walking together they had no distractions while they talked. She and Bill had come to know each other extremely well very quickly.

Finally she found her keys, which had slipped through the hole in her jacket pocket and into the lining.

"Here we go. I can put on a pot of—"

The bang of firecrackers echoed from nearby.

The animals went ballistic. Both of them frantically ran in circles at Brenda's feet, hopelessly tangling the leashes at the same time as making so much noise growling and barking and yowling that they were a blur of noise and flying fur.

"Help me!" Brenda screamed. "They're going to bite me!"

Heather dropped her keys on the ground and tried to grab Fluffy.

Bill tried to hold the plaque and the photographs under his arm while he scrambled to grab Fido.

"Ow! Ow! They're stepping on my feet!" Brenda screeched.

Another blast of firecrackers sent them into a total frenzy, knocking Brenda to the ground. With no constraint, they bolted.

Heather dropped to her hands and knees. "Brenda! Are you okay?"

Bill took off at top speed after Fluffy and Fido. Heather stayed with her sister, knowing that even though the animals ran faster than any human, the complex's outer fence would prevent them from going far. As soon as they settled down, Bill would have them back.

"I'm fine, just a few bruises. What are those kids doing with firecrackers?"

Heather stood and offered Brenda a hand up as a car drove past on the way to the exit.

"No. . ." Heather gasped and ran, deserting her sister. She didn't know where the animals or Bill were, but she didn't want to think of what would happen if they were near the gate when it opened. She could hear the barking and meowing of the animals, as well as Bill calling them as she neared the open gate.

The gate began to close, but it was too late. Under the glow of the streetlight, she saw Fluffy and Fido bolt onto the street. "Fluffy! Fido!" she called as loud as she could through her panting.

She reached the gate just as it clicked shut. Five seconds later, Bill arrived beside her, gasping for breath.

"I nearly had them," he panted, "but they were too fast."

Her eyes burned, and she didn't try to stop the tears. "What are we going to do? They're all tangled up together. They're going to be in trouble!"

"I know. I'll go looking for them, but I doubt I'll find them tonight. When they calm down, they'll probably come if we call them. Or maybe they'll just come home. With all the walks we've been going on, I know they know their way around the neighborhood."

Brenda suddenly appeared beside them. "I'm so sorry! I couldn't hold them. Don't worry, they'll come home. Or someone will find them and bring them home."

Bill gazed down the quiet street. "It's not your fault Brenda. We know that."

"I'd offer to help look for them, but they wouldn't come to me if I called them."

"We know. Now if you'll excuse us, I think Heather and I are going to start looking for them. Hopefully we'll find them before it gets too late."

Heather drove as fast as she could in the homebound rush-hour traffic. It had been the worst day of her teaching career. All she could think of was Fluffy and Fido, hopelessly tangled together, and hopelessly lost. They'd agreed that she would go to work in the morning while Bill took some more banked time off to look for their pets. She'd called him on his cell phone between every class and twice during her lunch break, only to hear the same results. Nothing.

Instead of going home she began driving around her neighborhood, hoping for the best, but instead of finding Fluffy and Fido, she found Bill walking around.

"Hop in!" she called through the window. "Have you eaten?"

She could tell by his expression when he opened the car door and caught the aroma of the fast-food hamburger and fries that he hadn't.

She turned off the ignition, they prayed for their meal and for help finding their beloved pets, gulped down the food, and Heather continued to drive around while Bill scanned the area. Every once in awhile Bill would call their names out the window, then listen for an answering bark, hoping to see them running happily toward them. Except for normal neighborhood stuff, all was quiet and still.

Over the course of the evening, Heather tried to calm her increasing anxiety. The closer it came to sunset, the less hope there would be of finding them. It had been nearly twenty-four hours since their disappearance, and she knew they both would be tired and hungry. Worst of all, tied together, they were helpless.

Just before nine, Bill's cell phone rang.

He smiled weakly at her as he pulled the antenna out. "I'm half expecting it to be you. You're the only one who's called me all day. I put my home number on call-forward to my cell, just in case."

She forced herself to smile, despite not feeling like it.

After he answered, he broke into a wide smile, said a resounding thank-you, and tucked the phone into his pocket. "I've got good news. They're at the SPCA, safe and sound. Let's go."

Heather made it to the animal shelter in record time. After they paid the fines and kennel fees, the staff member in charge complimented both of them on their pets' ID tattoos. She then told them that it was because of the tangled leashes that Fido and Fluffy had been easily recognized as lost, and some concerned teens had easily captured them and turned them in.

They weren't allowed to give out the teens' names, so Bill emptied his wallet of all his cash and instructed the clerk to give it to them as a reward with his utmost thanks.

Heather was so happy she barely kept herself from laughing at Bill, who had to sit with both Fluffy and Fido in his lap the entire drive home because both animals wanted to be held after their ordeal.

Even seeing Brenda's truck in the visitor parking space didn't dampen Heather's spirits. She first dropped Bill and Fido off in front of his townhouse, then drove home where Brenda was waiting, sitting against her front door.

Brenda broke into tears at the sight of Heather carrying Fluffy from the car and babbled behind her the whole time as Heather unlocked the door and went inside, straight to the kitchen, and opened a can of cat food.

While Fluffy gobbled down her food, Heather put on a pot of coffee.

"Sis, I have to talk to you."

Heather wasn't sure she wanted to hear what was coming, but knew she should listen. Over the past month she'd come to some difficult decisions about her sister, the first being that no matter how much Brenda had hurt her, and no matter what Brenda's intentions were, as a Christian, she would forgive her sister. No matter what happened, Brenda would always be her sister, and she had to love her just for that.

"I have to talk to you about Bill."

Now she knew she didn't want to hear it, but forced herself to remain silent.

"I want to tell you what a good man you have. I know I've been horrible to you in the past, especially with Jeff, and I want to say I'm sorry. I guess the reason I'm telling you this is that I met someone recently at the singles group at your church."

Her head was spinning with what Brenda was saying. "That's great, Brenda. Do you think it's serious?"

Suddenly, a fresh stream of tears poured down Brenda's face. "I don't know. That's why I'm so mixed up. With you, when a man starts to like you, it's that simple, he just likes you. But when a man likes me, I never know if it's because of my looks, or because of the way I flirt with all the guys and it's the excitement of the moment, or if it's because he just likes me for myself."

"I don't understand."

"I must admit that I made a play for Bill, just like Jeff, but I have to explain. The men who go to you are always such nice decent guys—guys I think I could trust. I couldn't help myself. I wanted them because they wanted you. And then when they dumped you for me, it made me think that they could dump me like that, too, when something better comes along. I couldn't live like that.

But Bill is different."

Heather smiled. "Yes, he is."

"Everything I did was pointless. He just wasn't interested, and it hurt. And that made me see how horrible I've been to you over the years. I've been so jealous, and that was wrong. I'm sorry."

Heather's mind went blank. All she could think of was that Brenda—beautiful, multitalented, ever-popular Brenda—was jealous. . .of her. She'd never once stopped to consider Brenda's troubles, but now she could understand, even if she didn't completely agree. "It's okay. I forgive you."

Brenda sniffled. "He loves you, Sis. I hope you love him, too."

Heather stared blankly through the window at Bill's back patio door. She'd never met a man like Bill. They were opposites is some ways and complementary in others, and the combination made her enjoy all their time together. He was a man of character and commitment and a man of faith. She also realized that he was waiting for her to make the first move in furthering their relationship, giving her time to work out her fears concerning her sister.

Heather stood. "The coffee's ready. Help yourself. I have to take care of something."

As fast as her feet would carry her, she ran to Bill's door.

"Heather? What are you doing here? Is something wrong?"

"Nothing is wrong, but I have to do something. May I come in?"

"Uh. . .certainly. . ."

Heather nearly laughed. It was the first time since she'd known him that he didn't appear sure of himself.

She stepped close to him and rested her hands on the sides of his waist. His eyebrows raised, but he didn't comment.

"Yesterday I think you wanted to kiss me good night. I'm here for a rain check."

She expected him to say something but before she knew it, she was enveloped in his arms, and she was rendered speechless by his kisses. The only time he broke contact was to say a quick "I love you," and again, his mouth covered hers.

Eventually they broke contact, but she remained nestled in his arms. "I love you, too," she whispered into the center of his chest.

He buried his face in the hair on top of her head. "Really?"

Heather snuggled in further. "Really."

"Well, in that case, I'll let you know what I've been thinking."

"Mmm. . . ," she mumbled into his chest.

"I don't think Fido or I will be able to stand it when you and Fluffy go off to visit your aunt Harriet this summer."

"But it's her birthday, and my holiday."

"I know. We should go with you to California."

She didn't have to think very hard to know what Aunt Harriet would say. Aunt Harriet was the most "people" person she knew. Some of the so-called nieces and nephews weren't related in any tangible way, but they still called her Auntie, and were just as close to her heart as her blood relatives. "I think Aunt Harriet would be delighted. It's a large house; I'm sure there will be lots of room for you."

"Oh, I don't want to stay in separate rooms. I want to get a room in a hotel."

Heather placed her hands in the center of his chest and started to push herself away. "Now just a minute!" She had said she loved him, but she wasn't about to share a hotel room and all that went with it.

He cupped her face in his hands. Heather froze, unable to break eye contact.

"I want to stay in the honeymoon suite."

"Honeymoon suite? But that means. . ."

His tender smile nearly brought tears to her eyes. "That's right. And your answer is?"

"I guess we can't separate Fido and Fluffy, can we?"

His heart pounded beneath her palms. "Didn't anyone ever tell you not to answer a question with a question?"

"Yes, Bill, I will marry you."

She melted into his arms, feeling a peace and love inside like she'd never known possible.

Bill's deep voice echoed in his chest as he spoke. "I don't care where we live after we're married, your townhouse or mine. But since both yards are set up for pets, wouldn't it be nice if our new neighbors had a dog?"

"You mean a cat."

"No, a dog."

"No, a cat. . ."

GAIL SATTLER

Gail is an animal lover, which is why she found writing this story so much fun. Gail has two dogs, one of whom frequently hangs out on the roof of her house surveying the neighborhood, as well as countless tropical fish, many of whom have names. When she's not looking after her pets, she's a mom to three busy boys and is active in her church where she is the Adult Worship Leader. Gail loves to compose love stories that are only possible with God in that happy ending. She has written a number of novels for Barbour Publishing's **Heartsong Presents** line and was voted favorite author for the year 2000. You are invited to visit Gail's website at http://www.gailsattler.com.

The Tail End

by Gail Sattler

Epilogue

A unt Harriet wants to do what?"

Harriet perked up her ears. She rested her fists on her hips and turned toward the group behind her. "I may be seventy years old, but I'm not deaf."

Kerry lowered her eyes, took in a deep breath, then turned to face her. "I know, Auntie. But really, are you sure you want to do this?"

"I did ask everyone to bring their pets with them for a reason, Dear."

Jake leaned to whisper in Kerry's ear, but since he had to speak over the volume of all the voices around, Harriet still heard his words. "From what you told me about your aunt Harriet, I don't think anyone is capable of stopping her from doing anything, once she sets her mind to it."

Harriet grinned and reached up to touch the brim of her latest choice of hats, a charming straw bonnet with a splash of flowers all around the brim—perfect for summer. As usual, Cheep sat on her shoulder. As she waved her arms over her head to get everyone's attention, he jostled closer to her neck and dug his talons into the hidden wooden piece she had sewn into her shoulder pad. "Hop into the cars, everyone! We're going!"

Harriet watched the mass exodus. She had rounded up everyone she knew with a van or large vehicle to transport all her nieces and nephews who had come from all over the continent.

"Yoo-hoo! Matt! Lynne! You take that big horse of yours and go in the big van!"

Matt grumbled as he walked past, but she still heard him. "He's not a horse. He's a Great Dane. And his name is Brutus."

Lynne neatly carried her stocky little Bamboo, who, of course, was quiet and very well behaved.

Cheep chirped from her shoulder as Heather and Bill approached with their dog and cat. "You two go there, in that car. Your dog will fit in back, and the cat can go in your lap."

On his way past, Bill stopped and reached out to tickle Cheep under his beak, but Heather pulled his hand away. "Watch it! That foul thing will nip your finger."

"I heard that, Dear," Harriet said softly.

"It's true, Auntie. Remember when Cheep nipped me last time I was here?"

"Yes. And how you've grown since then."

Bill laughed aloud and rested his elbow on top of Heather's head. "Not really."

Heather knocked his arm away and pulled him to the car saying something that Harriet couldn't hear. But it was no matter. She had too much to do to worry about it.

"Brian! Rachel! You come with me!"

She scrambled into her compact economy car, encouraging her nephew to ride in the back with their little dog so she could get to know her soon-to-be niece-in-law better.

Harriet led the armada of vehicles to the city park, knowing that this was going to be the best birthday party of her life.

After everyone found a parking spot, she directed them all to the picnic area where she'd tied the red balloons, discreetly reminded all who had dogs to get a cleanup bag from the dispenser, and instructed everyone to wait by the balloons until it was time for the annual SPCA Pet Walk to begin.

She'd seen other groups assembling, and not only were there dogs and cats galore but other birds as well. She'd also seen a ferret on a leash, a lop-eared rabbit, and even a couple of snakes. She was glad her own group had brought normal pets, but she would have been just as delighted if someone from her family had brought a turtle, although that would have been difficult to walk.

Harriet stood on top of one of the wooden benches so she could be seen in the crowd. "Attention everyone!" she called out, waving her arms.

"Cheep!" called Cheep.

"Let's play a little game!"

All her beloved nieces and nephews groaned, but Harriet ignored them.

"I want you to introduce your animals to each other, so you can all get to know everyone else a little better before the Pet Walk begins."

Everyone just stood around staring blankly, so Harriet marched up to the first group.

She removed the medium-sized mutt from Kerry's arms. "My name is Puddles!" she squeaked in her best imitation of a little doggie voice. "And I belong to. . .?"

Harriet held the dog back out to Kerry and Jake. Matt and Lynne laughed, Bill and Heather stared with open mouths, and Brian and Rachel tried to look elsewhere.

"Well?" she said, tapping her foot.

Jake accepted the dog and lowered him to the ground. "My name is Jake, and Puddles is Kerry's dog. . . though come to think of it, I guess he's mine now, too." Jake smiled at Kerry and winked. "You'll have to excuse me. This is still a little new to me. We're on kind of a belated honeymoon. And here we are in the middle of some huge park, about to walk the dog."

Kerry grinned impishly and slipped her arm through the crook of his elbow. "For a guy who would turn down a delicious, home-cooked meal on our third date to gorilla-sit, a honeymoon among a zoo of animals isn't all that surprising."

Heather and Bill snuggled up close and slipped their arms around each other, after making sure their pets' leashes wouldn't tangle. "This is Fluffy and Fido," said Heather. "We're on our honeymoon, too. He's Bill, and I'm Heather."

"My name's Brian, and this is Rachel. Oops, I mean this is Sparky. Rachel and I aren't married yet, but we will be soon. Right, Rachel? Uh. . .Rachel?"

Instead of listening to Brian, Rachel was intently

watching the cat and dog. Fido appeared bored, so he lay down, and then Fluffy walked in circles to snuggle into him, comfortably nestling against his side.

Harriet tapped Rachel on the shoulder. "He's talking to you, Dear."

"Oops! Sorry!" Rachel sputtered. "I was just looking at Fluffy and Fido together. It's amazing that they could be so friendly to each other. I thought cats and dogs were sworn enemies. And for your cat to be on a leash, too. Wow."

Harriet nodded. "Yes, I wish I could have brought my cats, but I could never get any of them to walk on a leash."

Bill gave a very halfhearted laugh. "It wasn't always this way, right, Honey?"

"I don't want to talk about it," Heather grumbled.

Lynne bent to pick up her cute little Corgi. "This is Bamboo, and I'm Lynne. And you can't miss Brutus. Right, Matt?"

"He does appear to be the biggest dog here, doesn't he?" Matt said as he studied the ever-growing crowd. "This is quite an event, isn't it? I have a great respect for anything the SPCA does. Back home, I'm involved in the Animal-Assisted Therapy Program. We get pet owners and their pets to visit people in nursing homes, kids in hospitals, stuff like that. I also got Brutus from the animal shelter. Although I can't imagine why they would have had trouble finding him a home."

Harriet forced herself to keep a straight face as she petted the dog, whose nose was as high as hers. "Not everyone wants a horse, Dear."

Brian smiled and bent to pet his dog. "That's great,

Matt. I got Sparky from the SPCA, too."

Harriet silenced everyone and waved her arms in the air again.

"Cheep!" called Cheep.

"The walk is about to start! Let's all keep together, please!"

Since they were the first large group to have arrived, they assembled closest to the starting point.

A man wearing a baseball cap with an SPCA logo stood on a small platform and raised a megaphone to his mouth. "Welcome to the Annual SPCA Pet Walk! We're glad to have so many participants this year, and I think that's mostly due to our longtime member, Harriet Davis."

Harriet felt herself blush as the crowd cheered and applauded. Cheep shuffled back and forth on her shoulder at the uproar of the crowd but settled down as the crowd hushed.

"We've provided maps of the walk route; Harriet is going to give them out. She's right there next to the banner at the starting line. You shouldn't need one—just follow the yellow markers, and everyone have a great Pet Walk!"

The crowd cheered louder this time.

Cheep shuffled back and forth again, making gurgling squawks. Harriet felt the movement change as Cheep began to flex his wings in nervousness.

"Cheep! Settle down!" Harriet whispered to the bird then smiled to the crowd.

"Cheep!" called Cheep.

Without warning, the bird took off, flying into the opening of the path, his brilliant colors almost fluorescent against the dark green of the trees.

"Cheep!" called Harriet.

Fluffy let out a loud meow and leapt forward when Cheep took flight, pulling Heather off balance. When the cat started running she pulled the leash out of Heather's hand.

Heather struggled to regain her balance then took off at a run behind her cat, who was running after the bird.

"Fluffy! Come back! Fluffy!" A chorus of barking drowned out all else.

Brutus charged through the crowd with Matt frantically pulling back the leash, to no avail.

Seeing another dog after his beloved cat, Fido strained against his leash, leaving Bill no choice but to run with him in the hopes of catching Fluffy.

Soon all the large and midsized dogs were loping behind. The owners, having given up, decided to go with the flow, at least for a little while, and jogged with their dogs.

The smaller dogs followed. Harriet could make out Brian with Sparky and Kerry with Puddles running, but not very fast. Short-legged Bamboo and Lynne scrambled along last.

"Everyone! Please!" the SPCA representative called through his megaphone. "This is a Pet Walk! Not a Pet Run! People!"

It was too late. Everyone had started, and no one was breaking the pace. Even the people not in Harriet's family jogged along the path. Not one person stopped to take a map from her.

When everyone was gone, she saw a few people still

standing by the starting line.

Rachel was pointing her finger and laughing at Brian and Sparky as they scrambled away, and Jake, always the veterinarian, was tending to a small boy's dog that had a bandage on his tail.

Harriet could hear laughing and happy chatter fading in the distance as the crowd rounded the corner.

She checked her watch. Cheep knew the path. Not only did she walk this path often, Cheep had flown it countless times, both with her and solo. In seventeen minutes he would be through the path, back to where it started, and back on her shoulder. Everyone else would simply take longer, except maybe Fluffy. She expected most people to take up to an hour, depending on when they could get their animals to slow down.

Harriet wiped a tear from her eye. This really was the best birthday party of her life. Not only had she lived to see her nieces and nephews grow up, but her favorite ones were either married or about to be. Best of all, they had all found good, Christian mates with whom to share their lives, and all were happy together.

She waited patiently, then smiled when Cheep landed back on her shoulder.

In her brief conversations with her favorite nieces and nephews, all four of them had met their partners through the wonderful world of pets. When the walk was over, she looked forward to being able to sit down and talk more with all of them and to hear their tales, or rather, their *tails of love.*

A Letter to Our Readers

Dear Readers:

In order that we might better contribute to your reading enjoyment, we would appreciate your taking a few minutes to respond to the following questions. When completed, please return to the following: Fiction Editor, Barbour Publishing, Inc., PO Box 719, Uhrichsville, OH 44683.

1. Did you enjoy reading *Tails of Love?*
   - ❏ Very much. I would like to see more books like this.
   - ❏ Moderately—I would have enjoyed it more if _____
   _____
   _____

2. What influenced your decision to purchase this book?
   (Check those that apply.)
   - ❏ Cover   ❏ Back cover copy   ❏ Title   ❏ Price
   - ❏ Friends   ❏ Publicity   ❏ Other

3. Which story was your favorite?
   - ❏ *Ark of Love*   ❏ *Dog Park*
   - ❏ *Walk, Don't Run*   ❏ *The Neighbor's Fence*

4. Please check your age range:
   - ❏ Under 18   ❏ 18–24   ❏ 25–34
   - ❏ 35–45   ❏ 46–55   ❏ Over 55

5. How many hours per week do you read? _____

Name _____

Occupation _____

Address _____

City _____ State _____ ZIP _____